Murder in the Blood

Murder in the Blood

Lesley Cookman

Published by Accent Press Ltd 2015

ISBN 9781783756940

Acknowledgements

It will be obvious to everyone who knows my regular holiday destination that part of this story is set in a very similar place. Here and there I have 'borrowed' the odd name, but have attached it to something else; for instance, the *Paradise* is not a boat in real life. I may have used the names of people I know – but I do that with English names, too. I have not based anyone or anything in my fictional village on anyone or anything in the real one – honest! Nor is my depiction of any of the criminal activities here based on anything but my imagination.

Special thanks go to Ella Preece, who patiently answered all my questions, and whose photographs inspire me all year round. Also to Lev Parikian for the name of my fictional village, and to my dear friend Alison Cottier, who named a bay for me.

A note for regular readers – and new ones. In the course of writing this book, I found that it linked up with several previous ones in the series, *Murder in Bloom*, *Murder by Magic*, and *Murder by the Sea*. To avoid spoilers, perhaps you should read those first!

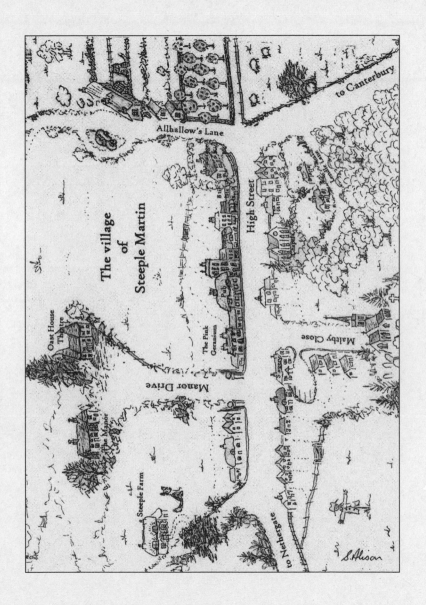

The village
of
Steeple Martin

Allhallow's Lane

to Canterbury

High Street

Oast House Theatre

The Pink Geranium

Pub

Malby Close

Manor Drive

The Manor

Steeple Farm

to Nethergate

S. Alison

WHO'S WHO IN THE LIBBY SARJEANT SERIES

From Steeple Martin

Libby Sarjeant	Former professional actor, artist and director of The Oast Theatre, resident of 17 Allhallow's Lane, Steeple Martin; owner of Sidney the cat
Ben Wilde	Libby's partner, son of Hetty Wilde, former architect, manager of The Manor Estate and architect of The Oast Theatre
Hetty Wilde	Widow, owner of The Manor
Peter Parker	Freelance journalist, co-owner of The Pink Geranium restaurant and life partner of Harry Price
Harry Price	Peter's life partner and co-owner and chef-patron of The Pink Geranium
Flo Carpenter	Best friend of Hetty Wilde
Lenny Fisher	Flo's partner and Hetty's brother
Adam Sarjeant	Libby's son
Ali and Ahmed	Owners of the eight-til-late in the village
Reverend Bethany Cole	Vicar of Steeple Martin
Joe, Nella, and Owen	of Cattlegreen Nurseries
Anne Douglas	Librarian; close friend of Reverend Patti Pearson, vicar of St Aldeberge's Church

From Nethergate

Fran Wolfe	Former actor, occasional psychic, Libby's best friend, and owner of Balzac the cat
Guy Wolfe	Fran's husband, artist and owner of the Wolfe gallery and shop; father of Sophie
Jane Baker	Assistant editor for the *Nethergate Mercury*; mother to Imogen
Terry Baker	Jane's husband and father to Imogen
Susannah Baker	Pianist and mother to Robbie the Kid
Emlyn	Susannah's partner and father to Robbie
Lizzie	Owner of the ice cream stall
George	Owner of the pleasure boat *Dolphin*
Bert	Owner of the pleasure boat *Sparkler*
Mavis	Owner of The Blue Anchor café

British Police Force

DCI Ian Connell	Kent Force
DS Bob Maiden	Kent Force
DI Michael James	Metropolitan Police
Commander Johnny Smith	Metropolitan Police

From Erzugan

Geoff and Christine Croker	Owners of The Istanbul Palace

Alcc Wilson	British ex-pat
Sally Weston	British ex-pat
Justin Newcombe	British ex-pat
Martha and Ismet	Owner of restaurant, Martha's
Mahmud	Owner of The Red Room
'Jimmy'	Owner of hotel, Jimmy's
Captain Joe	Owner of the *Paradise* pleasure boat

Visitors to Erzugan

Neal Parnham

Betty and Walter Roberts

Greta and Tom Willingham

Chapter One

The sea lapped gently into the granite cave, dark as ink. The moon, orange as a dying sun, touched wavelets and turned them into dull fire. Caught on an unseen finger of rock, the body bobbed gently to the surface.

There are secret places in the Mediterranean. Along the coast of Turkey, in the foothills of the Taurus Mountains, lie villages the tourists do not see. Ramshackle hovels of brick, breezeblock, and corrugated iron line the unmade roads, the odd discouraged goat tethered in a patch of dirt droops its head. Everywhere, acres of white-roofed glasshouses. Further inland, the pine-covered slopes rear up above the rusted metal hoops of abandoned polytunnels and half-built concrete houses left to the elements. Along the better surfaced roads, small groves of pomegranate and olive trees proclaim the more affluent villages, with their newly built villas announcing themselves to be 'Satilik' – For Sale, and a sudden clutch of billboards advertising hotels. There are still hovels, but the goats look more cheerful, and chickens cluck drowsily in the sun.

Women in headscarves and baggy trousers carry baskets and bundles through the tiny centre with its statue, pharmacy, and market, the road leads winding to the beach. And here are the small family-run bars and hotels, a few sunbeds on the beach, a few boats tied up to a leaning wooden jetty. It was to one of these villages that Guy Wolfe had brought his wife and friends.

Libby Sarjeant stretched her arms above her head and sighed. 'This beats the Isle of Wight.'

Ben Wilde, her significant other, smiled. 'At least we're not investigating murders and family feuds.'

From another sunbed, Fran Wolfe sat up suddenly and stared

1

at the sea.

Peter Parker lifted his sunhat from his face and gave his partner Harry Price a dig in the ribs. Five people watched Fran apprehensively.

Eventually, Libby could bear it no longer. 'What is it, Fran?'

Fran gave the appearance of someone jolted to reality. 'Eh?'

'What happened?' asked Guy.

Fran looked confused and shook her head. 'I don't know.'

Libby sighed. 'It was a moment, wasn't it?'

Fran's unwanted psychic gift often resulted in what her family and friends called her 'moments'. These ranged from seeing a picture of a plant to a vision of murder, sometimes with attendant feelings of suffocation.

'Yes,' said Fran slowly. 'Someone was drowning.'

The other five groaned.

'No, my lovely, please,' said Harry, sitting up and glaring at her. 'We're on bloody holiday.'

'I can't help it.'

'Don't worry about it,' said Libby, crossing her fingers. 'There must have been lots of drownings round here in the past. I expect that's what you saw.'

Fran smiled at her gratefully. 'That'll be it. Thanks, Libby.'

Guy stood up. 'I think we now deserve a drink. It must be nearly lunchtime.'

The little party stood up and gathered various belongings.

'Are we coming back to the beach after lunch?' asked Harry. 'Do we leave the towels here?'

'I thought Captain Joe said he'd take us out on the boat this afternoon?' said Peter, perching his hat on the back of his head.

'So he did.' Harry slung his towel over his shoulder. 'Come on, then, last one to the bar's a sissy.'

The tiny hotel sat right on the beach, its bar at the front. The six friends perched on bar stools and ordered the local beer. The owner, known to all British guests as Jimmy due to his unpronounceable Turkish name, handed them glasses frosted from the fridge.

'You enjoying your holiday?' he asked them, as he had

asked every day since their arrival. 'You glad Guy bring you?'

'Yes,' they all assured him. 'Very glad.'

Guy had mentioned the previous summer, when they were visiting the Isle of Wight, that he knew of a small bay in Turkey little-known by the general run of tourists. After the events of the past year, they had decided to award themselves a holiday, and even Harry had closed his beloved restaurant, The Pink Geranium. And Guy had been right.

The sweep of the bay, backed by the foothills of the Taurus Mountains, was dotted with twenty or so 'paynsions', hotels, and bars, and one supermarket. At least, that's what it called itself. Guy had seemed to know at least half the proprietors, and they had all greeted him with fond cries of recognition, even though his last trip there had been years ago, before he had met Fran. The other guests were mostly regulars, who guarded their little treasure jealously and were quite happy with the two-hour journey through the mountains from the airport, which put off the tour operators and all but the most intrepid holidaymakers.

Now they ordered soup and borek, the Turkish version of cheese straws – only more substantial – and salad, to see them through the afternoon boat trip. A couple of the other British guests joined them, and one, a solitary Englishman wearing a panama hat who rarely spoke, sat at the farthest table from the bar.

'Who is he, Jimmy?' asked Libby. 'Has he been coming here for years like the others?'

Jimmy shrugged. 'No. I do not know how he came here. He book over the phone. He know people in the village, I think.' He shrugged. 'Very quiet.'

One of the other guests leant forward. 'We gave him a lift into the village the other evening when we went to The Roma.' The Roma was a Turkish-Italian restaurant that provided a change from those in the bay. 'He barely said a word, but he seemed to know where he was going.'

'Oh, well,' said Harry, 'nothing to do with us.'

'No ...' said Libby thoughtfully, and was drowned out by protests from her friends. Libby's nosiness was legendary.

An hour later, and they were gathered on the wooden jetty while Captain Joe, bearer of another unpronounceable name, let down his little gangplank for them to board his boat, the *Paradise*. There were several small boats competing for trade from the tourists, all taking trips round the coast to visit bays only accessible from the sea, where one could swim, eat freshly caught fish, and drink beer or raki, according to taste. This afternoon Joe was taking them to a small bay, rarely visited, where there had been recent sightings of turtles.

The boat chugged off towards the headland, where a rocky island guarded the entrance to the bay.

'Reminds me of our Dragon Island in Nethergate,' said Libby to Fran, as they approached it.

'Same sort of shape,' agreed Fran. 'I love that someone's planted a Turkish flag on top.'

'They do that everywhere, don't they?' said Libby. 'I must say, I'm glad Guy brought us here. I want to come back, don't you?'

But Fran wasn't listening. Her back was rigid and she was staring at the sheer rock face rising from the sea. Turning her back on the island, Libby tried to see what she was looking at. And realised that Captain Joe was turning the boat slowly inshore.

The six friends stood together peering into the darkness of the cleft in the rock and saw what Fran had seen. Bobbing face down on the surface of the water – a body.

Chapter Two

'I am sorry, my friends,' said Captain Joe. 'The coastguard say I must stay until they arrive.' He shrugged and spread his hands wide. 'What can I do?'

Everyone assured him they understood and sat down with their backs towards the cliff.

'At least we weren't expected to haul it out of the sea,' said Libby.

Five voices protested.

Captain Joe appeared from the tiny galley. 'Tea?' he asked.

Everyone nodded, and Libby pulled out a packet of biscuits from her bag.

'What do you suppose they do now?' said Fran.

'With the –' Guy jerked his head backwards.

'The body. Yes.'

'I can't imagine they've got a morgue here,' said Ben.

'And don't they like to bury bodies really quickly?' said Harry.

'Nothing to do with us,' said Peter. 'The coastguard will pick it up and take it away to wherever it needs to go. We needn't hear anything more about it.'

'Tea.' Captain Joe appeared with a tray of tea glasses. 'Coastguard on the way.'

Libby opened her mouth and Fran and Ben both kicked her. She closed it again.

They sat in silence until the sound of a boat travelling at high speed reached them.

'Coastguard,' said Captain Joe.

The boat slowed and came alongside. Captain Joe proceeded to demonstrate, with many arm gestures, how they had come upon the body. From the looks directed towards them by the uniformed officer, the six friends got the impression that their presence was being questioned and possibly thought suspicious. Eventually, a notebook and pencil was produced and handed to Joe.

'He wants you to write down your names and the address of the hotel,' he said with a shrug.

'Why?' asked Libby. 'We're just tourists.'

'Witnesses,' said Guy, taking the pad.

They all wrote down their names, while activity on the other side of the coastguard boat suggested that the body was being retrieved. Sure enough, as Joe handed the notebook back across the gap between the boats, something was hauled aboard. Libby turned her back and Joe started the engine of the *Paradise*. The officer on the coastguard boat shouted and gestured again towards the friends.

'I'm sorry,' said Joe helplessly. 'He wants you to look at it to see if you know the person.'

'Why on earth would we? We aren't local,' said Ben.

'That's ridiculous,' said Peter, standing up suddenly and crossing to the rail. 'We're English,' he announced in stentorian tones. The officer simply looked at him with his eyebrows raised.

Joe broke into a torrent of Turkish and the officer slowly nodded.

'He says please the men look, but not the ladies,' said Joe, looking miserable.

The other three men joined Peter, and Libby and Fran looked at each other.

'This is extremely unpleasant,' said Libby.

'Not to put too fine a point on it, yes,' said Fran.

There was further conversation in Turkish and Peter, Harry, Ben, and Guy rejoined them.

'Nasty,' said Harry, and the others nodded.

'But we don't know him,' said Ben.

'I don't feel like a boat trip now,' said Libby.

There was murmured agreement, and Guy turned to Joe,

6

who unhappily agreed to take them back to the village.

'Not good,' he kept saying, shaking his head.

The little boat chugged slowly back into the bay and the wooden jetty. Under the tree where the boatmen sat, several heads turned in surprise. Joe and his passengers trudged up the sandy slope to tell them what had happened. There was much shaking of heads and pursing of lips.

'They say unlucky,' Joe told the friends. 'Very unlucky.'

'Especially for the victim,' muttered Guy.

'Do you want to come back to the hotel for a beer, Joe?' asked Peter.

Joe shook his head. 'No. I stay here. Coastguard say Jandarma will come.'

'Where will they land the body?' asked Fran.

Joe shrugged and shook his head.

'Come and have a drink later, then,' said Ben. 'Thanks for the trip anyway, Joe.'

As they walked the short distance to the hotel, Libby pointed out to sea.

'The coastguard boat's coming in to the other end of the bay.'

'So they'll take it off there,' said Harry. 'But where will they put it?'

'Perhaps they'll send a hearse or an ambulance to take it to a morgue,' said Fran. 'No idea how the system works in this country.'

When they got back to the hotel, the couple who had joined them for lunch were on sunbeds by the pool. The woman sat up.

'That was quick! Did Joe's boat break down?'

Fran and Libby went over to explain, while Harry began to commandeer other sunbeds.

'How horrible.' The woman had turned quite pale. 'I'm so glad we didn't come.'

Her husband sat up beside her. 'I wonder if we'll ever know who he was? Or what happened?'

Libby shuddered. 'I'd rather not think about it at all.'

Jimmy strolled over.

'The Jandarma will want to talk to you,' he said.

'But why? How could we have known anything about it?' asked Libby.

'In England the police talk to everybody, no?'

'Yes, they do,' said Ben. 'And we were on the boat, Lib. In their eyes, it was Captain Joe and us who discovered it.'

Libby sighed. 'Yes, I suppose it was.'

'I'm going to have a swim,' announced Fran. 'Take my mind off it.'

'Beatcha,' said Harry, and disappeared into the water with a splash.

'Too energetic,' said Peter, appropriating one of the sunbeds Harry had pulled into the shade of a large umbrella. 'I shall sleep.'

'I think I want tea,' said Libby.

'I bring you chai?' said Jimmy.

Ben smiled. 'I think she wants good old builders' tea, Jimmy.'

'Builders?' Jimmy looked bewildered. Guy tried to explain.

'Never mind.' Libby patted his hand. 'I shall go and make some in our room.'

By the time the friends met at the bar in the evening, the events of the afternoon had been discussed and dissected over and over. Several of the other guests of the hotel had also gathered for pre-prandial drinks and had to hear the story all over again, so when the bright blue van drew up and discharged three uniformed Jandarma officers it came as a an unpleasant descent into reality.

Jimmy's office was not large enough to accommodate nine adults, so the senior officer unwillingly took over a corner of the bar building and glared at anyone who dared come anywhere near it. As it happened, neither he nor his two underlings spoke English, so Jimmy had to leave his position at the bar to stand in as interpreter. Luckily, some of the other guests were long-term visitors and took over as temporary barmen.

After some obviously dissatisfactory verbal skirmishing,

8

Jimmy turned to his guests.

'The man was English,' he said. 'This officer thinks you know him.'

'Why?' asked six voices.

'Because you are English.'

General laughter. The officer looked thunderous.

'We don't know every English tourist here,' said Ben.

'He was not tourist. He lives in the village,' said Jimmy, darting an uncomfortable look at the three Jandarma.

'Oh, I see,' said Libby. 'Well we don't know anyone who lives here, I'm afraid. Only the people we've met since we arrived.'

Jimmy repeated this to the Jandarma.

'Has he got a photograph?' asked Fran suddenly.

Jimmy repeated the request. Grudgingly, the senior officer brought out a blurred photograph.

'Where did they get that?' asked Harry.

'His passport,' said Jimmy. 'In a bag tied to his ...' He indicated his waist.

Fran picked up the photograph, raising her eyebrows at the officer, who nodded. She pushed back her chair and went over to the bar. It drew the other guests in the bar like iron filings to a magnet. After a moment, Fran returned to the others with the lone Englishman, panama in hand, in tow.

'This gentleman says he recognises the picture,' she said, and sat down.

The officer waved a hand and spoke rapidly to Jimmy.

'He says you can go, but he will speak with this gentleman. Mr Parnham.' Jimmy sat down beside the newcomer, looking even more miserable.

'Well!' said Libby, as they retrieved their drinks from the bar. The rest of the guests milled round wanting to know what happened.

'I wonder,' said the woman they'd been talking to earlier, 'if that bloke knew the dead man? I said he looked as though he knew where he was going when we took him into the village, didn't I?'

'Perhaps he did,' said Ben.

'We'll ask him when he comes back,' said Libby. 'I'm Libby, by the way.' She held out a hand.

'I'm Greta Willingham. This is my husband, Tom.' Greta took the proffered hand and introductions were made all round.

'You said he was English?' asked someone else, as chairs were pulled up into a rough circle.

'So the officer said.' Guy sat down next to his wife.

'I bet Sally would know him,' said Greta.

'Sally?' queried Fran.

'Sally Weston. She's lived here for years,' explained Tom. 'She started by coming out on holiday and stayed.' Tom turned to Guy. 'You must have met her when you were coming here before.'

Guy looked worried. 'Don't tell me I met you and I've forgotten?'

'Only in passing,' said Greta. 'You were always with your little girl. How is she?'

'Sophie? All grown up now. Did an art degree at university.'

'Oh, you were an artist, weren't you?' said Tom.

'Yes, and I do apologise for not remembering you,' said Guy. 'So, no, I don't remember a Sally. Sorry.'

'Things have changed a lot in the past few years,' said a comfortably built elderly woman with pink hair. 'We've been coming for over ten years and things are very different.'

'So,' said Libby, determined to bring the conversation back to the dead Englishman, 'no one except Mr Parnham there recognised him?'

There was a mass shaking of heads.

'We don't know anyone except a few bar and hotel owners,' said the pink-haired lady. 'And we don't go far.'

'We go in to the market,' said Greta, 'and we have a drink in the village, sometimes with Sally.'

'Do you hire a car?' asked Ben.

'Oh, no, dear. We have a taxi,' said Greta. 'We use them to go to the river restaurants, too.'

'River restaurants? Libby turned to Guy. 'You haven't told

10

us about them?'

'I don't think I ever went there,' said Guy.

'Oh, there was only the one when you came here,' said Tom. 'There are three now. Lovely places.'

'We'll go tomorrow,' said Peter. 'Harry's very keen on trying as many different restaurants as he can.'

'Really?' Greta looked interested. 'You like food, then?'

'I'm a chef,' said Harry, with a grin. Several of the other people leant forward. 'I have a Mexican vegetarian restaurant called The Pink Geranium.'

'Nearly vegetarian,' said Libby.

'Yes, petal, nearly.'

'How, nearly?' asked the pink lady's husband, a short, bushy-moustached individual.

'I branched out,' said Harry. 'I now do a selection of non-vegetarian dishes in a separate kitchen.'

'Why separate?' asked Bushy Moustache.

'You can't cook meat – or even prepare it – in a veggie kitchen, dear,' explained his wife.

'Bloody nonsense,' said Bushy Moustache, and buried his face in his beer glass.

Mr Parnham left the table with the Jandarma officers and approached the group by the bar.

'Everything all right?' asked Guy.

Parnham frowned.

'I'm not sure,' he said. 'You see, I'd met him.'

Chapter Three

'Really?'

'Where?'

'Did you know him?'

The questions seemed to distress Mr Parnham.

'I – I don't know. Do excuse me.' He gave an odd little bow and walked swiftly away from the bar towards the beach.

'Oh, dear,' said Libby. 'We upset him.'

'Let's go and find dinner,' said Harry. 'It's really nothing to do with us, is it?'

The group stood up and said goodbye to their fellow guests, but as they stepped out on to the beach road, the senior Jandarma officer came up behind them with Jimmy trailing in his wake.

'He says he will want to talk to you again,' said Jimmy. 'Something Mr Parnham said.'

The officer gave a curt nod and strode past them to his blue van. His two cohorts scampered after him.

'What's Mr Parnham's other name?' asked Fran.

'Neal, I think. This is the first time he's been here.' Jimmy turned back to the bar. 'I shall see you later.'

'And what could Neal Parnham have said about us that would make the Jandarma want to speak to us again?' said Libby, watching the blue van turn round at the end of the bay to make its way back along the road and out of the village.

'Next time we see him we'll ask him,' said Ben. 'Come on woman. I'm starving.'

Fifty yards from the hotel, Abdi's tiny courtyard restaurant just about had room to fit them in.

'You eat outside everywhere here, don't you?' said Libby,

sniffing appetising smells wafting from the kitchen at the back.

'Except when it rains,' said Guy. 'I remember getting drenched here once.'

Abdi was another local who remembered Guy from years before. He handed round menus.

'He did. We took him into the kitchen.' He beamed round the table. 'Now, what would you like to drink?'

It was just as they were paying their bill that Libby spotted Neal Parnham on his way back to the hotel.

'I'm going after him,' she said, grabbing her bag and colliding with chairs.

She caught up with him just before he reached the hotel.

'Mr Parnham!' she panted. 'Neal. Can I have a word?'

He turned. 'What about?'

Libby frowned. 'Well, what do you think?' she said, breathing a little easier. 'You told us you'd met the – er – body, and now the Jandarma want to talk to us again. Because of something you said. What did you say?'

Neal Parnham's face lengthened even more.

'I – oh. It's so difficult when he doesn't speak English.'

'Or you don't speak Turkish. It's their country,' said Libby.

Parnham looked at his feet. 'Yes, of course. But he misunderstood – or Jimmy did. I said this man knew other English tourists in the village. The dead man, I mean.'

'And he thought you meant us? But you would have pointed us out, surely?'

'But I said I didn't know who they were.' Neal Parnham looked up. 'I'm sorry if I've put you in a difficult position.'

Libby sighed. 'Oh, that's all right. I see now how it happened. But how exactly did you come to meet him? Greta and Tom said they thought you knew someone in the village. It wasn't him, was it?'

'Not – well, not exactly.'

Libby noticed the others coming up behind. She took Neal's arm. 'Come on. Come in and have a drink with us. You look as though you could do with some company.'

He looked round at the six smiling faces and seemed to

relax. 'That would be good, thank you.'

Greta and Tom were sitting at a table with Lady Pink Hair and her bushy-moustached husband, who appeared to be taking no part in the conversation, merely looking as if he had a bad smell under his nose. Probably rising from his moustache, thought Libby.

Greta raised a hand and smiled, but Libby was already shepherding her party to a table near the pool.

'Tell us where you met the dead man,' said Fran, when they were settled in their seats and Peter and Harry had gone for drinks. 'You have a friend in the village?'

'Yes. Well, someone I met here, actually.' Neal sat back in his chair and took off his straw trilby. 'Before you came.'

'How long have you been here?' asked Libby.

'Three weeks. I'm on a sort of extended break.' Neal looked up and smiled as Harry put a beer glass before him. 'Thank you.'

'When are you going home?' asked Libby. 'Sorry if I'm being nosy ...'

'She's always nosy,' said Ben. 'Sorry.'

Neal, now looking much more relaxed, smiled again. 'Oh, I don't mind. It was just so horrible being questioned and ... well, when they showed me that photograph ...'

'A shock,' said Fran. 'Of course it was. So you met him –?'

'Chap I met on the beach, Justin, has a house in the village. He invited me for lunch and dinner a couple of times, and introduced us.'

'And he's an English resident?'

'Yes, there's quite a little group of ex-pats here.'

'And he knows other visitors?' said Guy.

'Oh, yes. They were talking about the regulars – the people who come back every year. I gather that those people do.' Neal indicated Greta and Tom.

'And did they know the same people?' asked Libby.

'Oh, there seem to be some who everyone knows. And they all have their particular hotels.'

'I always stayed here,' said Guy. 'Well, I only came twice,

but it was always to this hotel.'

'This is your first time here, is it?' Fran asked Neal.

'Yes. I came across it on the internet and thought it looked – well, quiet. Not touristy.'

'That's why people come back year after year,' said Guy. 'It costs more than a package holiday, but the fact that it's such a long way from the airport keeps most of the tour operators away.'

'The average punter doesn't like much more than a half-hour journey from airport to hotel,' said Harry. 'Must say, I'd come back if I could get the time off.'

'What do you do?' asked Neal.

'He's a chef,' said Libby. 'With his own restaurant. So he can't afford to close it often.'

'Did you tell the Jandarma about your friend Justin?' asked Peter.

'I had to, didn't I? I felt very guilty. That was why – well, I was a bit rude earlier.'

'You know,' said Libby, 'if this is a British-based crime, then I don't think the Jandarma are going to solve it.'

Neal looked startled, but everyone else groaned.

'Well, it stands to reason, doesn't it?' said Libby. 'They didn't know how to question us, and there's the language barrier ...'

'So you think you ought to investigate,' said Ben. 'How did I guess?'

'I think Libby could be right,' said Fran. 'After all –'

'Wait a bit!' interrupted Neal. 'Investigate? What do you mean?'

Libby looked embarrassed.

'At home, I'm afraid Libby and Fran have rather a reputation,' Peter started to explain.

'For looking into murders,' continued Harry.

'I don't believe it!' Neal Parnham's eyes were wide. 'That sort of thing only happens in books.'

'Well – yes,' agreed Libby. 'But we still do it.'

'Mainly Libby,' said Fran. 'I'm merely the back stop.'

'No you're not …' Libby broke off at Fran's warning look.

'Anyway, the police usually get the answer before we do,' Fran continued smoothly. 'But that's the British police. If this is a murder within the ex-pat community, the local forces are going to be at a loss, surely?'

Neal Parnham's lean face expressed wariness and doubt. 'I've no idea. I don't know anything about life out here.'

'It wouldn't hurt to talk to the people he knew, would it?' said Guy.

'But on what pretext?' asked Ben sensibly. 'Introduce Libby and Fran as private investigators? Hardly.'

'No – as the people who found the body!' said Libby triumphantly. 'Nobody would question that!'

'I don't know.' Neal looked down at the table. 'Seems a bit –'

'Intrusive,' suggested Ben. 'I know.'

A silence fell.

'Neal!' A new voice called from outside the bar. Neal looked up and smiled.

'Well, that solves that problem,' he said, standing up. 'Justin, come in. Have a drink.'

Everyone turned round. A tall, dark-haired man in a checked shirt and light trousers, a sweater thrown over his shoulders, hesitated outside.

'Please,' said Harry, also standing. 'Come in and have a drink.'

Neal Parnham moved round the table to take the newcomer's elbow and guide him to a chair.

'Justin, these are my fellow guests here at Jimmy's. They found the body this afternoon.'

'Libby Sarjeant.' Libby held out her hand. 'And we can't keep saying "the body". Who was the poor man?'

'Alec Wilson.' Justin shook her hand looking bewildered. 'Um …'

'Beer?' asked Neal. 'Anyone else?'

Ben and Guy went with him to the bar.

'I'm sorry if we've come as a bit of a shock. I'm Fran

17

Wolfe. That's my husband Guy, the one with the beard.' Fran smiled her gentle smile.

'Harry Price.' Harry stuck out a hand. 'And this is Peter Parker.'

The three men looked at one another and Libby realised that they'd recognised something in each other. Which, in turn made her look across at Neal Parnham at the bar. Harry followed her gaze.

'Didn't you realise?' Harry said with a grin. 'Getting slow on the uptake, petal.'

'I don't see why it should matter,' said Libby, somewhat huffily.

'I do,' said Peter. 'There could be another community under investigation here, as well as the ex-pats. And that might be even worse.'

Neal, Ben, and Guy arrived back at the table with drinks.

'Pete thinks there might be more at stake here than just the ex-pats,' said Harry bluntly. 'I agree with him.'

Neal and Justin exchanged worried looks, then Justin looked round at the company.

'I'm not sure I know who you are, or why you're interested. Neal says you found Alec's body – '

'Believe it or not, these two …' Neal paused, then indicated Libby and Fran, '*ladies* are real life Miss Marples.'

'Oh, please,' said Libby, disgusted.

Fran looked amused, shrugged and picked up her glass.

Justin looked at Peter. 'You think the gay community might come under suspicion?'

Ben and Guy looked surprised.

'Don't you?' Peter raised an eyebrow. 'I gather Alec was gay, too?'

Justin nodded.

'Did the Jandarma come to see you see you earlier?' asked Harry.

'Yes.' Justin glanced at Neal, who blushed.

'Sorry.'

'Couldn't be helped.' Justin turned to Libby. 'Do you know

18

how they knew who he was?'

'Yes, we do,' said Ben. 'He had a bag tied to his belt with his passport inside. We saw his picture. That was how Neal recognised him.'

Justin nodded. 'And they knew he lived here?'

'Neal told them he'd met him with you,' said Harry.

'Yes.' Justin turned back to Fran and Libby. 'Do you think there's something going on?'

'Well, he was murdered,' said Libby. 'Fran and I weren't sure that the Jandarma are equipped to tackle an investigation in the English – or rather, the ex-pat community.'

'You're right there.' Justin's mouth quirked up at the corner. 'They'll have to get someone from Kumlucca – and they haven't even got a mortuary.'

'Will they repatriate his body?' asked Fran.

'I wouldn't have thought so.'

'What about forensics?' asked Libby.

'Oh, they've got a regional crime laboratory.'

'They'll send the body there, then?' said Guy.

'If they can be persuaded to.' Justin sighed. 'The local Jandarma aren't used to dealing with this sort of thing, and as you know, over here, the bodies are buried as soon as possible.'

'They can't do that!' Libby burst out. 'Without any examination?'

'The consulate in Antalya,' said Justin. 'That would be where to start.'

'Had he any family in England?' asked Fran. 'They would be the people to ask, surely.'

'Well, now,' said Justin slowly. 'That's just the problem. He didn't have, but now, it seems, he has.'

Chapter Four

'What do you mean? Now he has?' asked Harry.

Libby looked across at him anxiously. It wasn't so long ago that Harry had found out about his own background.

'He was adopted,' Justin explained, 'and recently his birth mother found him.'

Peter, Libby, Fran, Ben, and Guy all looked at Harry.

'Yes, all right,' he said. 'I can relate to that. Something similar happened to me. So what did he do? Did he meet her?'

'Yes, he flew to England.'

'And what happened next?' asked Libby. 'Are they keeping in touch? Were there any brothers or sisters? What about the father?'

Justin looked taken aback. 'I don't really know. He didn't talk about it much.'

Neal frowned. 'Isn't that a bit odd? If he told you about her in the first place?'

'Maybe.' Now Justin was looking uncomfortable. 'But I wasn't that close to him, you know. Martha and Ismet were his best friends, really, apart from Sally. The Jandarma are going to talk to them, too.'

Libby looked round at her friends, who all shook their heads.

'You want to talk to them, too,' said Neal, watching her.

Libby felt heat rising up her neck and into her cheeks.

'I don't see how that's going to help,' said Justin. 'This lady doesn't know any of us, and didn't know Alec.'

'But now you know he has family in England, they ought to be contacted,' said Fran. 'Will the Jandarma do that?'

'I don't know.' Justin's expression had reverted to bewildered. 'Only if someone tells them about the mother, I suppose.'

'Well,' said Libby, 'someone ought to. He'll have told someone her name, surely?'

'Maybe Martha,' said Justin. 'He didn't have a partner, so there was no one close.'

'You ought to ask Martha to tell the Jandarma if she knows,' said Neal.

'And someone ought to tell the consulate in Antalya,' said Ben. 'And none of us can really do that.'

'Why don't you ring this Martha and talk to her now?' said Libby. 'I'm sure if the consulate knows about it, they could intervene if they thought the Jandarma wasn't investigating properly.'

'Do you really think so?' Justin looked round the table and shook his head. 'I only came down here to have a word with Neal.'

'I think they're right, though,' said Neal. 'Could you call Martha now?'

Justin finished his beer, set the glass down and took out a mobile. 'OK. Here goes.' He stood up and walked away from the table, and Libby, strain though she might, could overhear none of the subsequent conversation.

'I wonder what investigations they're actually making?' said Fran, staring thoughtfully out into the darkness.

'How do you mean?' asked Libby.

'How did the body get there, for a start. It had to be by boat.'

'And was he dead before he got there,' said Libby.

'Libby, it doesn't matter. It's not your problem.' Peter frowned over the rim of his glass.

Libby looked over to where Justin had wandered right down on to the beach. 'He's taking a long time.'

'Probably having to explain why a party of English tourists have got involved with people they don't know,' said Ben.

'I wish I hadn't got involved,' muttered Neal. 'I should never have recognised his photograph. After all, they already knew who he was.'

'I expect it was an automatic reaction – you know – "Oh,

yes, I've met him" – before you have time to think it through,'
said Libby.

'And it was your duty,' said Fran.

'What even out here? Neal doesn't even know the man,' said
Harry. 'It's not as if his saying he didn't know would have
hindered the Jandarma. They'd have questioned everyone in the
village anyway.'

'But they wouldn't necessarily have known he came from
here, unless he'd written his address in his passport. I never do,'
said Libby.

Justin came back to the table and stood, looking agitated,
beside it. 'Martha said the Jandarma have already seen her and
Ismet. She suggested the British Consul, but apparently the
Jandarma brushed it aside. She's going to ring them tomorrow.'

'All that man wants to do is bury the body and get on with
his life,' said Ben. 'I'm not normally in favour of sticking our
noses into places they don't belong, but that would be criminal
in itself.'

'But he'll want to solve it, won't he?' said Guy.

'I don't think they care much,' said Justin. 'I don't really
know – we get so little crime here.'

He jingled some coins in his pockets, staring out at the sea.
'Martha said – um – would you like to go up for coffee – or
something –'

'Yes,' interrupted Libby. 'We would. When?'

'Tomorrow? I don't think I can fit all you in the car ...'

'We'll get a cab,' said Libby. 'Where do we go and what
time?'

'Martha said about eleven. Before the lunchtime customers
start coming in. It's just called Martha's Place, on the river.'

'Oh, one of the river restaurants?' said Peter. 'We wanted to
try them.'

'Will you be there?' asked Harry.

'I suppose so.' Justin looked glum. 'Neal?'

'Do I need to?' Neal sounded nervous.

'I think so,' said Libby. 'After all, it was you –'

'Yes, all right, all right.' Neal stood up. 'And now I'm going to bed. I'll see you all down here at breakfast.'

He strode off, his rather long face longer than ever.

'I'll go too,' said Justin, pulling car keys out of his pocket. 'Er – nice to ɪeet you … ' He trailed off, gave a brief nod and disappeared into the night.

'Well!' said Libby, looking round at her friends. 'That was illuminating.'

'It was?' said Guy.

'Well, yes. We know who the body was, all about his mother trying to find him and that he's got friends in the village.'

'Some of whom are very uncomfortable,' said Fran.

'Who?' said Ben.

'Neal and Justin. They really don't want anything to do with it, do they?'

'No,' said Libby slowly. 'I wonder why.'

'We can walk,' said Neal Parnham the following morning. 'It's just at the other end of the bay and up the river road.'

'How far?' asked Libby. 'It's very hot.'

'And no shade along the bay,' said Fran.

'It takes me about half an hour,' said Neal, 'but I suppose it is hot. I'll walk and you can share a taxi.' He gave them a quick smile and loped off, Panama tilted forward.

'I'll go and ask Jimmy to book a taxi,' said Guy.

'He didn't want to come with us in the first place,' said Libby, as they waited in the shade of the bar.

'No. Do you think he'll turn up?' asked Fran.

'Debatable,' said Ben with a shrug. 'It doesn't really matter if he doesn't.'

'Of course it does!' said Libby.

'Not really,' said Peter. 'He didn't know the man. He's on holiday like us, this Alec Wilson was a casual acquaintance.'

'How casual?' said Harry. 'Could it have been …?'

'Sex? Possibly. I don't see that it matters,' said Peter.

'Here's the taxi,' said Guy.

Further along the bay, where there were no hotels or bars, just beach, sea, and mountains that ran down to the road, they passed Neal, striding along, head down. They waved, he looked up and lifted a hand.

'Not that overjoyed to see us,' said Ben.

'At least he's going in the right direction,' said Fran.

Martha's Place, the middle one of three restaurants on the shallow river that ran through the village, was reached by a bridge that looked a lot more unstable than it actually was. Trees lined both banks and shaded the tables that were set on pontoons in the water, attended by ducks and the occasional goose. Below them against the bank sat a row of köşks, the covered Turkish outdoor seating areas. Justin was waiting for them on the other side of the bridge at the head of the steps that led to the pontoons, a comfortable-looking middle-aged woman with plaited grey hair by his side.

'This is Martha,' said Justin.

'Hello,' said Martha, beaming at them. 'Come on down and let's get you something to drink. What would you all like?'

A small waiter was sent scurrying to procure coffee all round, and Martha led them to a table in the middle of the river.

'This is wonderful,' said Libby, gazing round. 'I've never seen anything quite like it.'

'Beautiful, isn't it?' agreed Martha. 'We're very lucky.'

'Have you been here long?' asked Guy. 'Only I was told that there was only one river restaurant when I came to the bay some years ago.'

'Yes, we were the first.'

'And you knew Alec Wilson,' prompted Fran.

The beaming face fell. 'We did. I can't believe ... any of this.'

'We felt the Jandarma weren't really concerned to look into the death properly,' said Ben. 'About his mother, for instance.'

Martha's face lightened. 'I've spoken to the consulate in Antalya this morning, and they are going to intervene. I don't think the locals were even going to do an autopsy.'

'But he was drowned, is there any point?'' said Harry.

'You know better than that, Hal,' said Peter. 'They need to know if he was dead before he went into the water.'

'And he must have been,' said Libby. 'No one could have tied that bag to his waist if he'd been alive – or conscious.'

'Do you know anything about his mother?' asked Fran. 'She ought to be told.'

'He never even told me her name,' said Martha sadly, shaking her head. 'He told me she'd found him, and that was all.'

Everyone except Martha looked at Harry, who smiled.

'They're all worried about me,' he explained. 'I found out about my childhood only last year, so it's a bit close to home.'

'Oh.' Martha looked mildly confused, but the moment passed with arrival of the small waiter and the coffee. 'English coffee,' she said. 'Not Turkish. Ismet likes the Turkish, but I can't stand it.'

'What did the consulate say about finding his mother?' asked Fran.

'They said there must be some evidence in his house, but they didn't know if it had been searched properly.' She shook her head again. 'Ismet says he's pretty sure it wouldn't have been.'

'What about how he got out to that cave?' said Guy. 'Someone with a boat must have taken him out there.'

'Alec had a boat himself, but the Jandarma said it was still beached.'

'Someone would have heard an engine though, don't you think?' said Guy.

'I doubt it. Unless they lived right by the water's edge. And a boat taken out at night wouldn't have gone from the part of the beach by the hotels.' Martha sighed. 'It must have been a local. Nobody else would have known where to get a boat, or how to take it round the headland.'

'Or how to get a body down to the boat,' said Libby.

'Unless the body was still alive when it got into the boat,' said Ben.

26

Chapter Five

They all looked at him in surprise.

'You mean he took himself out there?' said Libby.

'Why not?'

'But why on earth would he take a boat out at night with someone else?' asked Harry.

'To show them something? Is there anything around you could only see at night?'

'I don't think so,' said Martha doubtfully. 'They go night fishing sometimes, but I don't remember Alec ever doing it.' She looked up and waved. 'Here's Neal, look. Alec did show him around a bit, I think.'

Neal came down the steps to the pontoon, panama hat in hand. He bent to kiss Martha on both cheeks.

'We were just wondering, Neal,' said Martha, 'if Alec would have taken his boat out at night. Do you think he would?'

'I don't know. I never went out on his boat.' Neal pulled out a chair and sat down. 'I ordered coffee on my way down. I hope you don't mind.'

'Martha's been in touch with the consulate,' said Justin. 'They're going to intercede with the Jandarma. They need to trace Alec's new-found family.'

'They need to search his house, then,' said Neal. 'He didn't tell anyone the names of these people?'

'No. Unless he told Sally,' said Martha. 'She might know.'

'Somebody mentioned her last night,' said Libby.

'Where does she live?' asked Fran.

'Outside the village on the way to the coast road. I could ring her.' Martha stood up. 'I'll go and find her number.'

While they waited for Martha to return, they studied the menu which had been left on the table and decided to stay for lunch.

'No reply, so I've left a message,' said Martha, coming back to the table. 'Did you want to eat?'

After orders had been taken, and Neal had declined, he stood up again. 'I'm going back to the hotel. I'll see you all later.'

They watched him cross the bridge in silence.

'Well, now.' Libby sat back in her chair. 'Why did he bother to walk all this way, stay for five minutes, and go again? His behaviour really is peculiar.'

'I think the whole thing has knocked him for six,' said Peter. 'It looks to me as though he and this Alec were having an affair.'

'You could hardly call it that,' said Harry. 'He was here on holiday. It was a holiday fling if anything.'

'What do you think, Justin?' Libby turned to look at him. 'You introduced them, didn't you?'

Justin nodded.

'So did they see more of each other after that?'

'Yes, but I don't know anything more than that. Alec took Neal out a few times, but just to show him the country, really.'

'That's what it was, then,' said Libby confidently. 'An affair.'

During lunch the lady with the pink hair and her bushy-moustached husband arrived at restaurant. They stopped on the steps leading to the pontoon.

'I can't get down there,' said Bushy Moustache. 'Damn silly place for a restaurant.'

'We can sit here, then, look.' Pink Hair indicated a table on the same level as the steps. 'Then you won't have to use the steps.' She looked over and waved at the rest of the hotel contingent. 'Hello, there!'

They all waved back.

'Thank goodness he doesn't like the steps,' muttered Libby. 'Otherwise they might have joined us.'

'He's too grumpy to want to join anyone,' said Harry. 'Have you noticed, if there's a conversation in the bar he just sits and stares off into the distance and has to have everything repeated?

He just doesn't take any notice.'

'I think he's probably a bit deaf,' said Fran. 'And doesn't want to admit it.'

'That's charitable,' said Libby. 'But is it enough to make him so grumpy? He doesn't like anything, does he? Have you seen the way he turns up his nose when he's offered something? He doesn't like fish because of the bones, he doesn't like shakshuka because of the texture, and sometimes he just takes one look at a menu and says there's nothing there he could eat.'

'And yet they've been here before.' Peter shook his head. 'Makes you wonder. Why don't they just go and stay in Bournemouth?'

'Poor old Bournemouth,' said Guy.

'What exactly is shakshuka?' asked Ben.

'Aubergine, pepper, tomato, and potato, basically,' said Harry. 'Didn't you try it the other evening when Jimmy put out all the mezze?'

'No.' Ben looked sheepish. 'I'm as bad as him. I didn't fancy the look of it.'

'It's gorgeous,' said Libby, dreamily.

'I'm going to put it on the menu at home,' said Harry. 'They've said they'll teach me back at the hotel.'

Martha appeared beside the table with a tray. 'All finished?'

'Yes, thank you,' said Libby. 'Do you do shakshuka, too? Harry's going to learn it from the hotel.'

'Yes, we do it. You'll find several different versions of it out here, and of course, in other Middle Eastern countries it's served with poached eggs in the middle.'

'Really?' Harry looked interested. 'I'll have to look into that.'

'That and Alec's murder?' Martha looked amused. 'You will be busy!'

After they'd declined any more to eat and drink, and Martha had refused to take any payment, she promised to let them know at the hotel if she heard back from Sally Weston.

'I'm sure if Alec had told anyone about his long-lost family, he'd have told her,' she told them. 'They'd known each other ever since she first came out here, and were very close. Weren't they?' She turned to Justin, who'd been remarkably quiet during the meal.

'Yes.' He looked uncomfortable.

'What?' asked Libby. 'Don't you like her?'

Colour crept into Justin's cheeks. 'Yes, of course. I just thought … well, I thought they were a little too close.'

Martha's eyes widened. 'Don't be stupid, Justin! Alec was gay!'

Ben sensed Libby's immediate interest and trod on her foot.

Justin shrugged.

'Wouldn't be the first time that's happened,' commented Harry. Peter and Libby looked at him sharply, and Libby realised that Peter must know about Harry's foray into heterosexual sex, as she did.

'We must go,' said Fran, forever the calming influence. 'Thank you so much for lunch, Martha. And for the information. If we can find out about Alec's mother in England, perhaps we could go and see her when we go home.'

'I suppose it was England?' said Libby suddenly. 'She could have been from anywhere!'

'No.' Justin shook his head. 'I told you, remember? He flew to England to meet her.'

'But that could have been a sort of halfway house.' Libby was just warming up.

'Don't theorise ahead of the facts,' said Ben. 'Goodbye, Martha.' He held out his hand.

They crossed the bridge, leaving Justin behind with Martha. Pink Hair and Bushy Moustache had long gone, and it was only when they reached the other side they realised they hadn't ordered a taxi to take them back to the hotel.

'We'll just have to walk,' said Peter. 'Come on.'

'And that little shop down there sells hats, I bet,' said Guy. 'We'll all need one.'

Libby groaned.

The little shop did, indeed, sell a variety of hats, and supplied with mock panamas, baseball caps, and floppy straw numbers according to taste, they began the walk home.

'What do we think, then?' asked Harry as they turned on to the beach road. 'Was Alec Wilson murdered? And if so, was it because he was gay?'

'We don't know enough about him,' said Libby. 'He'd obviously lived here a long time, because he was already here when this Sally Weston arrived, and that was – what did they say? –ten years ago? And although Justin knew him, he obviously wasn't that close.'

'We need to meet the rest of the ex-pat community,' said Libby, taking off her new hat and fanning her face with it. 'How do we do that?'

'Libby!' protested five voices in chorus.

'Oh, come on, you're all as interested as I am. Poor bugger's dead, with only the local cops to investigate, who have no knowledge of British procedures –'

'Or sensibilities,' put in Fran.

'And somewhere in England – or elsewhere – there's some poor woman who's lost a son she's only just found. I think we owe it to her, if not to Alec.'

'I think you're over-justifying yourself, petal,' said Harry.

'I agree, though, Hal,' said Fran. 'And no one we've met here so far seems to have any knowledge of his English roots or family. We're the only ones.'

'And we didn't even know him,' said Peter.

'I know, I know,' said Libby, 'but we can talk to people who did, like Martha and Justin.'

'Who didn't seem to know much about him,' said Ben.

'But this Sally did,' said Libby excitedly. 'I bet she knows all about him. And if he had any enemies out here. I do hope Martha gets in touch with her soon.'

Twenty minutes later they arrived back at the hotel and Libby threw herself on to a sunbed. Jimmy waved from the back of the restaurant.

'Message!' he called.

Libby sat up.

Ben went over to Jimmy, then turned and gave Libby the

thumbs up.

'That looks as if Martha got hold of Sally.' Fran perched next to her friend.

Ben came back and sat on the end of another sunbed. 'Sally called Martha. Apparently she was a bit surprised, but she's happy to talk to you and she's given us her number.'

'Excellent.' Libby beamed. 'And now I'm going to have a swim.'

It was later in the afternoon on her way back to her room that Libby asked Jimmy if she could borrow the phone to ring Sally Weston. There was no reply.

'You should have done it when Jimmy gave us the message,' said Fran. 'She's obviously gone out again.'

'I'll try again when we come down for dinner,' said Libby. 'She can't always be out.'

But there was still no reply when they gathered in the bar for a pre-prandial drink.

'She's probably gone out to dinner now,' said Harry.

'So frustrating not having a mobile number,' said Libby.

'We managed to live without them for years,' Ben reminded her.

'But we don't now and we've got used to having them,' said Libby. 'We keep missing Sally because we can only use the phone when we come down here and ask Jimmy's permission.'

Just then Pink Hair and Bushy Moustache arrived in the bar.

'Hello!' Pink Hair gave them a little wave. 'Did you enjoy your lunch?'

'Very much,' said Peter. 'It's a lovely place, isn't it?'

'Beautiful. It must be nice to sit down there almost in the water,' said Pink Hair wistfully.

Peter turned to Bushy Moustache. 'I'm sorry you couldn't manage it down to the pontoon.'

Bushy Moustache grunted.

'Did you enjoy the food, though?' persisted Peter.

'Wasn't really anything there I liked.' Bushy Moustache waved at Jimmy's young assistant. 'Beer.'

Peter sighed and turned back to his friends. 'I don't know

why she puts up with him.'

Greta and Tom were next into the bar.

'Any news?' asked Tom as they waited to be served.

'Not really,' said Guy. 'No one seems to know anything about the poor man. We're waiting to hear from Sally Weston.'

'I said she'd know,' said Greta. 'You haven't spoken to her yet?'

'No,' said Libby. 'We went to see Martha today and she's spoken to Sally, but every time we ring she's not there.'

'Busy lady,' said Tom with a grin. 'Doesn't she teach a class somewhere in the evenings?'

'Oh, yes – jewellery or something?'

'English cookery,' called Pink Hair from across the room.

'Oh, that's right.' Greta smiled at the elderly woman. 'She teaches the hotel and restaurant chefs how to make roast beef and Yorkshire pud.'

'But we don't come out here to eat English food!' said Harry. 'We want proper Turkish stuff.'

'You might,' came the muttered grunt from the corner. They all turned to look at Bushy Moustache, but before anyone could reply, Jimmy hurried into the bar.

'Libby, Martha is on the phone for you.'

'Martha?' Libby was surprised. 'Oh, OK.'

She followed Jimmy into his tiny office and picked up the receiver.

'Hello? This is Libby.'

'Oh, Libby!' Martha sounded agitated. 'You'll never believe this. Sally's been murdered.'

Chapter Six

'Apparently,' Libby reported to the assembled guests in the bar, 'the Jandarma went to question her about Alec Wilson and found her.'

'When?' asked Ben.

'I don't know – this evening, I suppose.'

'She was still alive when she spoke to Martha – when?' Fran looked round at her friends.

'While we were on our way back here,' said Guy.

'It's got to be connected,' said Libby.

Greta shook her head. 'Poor Sally. I liked her.'

'She could be a bit much,' said Tom.

'In what way?' asked Fran.

'She was what Tom would call a ball-breaker,' said Greta, pulling a face. 'That doesn't go down too well in Turkey.'

'I've seen some formidable women out here,' said Peter. 'I'd say they rule the roost.'

'Within the family,' said Tom.

'Ah, family.' Jimmy came up behind the bar, shaking his head. 'Sally, she had no family.'

'So she was a bit independent?' asked Libby.

'Did it all on her own,' said Greta. 'Didn't need a man.'

'Course she bloody did,' came a growl from the corner. 'Stupid woman.'

Everyone in the bar turned to Bushy Moustache in surprise. Pink Hair sighed and rolled her eyes.

'He calls it "old world gallantry",' she said. 'I call it flirting.'

Bushy Moustache's face had turned almost purple. 'I will not sit here ...' he began, pushing his chair back.

'Fine,' said Pink Hair. 'I shall join –' she looked across at Libby's group, 'my friends.'

Bushy Moustache, stumbling a little, left the bar. Pink Hair stood up with a sigh and moved across to Libby's table. 'I'm sorry about that.'

'No, no, sit down,' said Libby, accompanied by murmurs of agreement. 'Libby Sarjeant.' She held out her hand.

'Betty Roberts. That's my husband, Walter.' Betty shook Libby's hand and then everyone else's, including Greta's and Tom's. 'I'm sorry about him. He's been getting worse and worse as he gets older. He still thinks a woman's place is in the kitchen and that a woman on her own is only looking for a man. And it's his place to help her along.' She shook her head. 'He tried it on with Sally and she put him in his place.'

'You were there?' asked Fran in astonishment.

'Oh, yes. He never cares about me. He never gets anywhere anyway, so it doesn't really matter.'

'Can I get you a drink?' asked Harry, standing up abruptly. Libby realised that he was moved by this stoic woman.

'I'd love a beer!' said Betty. 'He doesn't approve of me drinking beer.'

'Forgive me,' said Peter, leaning forward, 'but how do you put up with him?'

Betty laughed. 'Habit, I suppose. And where else would I go? I'm far too old to start again, and he'd never cope on his own.'

'Have you got children?'

'Yes.' Betty's face fell. 'They don't get on with him, so I hardly see them. My daughter always invites me for Christmas and birthdays, but she won't have him, so I don't go either.'

Libby's stomach clenched in sympathy. What an awful life this woman led.

Harry came back and put the glass of beer down in front of Betty and laid a hand on her arm. 'Enjoy.'

She smiled up at him. 'Thank you.'

'So you knew Sally, too?' asked Libby, attempting to put the conversation into less emotional waters.

'We met her a few years ago. One of the other restaurant owners invited all Jimmy's guests to a party to meet some of the locals. I thought she was lovely.'

'So did I,' said Greta, 'but she was obviously different with men.'

'Except Alec,' said Fran.

'But he was gay,' said Harry. 'That makes a difference.' He grinned at Libby and leant over to pat her arm. 'Doesn't it, my old trout?'

'He's right,' said Libby, avoiding Betty's wide-eyed astonishment. 'Justin knew her, too.'

'I'm hungry,' announced Harry suddenly. 'Are we eating here?'

'We didn't tell Jimmy we were,' said Guy, 'so he won't be prepared for us.'

'Do you know The Red Bar?' Betty asked diffidently.

Everyone looked at each other.

'No.'

'I've heard of it,' said Tom, frowning.

'It's at the other end of the village. I went there last year with one of the other guests here. Walter wouldn't go. It was lovely.'

'If we go there, will you come with us?' asked Fran.

Betty looked as if she'd been given a present. 'I'd love to.'

In the end, they all went: Harry and Peter either side of Betty, who had an arm linked through each of theirs, Greta with Fran and Libby and Tom deep in conversation with Guy and Ben. The beach road petered out into a dirt track, the beach on their left and scrubby vegetation leading to the foothills of the mountains on their right. As the headland loomed towards them though the dark, a small, lighted building came into view, with red neon lighting announcing The Red Bar.

They ate outside under a trellis of vines; simple grilled fish, caught that day, pide, the wonderful Turkish flatbread, and chopped mixed salad that only the Turkish seemed to be able to do. The family who owned the bar cooked, served, and ran around between the tables. The baby was brought out to meet

37

them, and Betty remembered from last year.

'And how is your friend? Joan, was it?' asked the handsome young man who appeared to be head of the family.

'How you can remember!' marvelled Betty. 'Yes, Joan. We only met out here. She was on her own so we palled up. We've kept in touch by email, but she couldn't make it this year.'

'A pity.' The young man turned to the others. 'And these are your new friends?'

Betty introduced them and he shook hands formally with each of them. 'And do you know anyone else here?'

The friends looked at each other awkwardly.

'Well, not as such,' Libby said eventually. 'We've met some people ...'

'They're the people who found the body at sea,' said Betty.

'Oh?' The young man suddenly sounded serious. 'Alec.'

'Yes.' Libby cleared her throat. 'And we – Martha and us, actually – were trying to find out about his British family. And then we were going to talk to Sally Weston.'

'British family? I didn't know he had one.'

'He'd only just found them, apparently,' said Fran. 'You knew him and Sally, then?'

The young man looked at her sharply. 'I knew Alec, yes, and I know Sally. She is a favourite with the children.'

The others exchanged glances. It was Betty who spoke in the end.

'I'm afraid Sally's dead, too.'

The young man seemed unable to speak. At last, he turned and called over his shoulder to his wife, who hurried forward with a bottle of red wine. He gestured for her to take a seat and pulled up a chair himself.

'You don't mind?' he said. Everyone shook their heads, and he offered wine all round.

'I am sorry,' he said, putting a hand on his wife's arm. 'Sally was a dear friend.' he spoke briefly to his wife, who promptly burst into tears and ran back to the kitchen.

'I'm sorry, too.' Libby felt wretched. 'I wish we hadn't had to tell you.'

He pulled himself up straight. 'We would have heard. Can you tell me anything else?'

Between them, they related the events of the last couple of days.

'Betty didn't tell us your name,' Libby finished up.

'I am Mahmud.' The young man bowed his head. 'And my wife – I must apologise for her – is Almas. Sally was very kind to her.'

'She had no enemies here, then,' said Guy.

'None. We all liked her, although she could be – ' he paused, frowning. 'I do not know the word.'

'Sharp?' suggested Libby.

'Prickly?' from Harry.

'Like a schoolmistress,' Mahmud came up with eventually. 'Alec was her special friend. I did not know him so well. But they came here a lot. We are one of the only restaurants open in the winter.'

'You know Justin, too, then?' said Ben.

'Yes. He comes with them sometimes, or with another friend. They are quite – ' he paused again, frowning. 'Quite close, the English.'

'The English who live here?' suggested Peter.

Mahmud nodded. 'Do you know Geoff and Christine?'

They all shook their heads except Betty.

'They own the Istanbul Palace,' she said.

'What's that?' asked Libby.

'A hotel. It stands on its own on the way to the river,' said Mahmud.

'I remember seeing it,' said Guy. 'I didn't realise it was a hotel. It doesn't have any signs outside.'

'No.' Mahmud shook his head. 'I don't know why. But it also stays open all year, and the English go there a lot. They will all be very shocked. I must telephone.' He stood and bowed to them all. 'Please – this meal is – what do you say? You must not pay.'

'On the house,' said Libby, 'but we must pay. We brought you bad news, not good. We shall pay.'

With the dispute amicably settled, the group finished the last of Mahmud's wine and left, with promises to come back.

'So Geoff and Christine's hotel is a sort of local for the expats?' said Libby, as they walked back to Jimmy's.

'Seems to be,' said Greta, 'but I don't think everyone gets on with them. We've only been up there once because someone suggested the food was good, but we didn't care for it, did we, Tom?'

'There were quite a few Brits up there, and the food seemed to be mainly English. They seemed a bit cliquey.'

'Hmm. Could be motives up there, then,' said Libby.

'We can ask Martha. We're going to see her again in the morning, aren't we?' said Fran.

When they arrived back at the hotel, they asked Betty to join them for a nightcap, but she refused. 'I might as well go and make peace with Walter,' she said, 'or else my life won't be worth living.' And she trotted off quite cheerily.

'Fortitude, that's what she's got,' said Harry. 'Great old girl.'

They were all surprised to find Justin and Neal sitting at the bar staring morosely into their glasses.

'Hello!' said Ben. 'Where have you been all day? Have you heard the news?'

'About Sally?' said Justin. 'Yes.'

'Did you manage to speak to her?' asked Neal.

'No. Martha did, though.' said Harry.

'When? This afternoon?' asked Justin. 'That will help them narrow down the time of death, won't it?'

'If they look into it that closely,' said Peter. 'No one seems to have any faith in the Jandarma.'

'But Martha said the Antalyan consulate was going to look into it, didn't she?' said Fran. 'Now with two Brits dead – murdered – they'll have to act.'

'This is awful,' Neal suddenly burst out. 'It almost seems as though it's my fault. I only came out here for a bit of peace and quiet, and now ...' He looked ready to cry.

'Don't be silly,' said Libby, patting his shoulder. 'You know

40

it's not your fault. Just because it happened while you were here – it could have happened any time.'

'But I'd met him.' Neal turned tragic eyes on Justin. 'And I seem to have set the police on to Justin and all their other friends.'

Justin looked uncomfortable. 'Nonsense,' he muttered.

'I suppose they'll go and question Geoff and Christine, too, won't they?' said Libby.

Justin now looked surprised. 'Do you know them?'

'No, but Greta and Tom have been there, and Mahmud at The Red Bar was telling us about them. It seems like a sort of local for you ex-pats.'

Justin pulled a face. 'Not for everyone. We don't get on.'

'Oh?' Libby glanced at Fran, eyebrows raised. 'Did Alec get on with them?'

'No. We weren't particularly welcome there.'

'Ah.' Peter exchanged glances with Harry. 'I don't think we'll be going there, then.'

'Just Fran and me, then,' said Libby, 'after we've seen Martha. Now, who wants a drink?'

Chapter Seven

Before the sun rose too high in the sky, Libby and Fran walked along the bay towards the river and Martha's restaurant.

'That must be the Istanbul Palace,' said Fran, pointing to an attractive red-roofed cream building set on its own amid acres of uncultivated vegetation. 'No signage at all.'

'Odd, isn't it?' said Libby. 'I wonder how you get to it? There's no entry from here.'

Martha answered the question for them as they sat sipping iced tea on the terrace above the restaurant.

'There's a turning off this road. You'll pass it on your right as you go back to the beach road. Very discreet little sign. It's almost as if they don't want any trade.'

'You don't like Geoff and Christine?' asked Libby, noticing Martha's expression.

'Oh, I don't mind them. They're just a bit – well, snobby, I suppose.'

'Snobby?' Fran's eyebrows lifted in surprise. 'I thought out here it would be exactly the opposite in an ex-pat community. A classless society.'

'Anything but,' said Martha with a laugh. 'Geoff is supposed to be ex-military and from a posh background and Christine is an ex-model. They think they're better than most of the rest of us.'

'They would have known Sally and Alec, though?'

'*Knew* them, yes,' said Martha with a sniff. 'I don't think they were on visiting terms.'

'Ah. We got that impression,' said Libby. 'Homophobic, are they?'

'They would say no, of course. But yes. They are. And many of their so-called friends are, too.'

43

'So there's a divided society out here? I mean, we've met Justin and you, and heard about Sally and Alec, and Mahmud at The Red Bar said they used to go there. There must be a whole other set of ex-pats we don't know about.'

Martha nodded. 'Except that they're all like Geoff and Christine, so unlikely to know anything about Alec's death – or Sally's.' She sighed. 'I can't believe it, you know. Sally was such a good person.'

'Mahmud said she was a family favourite,' said Fran. 'His wife was upset.'

'She would be. Sally babysat for them, taught the little ones English and played games with them. And they liked Alec, too. He was good with the children.'

'So it could be someone from the other group who had it in from them,' said Libby. 'Doesn't that seem likely?'

'I can't see how,' said Martha. 'If they don't have anything to do with them why would they kill them?'

'I think you can cut out extreme homophobia, Lib,' said Fran. 'And anyway, Sally wasn't gay, was she?'

'No, definitely not.' Martha smiled sadly. 'She frightened some men, but they all quite fancied her. Even my Ismet.'

'So what's happened with the consulate?' asked Libby after a moment. 'Have they traced Alec's mother?'

'No. They've been really helpful, and apparently they've managed to get the police – or whoever it is – to investigate more thoroughly, especially now Sally's dead. They saw the connection immediately. They have traced his flight back to England, but there's no joy there. He flew into Gatwick back in March, and flew back here ten days later. But where he was in between is anyone's guess.'

'They think Sally was killed because she knew something?' said Libby.

'I suppose. They were friends and were killed within two days of each other. Must be.'

'The mother. That's the reason,' said Fran. 'Alec told Sally about his mother.'

'But why would anyone want to keep that secret?' said

44

Martha, looking bewildered. 'I know he didn't tell any of us, but I expect it was because he was a private sort of person. I don't think he could have been going to make a thing of it.'

'Well, I still think it's worth us going to meet Geoff and Christine,' said Libby. 'Can you just go in for a drink?'

'You can, although they'd be surprised,' said Martha with a smile. 'It's usually only their regulars in the bar. They'll be open now.'

'Regulars is what we like,' said Libby with satisfaction. 'We'll keep you posted, Martha.'

'And I'll tell you if I hear anything from the consulate or the Jandarma. Or whoever's in charge now.' Martha stood up and waved away the offer of payment for their tea.

Libby and Fran crossed the bridge and wandered down the track towards the branch road. Sure enough, soon, on their right appeared two very new-looking pale stone walls, curving into a smooth drive. On one of the walls a small plaque announced 'Istanbul Palace. Hotel, restaurant and bar.'

'This is it, then,' said Libby. 'Come on, let's have a look at them.'

'Are you sure this is a good idea?' asked Fran, following her friend onto the drive, either side of which were planted night scented Melissa shrubs.

'We're just going for a drink. Holidaymakers do visit lots of different bars.'

'But why are we going?'

'To check them out, of course. I want to see what it is that divides opinion so much. And if there's any suggestion of a motive.'

'You're not just being nosy?'

Libby turned and grinned at her friend. 'Of course I am. It's what I do best.'

There were shallow steps running the length of the building when they reached it, leading to a covered terrace where several people sat at tables. Libby started up the steps. Immediately, a short, round man with a bald head and a cheerful expression appeared.

'Hello! Welcome to the Palace,' he called.

'Well, thank you,' said Libby. 'We've only come for a drink.'

He held out his hand as Libby reached the terrace.

'Geoff Croker, pleased to meet you.'

'Libby.' Libby took the proffered hand. 'And this is Fran.'

Geoff shook hands with Fran. 'Come along in then. Bar's in here.'

He led the way inside to a cool marble floored room where comfortable chairs were place around small tables. Fran and Libby exchanged glances behind his back.

'Now, ladies, what'll you have?' Geoff sidled behind the imposing polished bar.

'Two beers, please,' said Libby. 'Nice place you've got here.'

'Yes.' Geoff looked round the bar complacently. 'We like it.' He placed two frosted glasses on the bar and began to pour the beer. 'So what brings you here?'

'We were exploring,' said Fran, before Libby could speak and put her foot in it. 'We saw the building from the beach road –' she waved a vague hand '– and when we walked up here we saw the sign. We guessed it was the same place.'

'Ah.' Geoff pushed the glasses towards them. 'I only asked because we don't get many people coming in for drinks, only our guests who are staying here.'

'And the locals,' said Libby.

Geoff looked at her sharply. 'Locals?'

'Someone said this is the place to meet the locals.' Libby smiled, charmingly, she hoped.

'Really? Now who would that be?' Geoff's 'mine host' smile had stayed in place, but his eyes had narrowed.

'Mahmud at The Red Bar,' said Fran. 'We had dinner there last night.'

'Ah, Mahmud.' Geoff appeared to relax, and Libby wondered whom he'd expected them to name. 'Good food. Nice little family.'

'Yes. He was telling me Sally Weston was a good friend of

46

theirs,' she said.

Geoff's face froze again. 'Sally?'

'You did know, didn't you?' Libby covered her mouth with her hand and hoped she looked shocked. 'Oh, I'm so sorry ...'

'Oh – yes. Of course. Terrible thing. Poor old Sally.' Geoff's smile had gone now. 'Didn't know her well, of course.'

'Oh, really? I thought you would have done. Mahmud said all the ex-pats come here.' Fran sipped her beer and stared at him over the rim of her glass.

'Er – no. Well, not all of them. All know each other of course,' he added hastily. 'Sally had her own crowd.'

'Who don't come here? Oh, that's sad,' said Libby.

'Yes, well, each to their own.' Geoff's smile tried to come back but didn't quite make it.

A door opened at the far end of the room and a tall, blonde woman walked in. Libby instinctively took a dislike to her. Geoff greeted her with relief.

'My wife, Christine,' he said proudly. 'These ladies dropped in for a drink, Chris.'

As the woman approached, Libby was irresistibly reminded of a young woman she'd encountered in a supermarket car park back home. The woman had parked her huge American-style cruiser in a disabled parking bay. Her make-up and over-the-top clothes had been more suitable for nightclubbing than a trip to the supermarket, and her spoiled little girl had danced around irritating the other shoppers.

Christine Croker could have been her older sister.

She slid onto a bar stool next to Libby, crossing her legs and showing off her bejewelled high-heeled sandals, which revealed her toenails, each one a triumph of the pedicurist's art. She nodded at the women.

'Where are you staying?' Geoff held a lighter out to his wife as she put a cigarette to her glossy lips. Libby tore her fascinated gaze away.

'Where? Oh – Jimmy's,' she said.

Christine lifted her eyes to meet her husband's.

'Nice little place,' said Geoff.

47

Libby and Fran picked up their glasses and retreated to a table on the terrace.

'They knew who we were,' whispered Libby, once they were seated as far away from the bar as possible.

'He was just too quick off the mark, wasn't he?' Fran let her eyes drift across the terrace to where Geoff and his wife now stood with a group of people, all of them looking serious.

'So what's the problem?' Libby leant back in her chair. 'Have they got something to do with the murders? And if so – why? Even if this is a little outpost of homophobia, they surely wouldn't kill someone because of that.'

'I think they're just worried. If they didn't get on with either of the victims, it could bring the police knocking at their doors.'

'Well, it would in England, but it doesn't look as though the Jandarma would bother,' said Libby.

'I wonder if the consulate has had any joy in prodding them into action? I had a look on the tablet this morning and consulates and embassies don't actually have the power to intervene in local court cases or investigations.'

'But if the government – our government – decides it should help, they can send people over, can't they?' said Libby. 'They've done that before.'

'I suppose they might. Now it's two deaths.'

A head popped up over the balustrade and smiled at them.

'Quite right. And that's just what they've done. Johnny Smith, at your service.'

Chapter Eight

Libby and Fran just gaped.

'Sorry if I startled you.' The man followed his head up the steps and came round to their table. 'You are Libby and Fran, aren't you?'

The both nodded, still staring.

'May I sit down?'

Libby nodded again.

'I'd better explain, hadn't I?'

'Yes, please. How did you know who we were or that we'd be here? And why?' Libby had found her voice.

'Your friend Martha –' he jerked a thumb over his shoulder '– got in touch with the consulate in Antalya, didn't she? And it just so happens I'm spending a few weeks in Antalya and I have a friend on the staff. I come every year, so everyone knows me and they've asked me to have a quick look into things – not officially, you understand, but with the co-operation of the local Jandarma – as the two victims were both British nationals. I went to see Martha, and she told me something about you two and your friends and told me you were coming here. And as I came up the steps I heard you talking. So, no great detective work there.'

'Oh, I see.' Libby smiled at Fran. 'And there we were, thinking we could sort it all out. I'm Libby Sarjeant, by the way, and this is my friend, Fran Wolfe.'

'Pleased to meet you,' said Johnny Smith, extending a hand to each of them.

'How did the consulate persuade the Jandarma to give you their co-operation?' asked Fran.

Johnny's wide smile almost split his face in half. 'Because I was part of a team that came out here to train them years ago. I've kept my links. I'm actually staying with a rather senior member of the force in Antalya. Lucky, huh?'

'What a coincidence,' said Libby.

'Don't knock it. Coincidences happen far more in real life than they ever do in films or books.' He stood up. 'I'm going to get a beer. Would either of you like anything?'

They both refused, and watched as he made his way to the bar. Medium height, rather shabby shorts and shirt, with grizzled grey hair and a bit of a paunch, he looked like any other middle-aged man on holiday.

'I wonder what he trained them in?' murmured Libby.

'Let's hope it was detection,' whispered Fran.

'Right.' He returned to the table with a bottle and glass. 'Now, Martha tells me you have a bit of a reputation. Care to tell me?'

Libby cast an anguished glance at her friend.

'I don't know that you'll approve,' said Fran calmly, 'but we've been involved in a few cases in England. Strictly unofficially, of course.'

Shrewd grey eyes surveyed her. 'I expect I could find out if you don't want to tell me.'

'You're actually still in the police force?' asked Libby.

'Oh, yes.'

'Not the Met, though?'

'I didn't say that, did I?' He laughed and carefully poured his beer into the glass. 'Yes, still with the Met. So, as I said, I expect I could find out …'

'Oh, we'll tell you,' said Libby. 'You see it all began …'

Over the next twenty minutes they related the bare bones of some of their adventures.

'You've been lucky,' said Johnny Smith when they'd finished. 'I know forces who would have kicked your butts long before now.'

'Which is why we haven't said much about our wonderful local police.' Fran took a sip from her glass and looked away.

'Tell me,' said Johnny, after a moment. 'Is there a reason

50

you get involved? Are you used as specialists in some area?'

Libby looked quickly at Fran, opened her mouth, and closed it again.

'No,' said Fran coolly.

Johnny grunted and finished his beer. 'Right. Tell me what you've found out about these murders.'

'We haven't found anything out,' said Libby. 'But we were there when the first body was discovered.'

'By the way,' said Fran, still cool, 'we only have your word for it that you're who you say you are.'

The wide smile broke out again. 'I wondered how long it would take you.' He pulled a wallet out of his shorts pocket. 'Here. And I've got a letter from the consulate, but it's in Turkish.'

Fran picked up the wallet and held it open for Libby to see. They both gasped. Commander J D Smith was shown in uniform, looking a good deal smarter than he did slouching in the chair opposite.

'Sorry.' Libby felt herself flushing.

'What for? Not asking?' He laughed. 'Well, now we're straight. What can you tell me?'

They told him everything, from finding Alec Wilson's body and Neal Parnham's recognition of him, to their suspicion that Geoff and Christine Croker knew who they were.

'Hmm. Homophobia rife, then, is it?' Johnny leant back in his chair and scratched his chin. 'Lot of it at home, still, but mostly undercover.'

'Yes, we've come across it,' said Libby. 'Two of the friends we're on holiday with have had to deal with it personally and professionally.'

'They part of the community here?'

'Oh, no, but they recognised immediately that this Neal was gay, and that was how – we think – he got to know the victim.'

'And the other man who came to see him, Justin,' said Fran. 'And the second victim was close to the first victim. We don't think she was gay, though. And by all accounts the regulars here don't – or didn't – like any of them.'

51

'Not a reason for murder though.'

'No,' said Libby. 'But the main thing we were concerned with was finding this mother he'd only just found out about. Except no one seems to know.'

'And of course, the idiots haven't searched her place or his.' Johnny frowned. 'So we'll have to do it.'

'*Us*?' Two shocked voices rose as one.

'Oh, I expect we'll have to have a frowning bobby looking on, but they don't know how to search properly. I was hoping they'd let us have one of their Crime Scene Investigation teams – they've got 'em, you know – but we're not important enough, it seems. So it'll be us.'

'But we don't know how to search, either,' protested Libby.

'Now, don't tell me you wouldn't welcome the chance to get on the inside of the investigation?' He grinned at them both and stood up. 'Now I've got to go and present my credentials at the local cop shop. I'll ring your hotel to tell you what I've set up, shall I? Got the number?'

'No, but there aren't many here,' said Libby. 'It's Jimmy's. The Jandarma will know.'

'Right, ladies. I'll see you later.' He waved over his shoulder and set off down the steps.

'Well, he's not my idea of a commander of the Metropolitan Police,' said Libby.

'But he is one,' said Fran, 'and we're very privileged. Came up through the ranks, do you suppose?'

'Do they still do that? Don't they all have to have degrees and things these days?'

'Not when he joined the force, I should think. He must be sixty.'

'Then he'd have retired, surely.'

Fran frowned. 'I'm not sure. Ian could tell us.'

'But Ian's not here, and I'm certainly not going to phone him.'

DCI Ian Connell was the police officer in England who had facilitated the friends' involvement in various murder cases, sometimes for the reason Fran had chosen not to reveal to

Commander Smith – that she was a reluctant psychic.

'We can go now, can't we?' Fran stood up. 'Sitting here knowing those people are talking about us isn't pleasant.'

'Are they, though?' said Libby.

'Of course they are. We said we thought they knew who we were, and now we've had a strange man come and join us, we're the subject of all sorts of speculation. Lucky we can get down the steps here instead of having to go through them all.'

Libby followed her down the stairs, resisting the urge to look back at the group at the other end of the terrace.

'Odd, though,' she panted as she tried to catch up. 'This isn't a tourist hotspot by any means, but they do have summer visitors. Why did they assume we were who we are? If you know what I mean.'

Fran looked back at her and grinned. 'Well, once we'd mentioned "the locals" and Sally, it was a pretty foregone conclusion, wasn't it?'

Libby pulled a face. 'You mean once *I'd* mentioned it.'

'He was suspicious as soon as we appeared. He said himself they don't get many casual visitors, and if they all knew about Alec's and Sally's deaths and the British tourists who found Alec it would be a good guess. And we – or you, all right – confirmed it for him. There's something they know that we don't, but I don't think Geoff or his constructed Christine are murderers.'

Libby giggled. 'Constructed Christine! I like that. She was, wasn't she? I wonder what attracted her to bumptious Geoff?'

'Money,' said Fran.

'But out here? She's more Marbella than remote Turkish village.'

'Escaping something?' suggested Fran. 'In which case that could be the reason they're a closed community.'

Libby gasped. 'You mean like the Costa del Crime?'

'Don't they say ex-pats are often trying to escape something?'

'Yes – the weather, usually,' said Libby.

'Alec Wilson himself might have been trying to escape

something.' Fran stopped and looked at Libby.

'And whatever it was caught up with him?' Libby stopped too. 'Actually, that makes more sense than anything else.'

'I expect Commander Smith will look into his background,' said Fran, resuming her now slower pace down the drive, 'which the local force would never have done.'

'Do you think it's more likely to be someone or something from his past than something or someone from here?'

'It's as likely, anyway,' said Fran. 'I expect our Johnny will look into it.'

Back at Jimmy's they joined the others for lunch and brought them up to date on the morning's happenings.

'So now we've got a high-ranking British police officer involved,' said Ben. 'I don't know how you do it.'

'It wasn't us!' said Libby indignantly. 'It was the consulate.'

'And they felt it was necessary because?' asked Peter.

'The local force wouldn't have looked into his background, and we knew he's been in touch with his long lost mum, so we need to find her,' said Libby.

'Nothing to do with nosing out a murderer?' said Harry.

'The consulate want him to do that, of course,' said Fran, refusing to be roused.

'And he's actually asked you to help search the victims' houses?' Peter sounded incredulous.

'He says the Jandarma wouldn't do it properly.' Libby was defensive. 'And they wouldn't know if they found anything because they can't read English.'

'There is that,' said Guy. 'Did you tell him about your previous adventures?'

'Yes. Martha had already told him a bit,' said Fran, 'although I don't know why.'

'Because we were investigating,' said Libby. 'It was very sensible of her.'

'Because now you can be as nosy as you like,' said Ben.

'All right, all right.' Libby sighed. 'Don't forget you're all just as interested. Where's Betty? We ought to tell her. She took us to Mahmud's place.'

'Greta and Tom dragged her off to the village,' said Harry. 'Walter refused to go and is sulking down by the pool.'

Libby peered. 'So he is. I don't know how she puts up with it. He doesn't seem to like anything.'

'I went over and asked him if he'd like to join us for lunch, but he said no, he didn't eat lunch.' Peter shook his head. 'Which is a lie. We've seen him.'

'Oh, forget about him. We'll probably see Betty and Greta and Tom later. We'll tell them then.' Fran pushed back her chair. 'I'm going to lie on a sunbed, have a swim, and then a cup of tea.'

'Unless we're summoned, of course,' said Libby at exactly the same time as Jimmy called out from his office.

'Libby! Fran! There's a Mr Smith on the phone for you.'

Chapter Nine

'I'll pick you up in ten minutes. That OK?'

'Now?' said Libby. 'We are on holiday, Mr Smith.'

'But you were already asking questions, weren't you. So why not come along and give me a hand.'

Libby sighed and looked at Fran, who nodded. 'All right. But not too long, please.'

She handed the phone back to Jimmy. 'Thanks. We'll see you later.'

They went back to where the other four were carefully positioning sunbeds.

'We're off,' said Fran. 'Not really sure we're doing the right thing. Ian would never let us get this involved.'

'But this bloke is doing it more-or-less as an individual,' said Harry. 'He's not part of the police force.'

'That makes it worse,' said Fran. 'But at least he's a British police officer.'

'But not a Turkish one. It all seems very shambolic to me,' said Libby, 'but I suppose we might be able to help.'

Johnny Smith arrived in a silver hire car a few minutes later.

'Alec Wilson's first,' he said after they'd both climbed in to the back seat. 'See if we can find anything about this mother.'

'We were also wondering if he was running from something when he moved out here,' said Fran.

'Like that bunch at the Istanbul Palace,' said Johnny with a nod.

Libby gasped. 'You thought that, too?'

He turned and looked at her, swerving on the dusty road. 'Of course. I reckon we'd find something in the backgrounds of all those ex-pats.'

They were driving towards the village, past villas in varying states of completion or disintegration.

'Just up here.' Johnny slowed the car and peered to the left. 'There. See, between those two houses.'

Libby and Fran saw, in a gap between two matching villas, a smaller one almost set into the hillside.

'How do we get to it?' asked Fran.

'There's a drive, they said,' he muttered. 'Here.'

The drive was simply a gap between the two matching villas and the one next to them. It led to the side of Alec Wilson's villa, which was small and unpretentious. Johnny led them to a covered porch and unlocked the front door.

'No police tape,' said Libby.

Johnny smiled over his shoulder. 'No.'

Fran was following unwillingly. 'What's up?' whispered Libby.

'We shouldn't be doing this.'

Libby stopped and looked at her. Fran nodded.

'Is it the house?'

Fran shook her head.

'Is it him?'

Fran nodded. Libby let out a breath. 'Ah.'

Johnny was now at the top of the stairs that led to the main living area.

'Johnny, shouldn't we wait for one of the Jandarma to come?' Libby called. 'You said we'd have one of them overseeing us.'

Johnny's face appeared over the half-wall at the top of the stairs. 'They didn't much care.'

Libby walked up slowly. 'I can't help thinking we shouldn't be doing this. Not without some proper authorisation.'

'The Jandarma are fine with it.' He shook the keys in her face. 'They wouldn't have given me these, would they?'

Libby looked over her shoulder. Fran was still at the bottom of the stairs.

'Fran's not happy about this,' she said to Johnny.

He narrowed his eyes at her. 'I don't believe in all that sort of thing, you know.'

Libby was shocked into silence.

Fran came up the stairs to stand beside her.

'And how did you know?' she asked.

'You think I didn't make enquiries?' He chuckled. 'I must say, your DCI Connell is very protective of you.'

'You spoke to Ian?' Libby's voice came out as a squeak.

'Of course. I don't take people on trust, even if you do.' He folded his arms and surveyed them both. 'Although you're good to be cautious even if it is a bit late. So why are you,' he pointed at Fran, 'worried? Think I've got an agenda?'

'Yes,' said Fran.

He raised his eyebrows. 'Well, that's blunt. What is it?'

'I don't know,' said Fran. 'I just wondered why you're taking such an interest when you're not officially involved.'

'A favour, I told you. You wanted it investigated, didn't you?'

'We wanted to find his mother,' said Libby. 'And you haven't got any resources.'

'We've got our eyes.' Johnny turned back into the room and pulled on a pair of disposable gloves and held out two more pairs for Libby to take.

'Well?' she whispered to Fran, who shrugged.

'We'll go along with it, but keep an eye on him.' Fran pulled on the gloves. 'Don't let him take anything away.'

Alec Wilson's home was sparsely furnished and very tidy. Johnny had found a drawer full of bills and official documents, including his resident's permit, in the single bedroom, but apart from that there was nothing to give any sort of clue to either his personality or his relationships.

'It's as though he didn't want to exist,' said Fran, riffling through the few books on a shelf beside the television.

'Does anyone know what he did for a living?' Libby was taking china out of a cupboard in the kitchen area. 'Was there a computer?'

'No.' Johnny wandered back into the living room frowning. 'But there's what looks like a charger lead for a laptop. So either the Jandarma have taken it – which is what we would do

59

at home – or it's been stolen.'

'You know,' said Libby, 'his passport was in a little bag tied round his waist when he was found. What about a mobile?'

Johnny looked blank. 'No one's told me about a mobile.'

'Don't you think you ought to check with them?' asked Fran. 'They might have the computer and the mobile phone.'

'And if they have, why didn't they tell you when you went to get the keys?' said Libby.

Johnny stayed silent.

'So what exactly did you tell them?' asked Fran. 'Not the truth, apparently.'

'I showed them my Met ID and the letter from my friend in Antalya. They just handed them over.' He sighed and sat down heavily on the edge of a couch.

'And why did you really want to come?' Fran sat down opposite him. 'In the interests of a murdered British citizen?'

'Yes.' He looked surprised. 'Of course.'

'But that's not all?'

'I'd rather keep that quiet, if you don't mind.' He stood up again. 'Find anything?'

'No, nothing. Fishing equipment downstairs in the lobby along with scuba stuff,' said Libby.

'I'll check out the computer and mobile.' Johnny started for the stairs. 'Coming to see Sally Weston's house?'

Sally Weston's lovely villa with its own pool was more productive, although nothing they found in the way of letters was useful. Her computer was password protected, and there was no mobile phone in evidence. She'd been found by the pool, Johnny told them, and there had obviously been no time for the killer to search the upstairs living room before the alarm was raised.

'But she wasn't found until the evening,' said Libby. 'Was she killed during the day?'

'I don't know,' said Johnny, 'but it seems odd that the killer would leave possible evidence behind unless he or she was scared off.'

'Or just didn't have time,' said Fran.

'What do you mean?' asked Libby.

'If the killer had to be somewhere else – had to meet someone, perhaps.'

'To provide an alibi,' suggested Johnny. 'Yeah, that's good. Come on, you ladies have another look through her bedroom and then we'll get you back to your hotel.'

'I don't like this,' said Libby, riffling desultorily through a drawer in the bedside table a few minutes later. 'She was on the pill.'

'I thought she was older than that,' said Fran.

'Obviously not.' Libby picked up a framed photograph. 'See – this is her.'

A blonde woman smiled out at them, her arm round the shoulders of a slight, prematurely grey-haired man.

'I wonder if that's her with Alec Wilson,' said Fran. 'There were no photos in his house, were there?'

'No, but it looks as if that was a much more planned killing, doesn't it? Taking the body out to sea and going back to clean up?' Libby sat on the bed and tapped her chin with the photograph. 'Whereas this was a panicky murder. Which means that Sally definitely had some kind of knowledge the killer didn't want made public.'

'Like who he or she was,' said Johnny, coming into the room. 'Find anything?'

Libby held out the photograph. 'Is that Alec Wilson?'

'No idea. There were no photographs at his house, were there?'

'Haven't you seen the body?' asked Fran.

Johnny looked startled. 'No. But you have.'

'Not really to look at. It was face down, anyway.' Libby shuddered. 'Vile. So you don't know what he looks like?'

'No.'

'From his passport photograph?' said Fran. 'The Jandarma showed it to us.'

'Then can't you say if that's him?' Johnny was frowning.

'No,' said Libby and Fran together.

'Are there other photographs?'

'Not in here. Probably somewhere, though.' Libby stood up. 'Let's have another look.'

Finally, Fran came across a shoebox tucked into a cupboard in the kitchen, but it was obvious that the photographs were at least ten years old.

'No one takes ordinary photos any more,' said Libby. 'They're all on phones.'

'But often transferred to computer,' said Johnny. 'I'll take hers with me.'

He dropped them back at the hotel in time to find the rest of the guests preparing to return to their rooms for tea and showers.

'Anything?' asked Ben.

'Fran's suspicious of him,' said Libby.

'And he does have some kind of agenda,' said Fran with a sigh. 'He virtually admitted it.'

'And he's taken Sally Weston's computer,' added Libby.

'Are you sure his Met ID was genuine?' asked Peter.

'It certainly looked it,' said Fran, 'and if it wasn't, how did he know about Martha's enquiry to the consulate and how did he get the keys from the Jandarma?'

Harry was staring at the sky. 'You said he was a commander?'

'Yes.' Libby turned to look at him.

'In the Met they have commanders in charge of different sections of the force,' said Harry. 'I wonder which section he's in charge of?'

They were all silent, looking at him.

'Are you thinking spies?' said Ben eventually. 'Or whatever that would be called today?'

'It occurred to me that maybe the British authorities knew he was here. That's why there's suddenly a senior Met policeman on the scene only a couple of days after he died.'

There was a further silence.

'It fits,' said Fran at last. 'But why would he involve us?'

'Partly to see what you knew,' said Harry. 'After all, he went straight to Martha, didn't he? She told him about you

62

two – and us – and then he went hotfoot after you. *And* he's spoken to Ian. He's got lines of communication we could only dream of.'

'Why did he ask us to go with him this afternoon, then?' asked Libby.

'Camouflage,' said Fran.

'Eh?'

'Two English tourists he could ask about the deaths,' said Ben.

'Except we didn't know them,' said Libby.

'He probably thought it would look better than just one strange bloke going into other people's houses,' said Harry.

'How do you know so much about it, anyway?' asked Guy.

'I lived in London, didn't I? On the streets, some of the time.' Harry picked up his towel. 'Right, I'm off to the shower. Coming, Pete?'

'He could be right,' said Libby, watching Peter and Harry stroll off down the path to their room.

'If he is, I doubt if we'll find out anything more about it,' said Fran. 'He's used us for whatever reason, and that will be it.'

'How infuriating.' Libby shouldered her basket. 'Do you think he'll talk to Justin and Neal?'

'If he's really investigating, yes, I would think so.' Fran began to walk down the path after Peter and Harry. 'He'll have got a list of people from the Jandarma, won't he?'

'If Neal comes into the bar tonight you can ask him,' said Ben. 'Now, come along woman and make me a cup of tea!'

But there was no sign of Neal Parnham when they assembled in the bar that evening. Betty and Walter were sitting with Greta and Tom, although Walter didn't look as if he was enjoying himself very much.

'Have you heard any more?' Greta called over to them.

'No,' said Libby and Fran together, having decided there was no point in relating their adventures of today.

'We were wondering if you felt strong enough to go out on a boat trip again?' said Betty. 'I'm dying to go, but Walter isn't keen.'

'Surprise, surprise,' muttered Ben.

'I don't like the fish,' said Walter.

Everyone stared at him. 'It's the bones,' he said and shifted awkwardly in his seat.

'You don't have to have fish,' said Fran. 'You can always ask for something else. Were you thinking of going with Captain Joe?'

'Yes,' said Tom. 'He's said he's free.'

'All right,' said Libby, looking round at her friends. 'I think it's about time we got back on the horse, don't you?'

Chapter Ten

'Do you suppose we're waiting for more passengers?' asked Fran the following morning, as the *Paradise* bobbed gently at its moorings. 'It's nearly half past ten.'

'I hope we aren't waiting for that one,' said Libby, squinting along the beach.

Fran turned to look. 'Oh, no.'

But Johnny Smith had raised a hand to them and beaming, approached the gangplank.

'Just wanted to have a look at where you found the body,' he said. 'No need to explain that to the other passengers, though, eh?' he winked and moved along to the fo'c'sle.

'Is he going to leave us alone?' asked Libby, watching as he nodded a greeting to those already established on mattresses. 'I'm going to stay here out of his way.'

'Wouldn't we be better with the others? Then he couldn't talk to us,' said Fran. 'They're up on top.'

'As long as Joe puts the shade up,' said Libby, getting to her feet and making for the ladder to the top deck.

But Johnny Smith didn't come near them. They heard him talking to Captain Joe, but the *Paradise* chugged on past the little island and the cave where Alec Wilson's body had been found. Nobody dared to discuss recent events in case he could overhear them, so they spent a relaxed day sunbathing and reading. At lunchtime Joe served up the customary grilled fish, rice-stuffed peppers, and onions, salad, and the inevitable chips, and Johnny sat with a couple whom the hotel contingent didn't know. Walter had been left behind, and Betty was thoroughly enjoying herself. She was even persuaded into the water when they reached Turkuvaz, one of the more sheltered bays where the water was shallow enough to wade ashore, and as turquoise as its name.

Libby was pottering along the shoreline looking for shells when a voice spoke behind her.

'Had any more thoughts, then, Libby?'

She turned and looked at Johnny Smith. 'About Alec Wilson? No. I didn't know him.'

'Or Sally Weston?'

'I didn't know her either. We never met either of them, I told you. Have you had her computer analysed?'

'It's gone to the lab. And we have no mobile for her or for Wilson, so we're up a gum tree.'

Libby frowned at him. 'I bet you're not. And Fran and I don't want to get any more involved, either.'

'Fine.' He shrugged. 'Now, tell me, the bloke who recognised Wilson's picture. He's at your hotel isn't he? But not on the boat?'

'No. He's friends with people in the village. He doesn't do tourist things.'

'What was his name?'

'Why do you want it?' asked Libby, feeling uncomfortable.

'He might have known Wilson. He might have confided in him.'

'He only met him in the last couple of weeks,' said Libby.

'So?' Johnny shrugged again. 'Who are his friends?'

'Look, I've said – we don't want to get involved. All we wanted to do was find his poor mother.' Libby was getting annoyed now.

'OK.' He smiled and stuck his hands in his pockets. 'Somebody'll tell me.'

Libby looked up and waved as Ben started down the gangplank into the water. 'I'm sure someone will,' she said to Johnny and went to meet Ben.

'He's still poking around,' she told the others, when Joe had started the boat's engine for the homeward journey. 'I wouldn't give him Neal's or Justin's names.'

'Surely he'd have been able to get them from the Jandarma,'

said Guy. 'He's just testing.'

'Well, it's making me cross,' said Libby.

When they arrived back at the bay in the late afternoon, Johnny Smith was the first off the boat, striding away in the direction of the village.

'Good riddance,' said Libby. 'Let's hope he doesn't come back.'

That evening they were surprised to be joined by Neal Parnham and Justin.

'Thought it was about time I treated Justin to dinner here,' said Neal, with a pale smile. 'He's been feeding me for the last few days.'

Libby opened her mouth to ask him if he'd seen Johnny Smith. Ben dug her in the ribs and Fran trod on her foot under the table. She glared indignantly at them.

'We went to The Red Bar the other night and met Mahmud,' said Peter. 'He said you often went there.'

Libby couldn't remember if Mahmud had said that or not, but she accepted the gambit as a possible way into the conversation she really wanted.

'You took me there, didn't you?' Neal asked Justin.

'Yes, last week. Nice little place and not touristy.' Justin carried two beers to the table. 'May we join you?'

'Of course,' said Ben, shifting his chair.

'But nowhere here is really touristy, is it?' said Harry. 'Not like Bodrum or Dalaman.'

'Nowhere catering solely for English or German tourists,' put in Libby hopefully.

'I thought you'd been to the Istanbul Palace?' said Justin.

'Er – yes.' Libby's eyes slid sideways to meet Fran's. 'Who told you?'

'Martha, of course.' Justin sounded surprised. 'She said that Johnny Smith went to find you there.'

'He did.' Libby sighed.

'He's spoken to you then?' said Fran. 'What did you make of him?'

'I was puzzled,' said Neal. 'He's supposed to come from the

Met, but how did he get here so quickly simply for a couple of unknown British nationals?'

'He told us he was on holiday with a friend who is some high-up in the Jandarma,' said Libby. 'What did he tell you?'

'Nothing,' said Justin.

'Wait a sec,' said Libby. 'When did you see him?'

'Yesterday evening,' said Justin. 'Why?'

'Because he asked me for your names today. I didn't give them to him.'

'And he already knew,' said Neal, frowning. 'What's he playing at?'

'Trying to find out if anyone knew anything more than appears on the surface, I should think,' said Ben.

'Is he more interested in Alec Wilson than Sally whats'ername?' asked Harry. 'If so, that's significant, isn't it?'

'How?' asked Justin.

'Something must be – as they say – *known* about him.'

'You mean known to the police?' Neal's eyes were wide. 'Do you mean he was a criminal?'

'Not necessarily,' said Guy.

'But that would explain his murder, surely?' said Neal.

'But if he was a criminal who had fled here from Britain, it would mean someone had come over here to find him.' Harry looked round the group with a gleeful grin. 'So it could be any one of us!'

There was a chorus of amused approval for this statement.

Jimmy helpfully directed a couple of his 'boys' to put several tables together, so all the guests could dine together. Betty forced the recalcitrant Walter to sit at the end of the table, where he faced away from everyone and pretended not to hear if anyone spoke to him, and she was able to join in the general conversation. Which, of course, revolved around the murders. Fran and Libby said nothing about helping to search the victims' properties, but joined in the speculation about the involvement of Commander Johnny Smith.

'You actually saw his ID?' said Greta, awestruck. 'A real commander?'

'That's what it said,' agreed Fran.

'Don't you believe him?' said Betty from the end of the table.

'He's definitely got connections,' said Libby. 'He was on to the UK about us as soon as he met us.'

'So was this man a criminal?' asked Tom.

'That's what I said.' Neal nodded.

'What did he do for a living?' asked Libby suddenly. Everyone turned to Justin.

'I don't think he did anything,' said Justin, looking bewildered. 'I just assumed he had some kind of private income – or he'd retired early.'

'How old was he, then?' asked Harry.

'I don't know exactly.' Justin was frowning. 'In his fifties, I suppose.'

'I thought he was younger,' said Neal. 'Late forties?'

'And he's been here ten years?' said Libby.

'Oh, more than that,' said Justin. 'He was here before me and Sally.'

'Then he was probably in his thirties when he arrived. A bit early for retirement,' said Ben.

'Did he never mention a job? Anything?' said Fran.

'No, none of us did,' said Justin.

'What do you do?' Peter fixed him with a gimlet eye.

Libby was interested to see the sudden colour rush in to Justin's face. 'I – er – well, nothing much. I do odd jobs for people.'

The image of Justin with a hammer and nails didn't fit with Libby. 'What sort of odd jobs?'

'Accountancy,' said Neal. 'That's what you said, didn't you?'

'Ah,' said Libby. 'But you didn't do anything for Alec?'

'No.' Justin's colour was receding. 'And what does that have to do with anything?'

'Trying to work out how he made his living. He must have had private money, as you said.' Libby turned her attention to her plate.

Conversation became more general, and eventually even Neal began to open up and smile. At last only the six friends were left in the bar.

'That was illuminating,' said Libby, watching Justin's back disappearing along the beach road.

'What was?' asked Harry.

'The fact that no one here has a job.'

'No one?' repeated Guy.

'The ex-pats, I mean. Justin, Alec, and Sally.'

'Sally gave cookery lessons, didn't someone say?' said Peter.

'Well, Alec and Justin, then.'

'And Justin does "odd jobs" for people,' said Fran.

'Fiddling their books for them, I would think, wouldn't you?' said Libby. 'I suppose he has private money, too.'

'Does he fiddle the books for that crowd up at the Istanbul Palace?' said Harry. 'You reckon they're all criminals.'

'I think they've all run away from something. It needn't be criminal. Johnny Smith thought so, too.'

'He probably knows,' said Ben.

'Well,' said Harry, 'I think Alec Wilson was a spy.'

'Here?' Libby was incredulous. 'What on earth would he be spying on here?'

'He was just waiting to be activated,' said Harry. 'Betcha.'

'I don't suppose we'll ever know,' said Ben. 'I can't see your friend the commander telling you any more about the case, unless he thinks he has a use for you.'

'He won't now,' said Libby. 'I refused to give him Neal's name and it turned out he already knew. He must realise by now that we don't know anything.'

And so it appeared. Neither Commander Smith nor the Jandarma were seen on or near the beach or the hotel. Neal reported that Justin had seen the Commander briefly in the village, but days went by and the whole subject of the murders was, if not forgotten, no longer discussed.

On Neal Parnham's last night, he bought his fellow guests a drink at the bar.

'Quite an eventful holiday,' he said, raising his glass. 'Cheers.'

'And we still haven't got any answers,' said Libby.

'Justin's promised to email me and let me know if anything happens.'

'Martha's said the same to us,' said Libby, 'although it looks as though there won't be anything.'

'And we don't even know if they found his mother,' said Neal. 'That's sad.'

'We did our best,' said Fran. And they all agreed.

Chapter Eleven

Kent was enjoying a perfect late June. Libby was glad to be back home, reunited with Sidney the silver tabby, who had been on holiday at the Manor with Ben's mother Hetty, and Fran was back in Coastguard Cottage in Nethergate with its view of the sea, Balzac the cat in his usual place on the window seat. Things were back to normal.

But Libby was troubled. None of the investigations in which she and Fran had been involved had ever fizzled out into nothing as this one had, and with no prospect of them ever finding anything further. All she had to look forward to was organising the summer show for The Alexandria, Nethergate's restored Victorian theatre. Since The Oast's company had been invited to fill a gap in the summer season a few years ago, it had become a regular feature, visitors to the little town flocking to see the old fashioned end-of-the-pier style entertainment.

The Oast Theatre, owned by Ben and his mother and converted by Ben in his former life as an architect, was run by Ben, Libby, and Peter, Ben's cousin. They had a fluid company of players, some amateur, some professional, the theatre played host to one-nighters, both comedy and musical, small visiting theatrical productions, and their own hugely popular pantomime each year. Pantomime and music hall being closely allied in their Victorian and Edwardian traditions, the regular pantomime performers were only too happy to turn themselves into seaside entertainers for a few weeks in the summer. All Libby had to do was find the material. To take her mind off the unfinished business in Turkey, she called Susannah, her musical director.

'Come over,' said Susannah, 'and we'll go through some music.'

'Can I ask Fran to come, too?' asked Libby.

'Of course. I have cake.'

Susannah lived not far from her brother and sister-in-law, Terry and Jane Baker, in a lovely Art Deco house on top of the cliffs in Nethergate, with a view across the little town to the island and the lighthouse on the headland. It was Terry who had introduced Susannah to the Oast theatre, when Libby and Ben held a birthday party in the theatre for Hetty's birthday, and she had come to play for them.

Libby and Fran spent a happy hour in the lovely sitting room, where Susannah's grand piano stood in front of double doors that led out to the shallow steps leading to the terrace. Susannah had spread out a small forest of sheet music, and even found some online clips of the items in performance, so they quickly had almost too much material.

'Right, tea outside now,' said Susannah, 'then I'll chuck you out. I've got to pick up The Kid from school.'

'This is a beautiful house,' said Libby, when they were settled on the terrace.

'I know.' Susannah smiled smugly. 'It was so lucky that Emlyn and I got back together after The Kid was born. Neither of us could have afforded anything like this on our own. So tell me all about this thing that happened on holiday.'

Libby sighed. 'It was a bit of a disaster, really. Oh, not the holiday, that was lovely, but we didn't find anything out about the victims or anything.'

'What we really got annoyed about was that there was no attempt to trace the victim's mother,' said Fran.

'His mother? How do you mean?'

Fran explained the circumstances of the murders.

'Couldn't you look up his birth certificate?' asked Susannah, when she'd finished.

'We don't know how old he was or his birthday,' said Libby, 'and Alec Wilson's quite a common name. I bet there are thousands.'

'Anyway, it would have been replaced by an adoption certificate,' said Fran. 'And nobody but the adoptee themselves can apply for the details.'

'Than how did the mother find him?' asked Susannah.

'I expect she went to one of those specialist services,' said Libby. 'Or a television programme.'

'Not a TV programme,' said Fran. 'That would have been too public. And I'm sure they would have filmed him in Turkey, so everyone would have found out about it.'

'That's true. It's still odd that he didn't tell anyone about it.'

'He did, though. Justin knew about it, just not who she was. And we're pretty sure Sally Weston knew, aren't we?'

'If you're that concerned, have you tried googling him? Putting it out on social media?' suggested Susannah.

'"Do you know this man's mother?" sort of thing?' said Libby. 'I suppose we could.'

'And what about this man Smith. Was he genuine?'

Fran and Libby looked at each other. 'We think so. He actually got in touch with Ian to verify our credentials, if you can believe it,' said Fran.

'You mean your nice Inspector Connell?'

'Chief Detective Inspector, please!' said Libby with a grin. 'Yes, him. Actually, Fran, perhaps we ought to ask him what he knows about Smith.'

'I suppose we could,' said Fran slowly. 'In fact I'm surprised he hasn't been on to us already asking us what the hell we were doing.'

'Good idea!' Libby brightened. 'Let's do it now.'

'We'll go to my house,' said Fran. 'Susannah's got to do the school run.'

Libby gave Susannah a lift to the school gates on her way to Coastguard Cottage, and waved to Guy in his gallery/shop as she drove past. Fran had left the front door open, and Balzac drifted forward to meet her with a soundless miaow.

'Who's going to ring?' asked Libby, sitting down on the window seat with Balzac.

'Doing it.' Fran held out her phone. 'Personal first.' She returned the phone to her ear. 'Voicemail.'

She left her message and joined Libby on the window seat.

'I wonder when he'll pick it up?' said Libby. 'Should we call the work number?'

'No,' said Fran. 'This is personal, not work. And we don't know what he's involved with at the moment.'

'Hmm.' Libby thought for a moment. 'Sally Weston. I wish we knew more about her.'

'Maybe we could.' Fran stared at a corner of the ceiling. 'If Martha knows her birthday.'

'Yes!' Libby clapped her hands and frightened Balzac.

'I'm not calling her, though.' Fran stood up. 'Have you got her email address?'

'Yes.' Libby reached down for the basket. 'It's in my book. I got everyone's email addresses, even Betty's.'

Libby's book had once been rather a glamorous affair with a linen cover. It was now somewhat battered, having been carried round in various bags and baskets for several years, and had become a social documentary of the early twenty-first century.

Fran collected her laptop from the kitchen and Libby read out Martha's email address.

'Now we just have to wait. I don't suppose Martha checks her email very often.' Fran closed the laptop just as her phone began to ring.

'Ian,' she mouthed to Libby.

'Hello, Ian,' she said out loud. 'No, we just wanted to ask –'

After a moment of listening, she raised her eyebrows at Libby. 'Told off,' she mimed.

'All right – yes, she is. I'll ask.' She put her hand over the phone. 'Ian wants to know if you're going to the pub this evening.'

'Is it Wednesday?' said Libby in surprise. 'Oh, no it isn't. Still, I suppose we can.'

'Yes,' said Fran into the phone. 'Yes, all right, I'll come up as well, yes, and Guy. See you later.'

She ended the call and made a face. 'He didn't sound pleased.'

'But wants to talk to us. That's encouraging,' said Libby.

'Well, yes.' Fran frowned. 'And now I've committed Guy

76

and me to driving up to Steeple Martin tonight.'

'I expect Guy's been having withdrawal symptoms not having his mate to chat to,' said Libby with a grin.

'We've only been home a few days,' said Fran. 'I think he could survive a bit longer.'

'Why don't we see if Harry can fit us in at the caff?' suggested Libby. 'Then it'll make it worthwhile.'

Harry could indeed fit them in, and they met in The Pink Geranium a few hours later. Ben and Libby arrived to find Fran and Guy ensconced on the sofa in the left-hand window of the restaurant while they waited for their table.

'I had a reply from Martha,' said Fran, as Guy poured wine for the newcomers.

'You did? Why didn't you ring me?'

'Because I got it just before we left and I was going to see you in about twenty minutes,' said Fran. 'Honestly, Lib.'

'Oh, all right.' Libby settled back in her chair. 'What did it say?'

'Sally's birthday was the twenty-eighth of December and Martha thinks she was forty-three or four. She remembered her fortieth birthday party a few years ago, but wasn't sure.'

'And did we know if she'd been married? Was that her maiden name?'

'Libby!' came the chorus of three voices.

'Well, all right, I only wondered. We can try with what we have, I suppose. Or do you think we could ask Ian …?'

'No!' said the three voices.

Harry had introduced some new Turkish recipes to his menu, kindly donated by Jimmy's chef at the hotel, and the obliging Mahmud at The Red Bar, and he insisted that his guests try them.

'Lovely,' said Libby, finishing her shakshuka and mucvar, the courgette fritters so popular as mezze, 'but it doesn't taste the same, somehow.'

'That's because you're not eating outside in a temperature of thirty degrees,' said Harry, coming to see how they were enjoying his efforts. 'Acceptable, though?'

'Gorgeous, Hal,' said Fran. 'You haven't got baklava for dessert, have you?'

Harry looked smug. 'Oh yes I have.'

They were all suitably grateful.

'So Ian's coming to put you through the wringer?' Harry absently poured himself a glass of red wine from the bottle on the table. 'Do Pete and I get to come?'

'I don't see why not. We don't even know what time he's coming, but we assumed it would be after ten, as it usually is on Wednesdays,' said Ben.

Wednesday night was a regular meeting night in the Steeple Martin pub. The Oast theatre company often rehearsed on Wednesdays and would repair to the pub afterwards; their friend the Reverend Patti Pearson came over to see her friend Anne Douglas, have dinner with Harry, and then go to the pub, and Ian would drop in on his way home from the police station or whatever case he was working on. They'd never worked out exactly where he lived, and even after several years of friendship, he'd never told them.

'OK,' said Harry. 'Baklava all round?'

But to their surprise, when they arrived in the pub at nine thirty, Ian was already there talking to Peter, who hadn't joined them in the restaurant.

'Are we in for a telling off?' asked Libby, as they settled at the corner table by the fireplace. 'Because we didn't do anything, I promise.'

Ian smiled. 'Apart from getting mixed up in murder in a foreign country, you mean? Oh, no, nothing at all.'

'We couldn't help it, Ian,' said Ben gently. 'We all saw the body. We could hardly avoid it.'

'No I appreciate that,' said Ian. 'I was more concerned about what you did next.'

'We were told the victim had been traced by his birth mother and one of his friends called the consulate.' Libby eyed him warily. 'We met the friend.'

'And then surprise, surprise, up pops a commander of the Metropolitan Police all ready to coerce you into helping him.

78

And who actually managed to get in touch with me to make sure you were who you said you were. All of you, in fact.'

'All of us?' said Guy.

'Oh, yes. Alec Wilson was a false identity.'

Chapter Twelve

After a shocked silence Libby said, 'Do you mean he was in the witness protection scheme? Or he was a spy or something?'

'As far as I'm aware it was the witness protection scheme, but I'm not privy to all the information.' Ian sat back in his chair and sipped his coffee.

'Why?'

'What for?'

'What had he done?' The questions all came out at once.

'I can't tell you. Commander Smith didn't confide in me, but I had to provide as much information as I could about you all in case you knew Wilson's real identity.'

'Golly,' said Libby. 'So we really were suspects?'

'I doubt if you're off his radar even now,' said Ian, with a grin. 'He's actually got a team out there now investigating.'

Libby hit the table. 'And we missed it!'

'It wouldn't have been pleasant,' said Ian. 'I should imagine all the ex-pats out there are having their lives pulled apart.'

'We were under the impression that some of them were there to escape from something,' said Fran. 'We were right.'

'We don't know that,' said Guy. 'Only about Alec Wilson – and we never actually met him.'

'That lot at the Istanbul Palace were definitely escapees,' said Libby. 'Johnny thought so, too.'

'Johnny?' Ian looked amused. 'Commander Smith?'

'He introduced himself as Johnny,' said Fran. She looked round the circle uncomfortably. 'And I don't know whether you know, Ian, but he asked Libby and me to help search both victims' homes.'

Ian's eyebrows shot up. 'Did he, now. Why?'

'He had no other help at the time, and the Jandarma weren't really interested.'

'Nothing's appeared in the media about this,' said Guy. 'Usually if the British police go to assist in the overseas murder of a British national it's all over the place.'

'Not when the victim is virtually under police protection.' Ian looked round at them all. 'And the story of a mother finding him is extremely suspicious. How would a birth mother find him if he'd been provided with a completely new identity? His old one would simply vanish when the new one appeared.'

'With nothing to link the two?' said Ben.

'No. So you see why it raised suspicions.'

'Why would he have said anything about the birth mother, then?' asked Libby. 'That seems rather odd. After all, she didn't go out to Turkey to see him, he came to England to see her, so nobody in the village would have met her.'

'And he seemed to have told no one who she was or anything about her,' said Fran, 'so why did he mention her at all?'

'As a cover of some sort?' suggested Peter, joining in for the first time.

'But he was only going back to England. Everyone knew that's where he came from,' said Ben.

'Did he go back frequently?' asked Ian.

'We don't know,' said Libby. 'The people we spoke to didn't seem to know an awful lot about him even though they'd known him for at least ten years. It was the other victim they said knew him best.'

'So was she killed because she knew something about his real identity?' asked Peter.

'If,' said Fran slowly and thoughtfully, 'he'd told people he had no family or friends left in England he would need an excuse to go back. So inventing an unknown birth mother would do very well.'

'I still don't see why he needed an excuse to go back,' said Libby. 'He could have just wanted to see the old place again. Making up what is quite an elaborate story seems a bit excessive.'

'It could, of course,' said Ian, 'be true.'

Everybody spoke at once.

'But you just said –'

'How?'

'It could?'

'Suppose somehow his real mother had found him. Perhaps when he was given his new identity he managed to tell her and she suddenly needed to see him.'

They all looked at each other.

'It's possible,' said Ben. 'But pure speculation.'

'That's what you're all so good at,' said Ian. 'Anyway, be warned that you're likely to be visited by either your Johnny or his minions. He isn't happy about this.'

'Was Wilson a criminal?' asked Libby. 'Can you tell us that at least?'

Ian shook his head. 'Not even that.'

'I've just thought,' said Fran. 'You know his passport was tied round his waist? Suppose it was there so that he would be identified if found?'

'Do you think he was meant to be found?' said Ian.

Fran looked at her friends. 'How likely would it be that the body caught on that piece of rock? If he'd been pushed off a boat, say?'

'He might have drifted into that little cave,' said Guy.

'And hooked himself up onto the rock?' said Fran. 'There are no tides in the Mediterranean.'

'A warning?' said Ian. 'Someone who wanted him investigated?'

'If that was the case, they didn't have to kill him,' said Libby. 'They could have sent an anonymous letter or something.'

'To whom, though?' asked Ian. 'No, killing him would make sure there was an investigation.'

'Which nearly didn't happen,' said Libby. 'The Jandarma weren't doing much good.'

'So it's thanks to you there is one,' said Ian.

'Not really. It's thanks to his friend Martha, who was worried about his newly found mother not knowing,' said Fran.

'Except that you two went and pushed her,' said Ben.

'Suppose you tell me everything that happened,' said Ian, sitting forward. 'As if you were giving me a witness statement.'

'Why?' Libby was wary.

'I told you. I think you'll be questioned again, and if I can give your commander statements while his investigation is still centred in Turkey, at least he'll have something to go on.'

'But he knows everything already,' said Libby.

'Did he take notes?'

'Well, no …'

'And you are no longer there for him to ask.'

'All right,' said Libby, 'but not now, surely?

The door swung open.

'Hello! What have I missed?' asked Harry.

The following morning, Ian and Fran arrived on Libby's doorstep at the same time.

'I thought we'd sit in the kitchen,' said Libby, leading the way. 'It seems less cosy than the front room.'

'And better for me to take notes,' said Ian.

'Yes,' said Libby with a sigh.

After they had settled at the kitchen table and Libby had provided coffee, tea, and biscuits, Ian took out his notebook.

'Now,' he said. 'From the beginning.'

Between them, Fran and Libby related the events that followed the discovery of Alec Wilson's body.

'It feels as though we've been through this a million times,' said Libby. 'And it doesn't get any easier.'

'I looked up the witness protection scheme online,' said Fran. 'It's part of the National Crime Agency.'

'Yes.' Ian sounded wary.

'Usually people are part of an investigation of serious crime, or possibly honour killings. I wouldn't have thought Alec Wilson was involved with honour killings.'

'So, serious crime?' said Libby. 'Organised crime?'

Both women looked at Ian.

'It's possible. I told you, I don't know the details. The Service works independently of local forces, although there are regional Protected Persons Units. But the whole idea of the service is that nobody knows where the person is.'

'But if there's a threat to the person in their new identity someone must get to know about it,' said Fran.

'There's a flagging system, of course,' said Ian, 'but you don't need to know about that.'

'And Wilson was flagged?' said Libby.

'When the restaurant owner called the consulate, yes. All the flag meant was that they had to inform the Met, which they did. As it happens, Commander Smith really was staying with one of the Jandarma chiefs at the time, so he was able to take over immediately.'

'But that would mean whoever killed him wasn't a local. We said that, didn't we?' Libby turned to Fran. 'It must have been someone who went out specially.'

'Not necessarily. After all, the other victim was a local. It could just as easily be someone he'd annoyed out there – nothing to do with any previous connection to crime.'

'I wonder if they found the computer and mobile phones,' said Fran. 'And if so, what was on them.'

'You'll never know, sadly,' said Ian with a grin. 'I'll get this typed up and send it across to Smith. Do you think there's anything in there you wouldn't have told him?'

'I wouldn't give him the names he asked for, but apparently he already knew them anyway. But we've all come home now – the holidaymakers, that is. Neal Parnham, Greta, and Tom, and Betty and Walter Roberts – they all left before we did, and we didn't see anything more of either Smith or the Jandarma after that.'

'Well, be prepared for him to descend like a ton of bricks. I hope this might keep him off, but I have my doubts.' Ian stood up. 'If anything else happens, let me know.'

Fran and Libby took fresh cups of tea and coffee into the garden after he'd gone.

'I wonder what sort of crime it was,' said Libby. 'Remember how worried Neal was when he thought Wilson was a criminal?'

'If he'd had a holiday fling with him, I'm not surprised,' said Fran. 'And we don't know that he was a criminal, remember. Far more likely he was a witness.'

'Or a gang member who turned on the gang and gave evidence. Much more likely.' Libby looked up through the leaves of the cherry tree. 'Do you think we'll ever go back there?'

'I'd like to,' said Fran, 'but we may be unwelcome.'

'Why?' Libby was indignant. 'We didn't do anything! We just found the body. With a local.'

'And asked questions, and encouraged Martha to inform the consulate,' said Fran. 'And don't forget the Istanbul Palace. They all saw Smith come to see us, and they will know by now who he was. He's bound to have questioned them all.'

'Hmmm.' Libby resumed her contemplation of the leaves. 'I wish we could find out what's going on. I wonder why Martha didn't say when she replied to your email.'

'I don't expect she's got time to write reams in emails,' said Fran. 'The restaurant seemed to be getting very busy by the time we left.'

'We've got email addresses for most of the others, haven't we?'

'Greta and Tom and Betty, yes. And Harry got Justin's, I think.'

'I wonder what Peter thought about that?' said Libby.

'I don't suppose he minded. More a solidarity sort of thing, I think.'

'And didn't Neal say Justin was going to email him if anything happened?' said Libby. 'So we're all in touch in a roundabout way. Shall we ask them all what's been going on? See if anyone's heard anything?'

'We could.' Fran tapped a finger to her lips thoughtfully. 'I could email Martha again.'

'And Hal could email Justin. And I'll do Greta and Tom and

Betty, although I don't suppose they'll know anything.'

'And we might as well ask Jimmy, too,' said Fran. 'I'll ask Guy to do that, as he knew Jimmy from way back.'

'Astonishing that they all remembered him, wasn't it?' said Libby.

'I think it's such a small place they're able to remember visitors. If it was a great big resort they wouldn't.' Fran sat up straight. 'Of course, there's social media as well! Jimmy's had a page, didn't it? If we went on to that we might be able to get in touch with other people.'

They went inside and Libby located the Facebook pages for Jimmy's hotel, Martha's, and even The Red Bar.

'Look! Greta and Tom are members,' said Libby. 'Let's put a post on there. Jimmy will probably see it, too.'

'It's a bit public,' said Fran. 'We don't necessarily want the world to know what's going on. I mean, we're not even supposed to know Wilson was in the witness protection scheme.'

'Oh.' Libby's face fell. 'Well, just put a post up saying "how is everyone" sort of thing?'

'That's suitably vague,' said Fran. 'Go on then. Someone might get back to us. It doesn't look as though Martha and Ismet use their page very often, so I'll email her when I get home. And then we'll wait and see who gets back to us first.'

'If anyone,' said Libby, beginning to type.

But the first person to get in touch with either of them was neither holidaymaker nor local resident. It was Commander Johnny Smith.

Chapter Thirteen

'Ah! Both of you together. That's lucky.'

Libby and Fran gaped at the man getting out of a large black Mercedes parked behind Fran's Smart car. He beamed at them as he trotted across the lane.

'Quite informal, I assure you,' he said, arriving slightly out of breath at the door. 'Just thought I'd have a quick word.'

'And you came all the way from Turkey to Steeple Martin to have it?' said Libby, finding her voice.

'Not quite. I've been in London since the day before yesterday.'

'DCI Connell told us you had a team out in Turkey,' said Fran, narrowing her eyes at him.

'I have,' he said cheerfully. 'Well, aren't you going to ask me in?'

Libby looked at Fran, who shrugged. She stood aside slightly unwillingly.

'Thank you.' He followed Libby into the sitting room with Fran bringing up the rear. Sidney ran between his legs and disappeared into the kitchen.

Libby and Fran sat side by side on the sofa and Libby gestured Smith into the chair opposite.

'So what's all this about?' she asked.

'First, can I ask why you were talking to DCI Connell?'

'No, you can't,' snapped Fran. 'He's a friend of ours.'

'Ah.' Smith nodded. 'And he wanted know what sort of trouble you'd got yourselves in to have questions asked by the Met?'

'Well, yes,' Libby agreed reluctantly.

'So he told you – what?'

Fran and Libby registered surprise.

'Nothing. He said there wasn't anything he could tell us,' said Fran.

'Hmm. When did you see him?'

'He left about half an hour before you arrived,' said Libby, 'but really, we do *not* have to answer your questions. This looks a little like harassment, to me.'

Smith sighed and shifted in his chair. 'I'm sorry. But we're getting nowhere fast out in that God-forsaken place and I needed to ask you some more questions.'

Fran sat up very straight. 'I would thank you to remember that some of those people out there are our friends, and I'm sure they've answered all the questions you asked them.'

'I thought you'd only just met them?'

Libby watched Fran's face go pink. 'That doesn't mean we didn't make friends with them,' she said.

'Hmm,' said Smith again.

'Actually,' Libby said, taking a deep breath, 'DCI Connell was here taking detailed statements from both of us to send you in case you needed to ask anything more. I think he was going to email it to you.'

'Well, that was very considerate of him, wasn't it? And here I am with all those little questions.'

'Well, I've got one first,' said Fran. 'We've told you absolutely everything we know, we helped you search those premises, which I'm pretty sure was illegal and now you're pestering us – with no warning – back at home. By what right are you doing this? If this is an official investigation we should be told.'

Smith looked at her consideringly for a moment.

'Oh yes,' he said eventually, 'this is an official investigation. And a serious one. But I came here informally, rather than officially with attendant sidekicks, in order not to alarm you too much. It seems I failed.'

'You certainly did,' said Libby. 'All you've done is put our backs up. Now you'd better carry on and tell us what it's all about – although I have a shrewd idea.'

Smith's face showed a flash of anger. 'What did Connell tell you?'

'Nothing. We've told you, he said he couldn't.'

Smith sat staring at his shoes until Libby let out a huge sigh and began to fidget.

'I'm going to have to trust you,' he said at last. 'I need to know if you could have known Alec Wilson years ago, before he went out to Turkey.'

Of course not,' said Fran. 'I've never known an Alec Wilson, and from what we could see in the passport photo, he didn't look at all familiar. Did he to you?' She turned to Libby.

'Same here,' said Libby. 'And surely we would have told the Jandarma when they first came to speak to us? The only one who recognised him at our hotel was Neal Parnham, and he'd only met Wilson a few days before.' She looked briefly at Fran, then back at Smith. 'Does this mean Wilson wasn't his real name?'

Smith was watching her carefully. 'Possibly,' he said.

'I knew it,' said Libby. 'Was he a criminal? That's what Neal thought.'

'And Harry thought he was a spy,' said Fran with a laugh.

'You're sure none of your party knew him?'

'As sure as I can be,' said Fran. 'Libby's known everyone much longer than I have.'

'I'd know,' said Libby confidently. 'I've known Ben, Peter, and Harry for twenty years and Guy for at least ten years.'

Smith sighed. 'I had to be sure.'

Libby frowned. 'But if that's what you were wondering, surely you'd have looked into our backgrounds thoroughly with all your resources.'

He looked up cheerfully. 'Oh, I have.'

'Oh!' said Libby and Fran together, slightly shocked.

'As far as we can find out, none of your party nor the other British visitors has so much as a speeding ticket. Young Justin was a different matter, but we can't see any link to Wilson.'

'What had he done?' asked Libby. 'We thought he'd probably been done for fraud.'

It was Smith's turn to look shocked. 'What made you think that?'

'We were told he'd been an accountant, I think,' said Libby. 'It was only a guess.'

'You're obviously far too good at guessing,' said Smith. He stood up. 'If I have any more questions, can I call you? I know I'll get DCI Connell's statement, but there might be things that arise from that.'

'I don't want to prejudice my own case,' said Libby as she saw him to the door, 'but would either of us have told you if we'd known Wilson in a former life?'

He turned and grinned at her. 'No, you wouldn't. But I don't think you did.'

Fran and Libby watched him turn the car and drive down the lane.

'Well, we got away with it,' said Fran. 'I was terrified we'd drop Ian in the soup.'

'And we didn't tell anything but the truth.' Libby sighed. 'And it's all getting even more interesting.'

'Frustrating,' said Fran. 'We can't do a thing.'

Libby laughed. 'Come on, it's me that usually says that!'

Fran smiled. 'You're right there. Anyway, we can do what we decided earlier, can't we?'

'We could look and see if anyone's answered our post on Jimmy's page,' said Libby, 'and then you'd better go home or Guy will start fidgeting.'

Fran raised her eyebrows. 'Why would he do that?'

'He'll think we're getting involved again.'

'We are.' Fran grinned and gave Libby a gentle shove. 'Go on, open the laptop.'

There were no replies on Jimmy's page, so Libby called Harry and asked him to email Justin.

'Why?' The sound of chopping filtered down the line.

'What are you doing?'

'Prepping for lunch, what do you think? Now, why do you want me to email Justin? Is it something to do with you seeing Ian this morning?'

'Yes. There's a team still investigating out there and we want to know what's happening, especially as we've just had a surprise visit from Commander Smith.'

'What?' The sudden clatter suggested Harry had dropped a knife.

'Yes. I'll tell you all about it when you aren't busy.' Libby grinned at Fran.

'Tell me now. Is Fran still there? Come over and I'll give you soup and stuff.'

Libby rang Ben to include him in the invitation; as she told Fran, Harry would certainly have asked Peter. When they arrived at The Pink Geranium, sure enough Ben and Peter were already at the big table in the right-hand window. Harry joined them bearing a cafetière and a bottle of red wine, and Libby launched into her story.

'So the upshot,' said Harry when she'd finished, 'is that Smith confirmed Alec Wilson was definitely a false name and was either a criminal or a crucial witness in a criminal case, and Smith is worried that someone who knew him before his name change has got at him.'

'It seems like it. Smith's left his team in Turkey, presumably while he looks into the English end. So we want to know what's going on over there.'

Ben frowned at her. 'But there's nothing you can do. Don't get involved.'

'It seems that we're already involved,' said Fran. 'Smith has looked into all our backgrounds.'

'What?' Peter looked affronted. 'A police check?'

'Fraid so,' said Libby. 'In case there was anything in our pasts that might have linked us to Wilson or this case, whatever it was.'

'But we don't even know what it was,' said Peter.

'So if we'd shown any sort of knowledge he would have jumped on it,' said Libby.

'There's the other alternative,' said Ben, thoughtfully stirring coffee. 'He could have been a "sleeper".' He turned to Harry. 'You were the one who suggested it.'

'I did?'

'You said he could be a spy.'

'But who on earth would plant someone somewhere like our village?' said Libby.

'Unless something was known about it and they needed a watch on it,' said Peter.

'Smuggling? The coastguard would deal with that, surely?' said Fran.

'Unless it was people or things from Britain … ' Harry tailed off. 'I know! People smuggling. Not *in* to Turkey, but *out*!'

'It could be,' said Fran, 'but why would he have been planted there ten years ago, or more?'

'Oh, I don't know,' said Harry with a gusty sigh. 'None of it makes any sense. Anyway, I'll send Justin an email and see if they know anything out there.'

'And I'll email Martha when I get home,' said Fran. 'Where's this soup, then?'

Ben walked back to Allhallow's Lane with Libby after lunch.

'I wonder what the story really is,' he said, as they passed the vicarage on the corner.

'We're never going to know,' said Libby. 'If it's that hush-hush, it'll be swept so far under the carpet even the spiders won't find it.'

'Then why did Smith make such a business of involving you two while we were out there?'

'Partly what Fran said, camouflage, and partly to find out if we knew anything. If we had, I wonder what would have happened?'

'I expect you would have quietly disappeared,' said Ben with a grin.

'And how would he have explained that?' Libby shook her head. 'I expect that's what they're doing out there now, making sure there are no loose ends flapping around.'

'Not looking for the murderer?'

'I got the impression that wasn't top of the priorities. And poor Sally Weston is simply collateral damage.'

Back at number seventeen, Ben went into the garden to carry on painting his new shed, and Libby went into the conservatory to do a little desultory painting. She produced small pictures of the local area, particularly Nethergate, for Guy to sell in his gallery and shop. A noted artist, Guy's original paintings commanded larger sums, but were reproduced on postcards and greetings cards, which he also stocked in the shop. During the summer season, Libby's pictures sold well, and Guy was always urging her to do more, but even though they were only 'pretty peeps', she struggled to manage more than one a month.

Now, after adding a stroke or two to the current masterpiece, she decided to check and see if anyone had commented on Jimmy's Facebook page.

We have a new policeman here, Jimmy had posted, *after your Englishman left.*

'I thought Smith said he'd left a team out there,' said Libby, showing it to Ben. 'Not just one person.'

'Jimmy's English isn't that good. He might not mean just one.'

But when Harry received a reply that evening from Justin, Libby got an explanation.

'He says it's a Turkish policeman. And the English team seem to be trying to put him off.'

Chapter Fourteen

'How do you mean?'

'I can't talk now,' said Harry against a background noise of clattering pots and pans, 'I'm right in the middle of service. Are you rehearsing tonight?'

'Yes – in about half an hour.'

'Come in when you've finished. If I'm not free by then I'll meet you in the pub.'

Libby ended the call. 'Harry's heard from Justin. He says he'll tell us about it after rehearsal.'

Ben sighed. 'For goodness sake, don't try and start conducting an investigation from here.'

'Of course not – I couldn't, could I?' Libby collected a folder of music and tried to look innocent.

The walk to the theatre took them past The Pink Geranium and Libby peered in to try and see Harry, but he was obviously busy in the kitchen. Libby's son Adam, who helped out occasionally, was serving, wearing his long Victorian apron. He waved.

The doors to the theatre were already open, and they found Peter up in the Sound and Lighting box.

'Susannah's here, too,' he called down.

'Did Harry tell you what Justin said?' Libby called back.

Peter appeared at the top of the spiral staircase leading down to the foyer. 'No. What's happened?'

Libby repeated what Harry had told her.

'He must have called him,' said Peter, sitting down on the top step. 'Hal put his phone number in the email, but I wouldn't have expected him to ring back. I suppose we'll have to wait until later.'

Libby pushed open the doors to the auditorium and went to say hello to Susannah. Ben had disappeared backstage to check on the workshop.

Gradually members of The End Of The Pier Show cast drifted in and were given their music. Susannah put them through their paces in some of the chorus numbers, some old favourites, some new to the cast, and Libby worked out who could be in the various comedy set pieces. It was familiar and soothing, and when at just after half past nine she felt some of her cast getting restless, she packed them off home – or to the pub, where most of them would go first.

Ben went round checking all doors were locked and Peter shut down all the lights, then they walked down the Manor drive towards the high street, turned left and stopped in front of the restaurant. Harry was sitting on the sofa in the left-hand window and waved.

When they were settled and Adam had supplied them with their drinks of choice, Harry began.

'I'm glad we'd finished service,' he said, 'I didn't want to tell you in the pub with your theatre crowd all there. I emailed Justin this afternoon, and I put my phone number on there. I don't really know why I did that – I didn't really expect him to ring.'

'Yes, Peter told us that,' said Libby.

'So then he rang, just before I called you.' Harry frowned at his coffee mug. 'He sounded quite upset. Apparently, these British cops have been quite polite, but have been concentrating on Wilson's and Sally Thing's houses, when suddenly this plain clothes bloke from Antalya turns up. And he's been going round asking all the same questions and more. And the British cops don't like him, but they can't stop him.'

'Goodness!' said Libby. 'So why is Justin upset?'

'He seems to be certain the murderer is in the village. And he's been asking about all the boats, and who is good enough to take a boat out at night. The crowd at that hotel you went to –'

'The Istanbul Palace,' supplied Libby.

'Yeah, that one, well they're getting very twitchy, Justin

98

said. Martha's the only one who seems calm about it all.'

'She was only worried about the mother aspect,' said Peter. 'And what do we think about that now?'

'If he's in the witness protection scheme or a sleeper it can't be true,' said Ben. 'No one could have found him.'

'So it was a ploy,' said Libby. 'Do you suppose he wasn't allowed to come back to the UK, and he snuck in secretly?'

'He'd have had to have a passport – which we know he had,' said Ben, 'so I don't suppose his travel was restricted.'

'Anyway,' said Harry, 'he's passed on Neal Parnham's email. He's been asking Justin questions, too.'

'I'll do a group email to him, Greta and Tom, and Betty,' said Libby. 'They'll want to know.'

'Do we tell them about Ian questioning you?' asked Harry.

'Perhaps not, but I'll tell them Smith came sniffing round.'

'He wants to cover up the truth, the Turkish policeman wants to uncover it,' said Ben. 'It could turn into an international incident.'

'Smith took Sally Weston's computer, and he said he was going to get Wilson's from the Jandarma,' said Libby. 'Will the Turkish policeman make him give them back?'

'No idea.' Ben shook his head. 'I wonder if there will have to be diplomatic intervention?'

'It can't be that important,' said Peter. 'Wouldn't there have been something in the press?'

'Smith won't want his cover blown,' said Harry. 'Right old mess, isn't it?'

Ben persuaded Libby not to call Fran then and there, but to wait to do that and send the email in the morning.

'It's Saturday, and I'm going to take Mum into Canterbury,' he said as they walked home. 'Do you want to come?'

'No, I'll ring Fran and send the email. Will you have lunch in Canterbury?'

'I expect so. Are you trying to keep me out of the way?'

'No! I just want to know if I ought to prepare something. Tell you what, I'll cook for you both tomorrow night. Hetty will be expecting us to lunch on Sunday, won't she?'

Sunday lunch at the Manor was an unvarying tradition, attended by as many people as Hetty could round up.

'I'll ask her,' said Ben. 'Now, do you want a nightcap?'

After Libby had seen Ben and Hetty off in the morning, she called Fran to read her the text of the email before she sent it, and to tell her Harry's news.

'I expect the Turkish people are cross that the British have taken over,' said Fran. 'We wouldn't like it if one of theirs came over to investigate here, would we?'

'I suppose not. I don't see how they're going to ever solve it now. They'll be working against one another.'

'It's not solving it Smith's trying to do,' said Fran.

'That's what Ben said. He's trying to cover it up, the Turks want to uncover it.'

'Well, no doubt we'll find out. Ian might even tell us,' said Fran. 'Now, I'm supposed to be helping in the shop, so I'd better get on with it.'

Libby sent the email to all her former fellow guests at Jimmy's, then went and peered once more at the painting in the conservatory. All she had to do now was wait.

It wasn't until Sunday morning that a reply was received from any of the residents of Erzugan or its visitors. Ben had made tea and brought it up to bed and gave Libby his smartphone to check her emails.

'Greta says she hasn't heard from anybody, and so does Betty,' Libby said, scrolling through messages. 'Nothing on Jimmy's page, but Martha's replied. She says this Turkish policeman has been prowling around, and is upsetting the people at the Istanbul Palace. Geoff Croker even went over to see her the other day.'

'Why would he do that?' asked Ben.

'Getting all the ex-pats on side, I suppose. Martha doesn't like the Crokers, though, so it's a bit odd.'

'Nothing from Neal or his pal Justin?'

'No, but I haven't got Justin's address – it was Harry who emailed him. Neal hasn't replied.'

'Where do they all live?' asked Ben.

'Greta and Tom live Leicester way, I think, and Betty near Manchester. I'm not sure Neal ever said where he lives. Why?'

'I just hoped we weren't going to be surprised by visits from them.' Ben slid back down under the duvet.

'Oi! Don't go back to sleep,' said Libby.

He grinned up at her. 'I wasn't intending to.'

Libby phoned Fran to pass on the information she'd received before walking up to the Manor for lunch. On the way, she and Ben met Flo Carpenter and Lenny, Hetty's brother, also bidden for lunch.

'Tell us all about yer 'olidays, then,' said Flo, as they all settled at the huge kitchen table. 'Even managed a murder out there, then?'

'Hardly our fault, Flo,' said Ben, wrestling with the cork of a venerable bottle of claret from Flo's excellent cellar. She had inherited it from her late husband, a considerable wine buff, and had added to it wisely over the years. Hetty's own cellar was good, but nowhere near as good as Flo's. Libby knew nothing about wine, other than preferring red to white and that some she liked and some she didn't.

'Attracts trouble, that gal.' Flo indicated Libby with a jerk of her thumb.

Libby made a face at her.

'There was a bit in the paper about somebody who'd been murdered in Turkey,' said Lenny suddenly.

'Which paper?' asked Libby.

'The local. The one your friend Jane works on.'

'She technically works for the *Nethergate Mercury*,' said Ben, 'but I think she's syndicated through the whole group. Did she write it, Lenny?'

Lenny looked surprised. 'I dunno, boy. Just about some woman whose daughter was killed out there.'

Ben and Libby looked at each other.

'It couldn't be,' said Libby.

''Ere. Just about to wrap the peelings in it.' Hetty handed over the paper and returned to her vegetables.

'Give it 'ere,' said Lenny, and began flipping through the

101

pages. 'There.' He handed the paper to Libby and Ben.

'Cherry Ashton!' they both said.

'What?' Flo scowled at them. 'Go on then – what d'yer mean?'

'The mother of the woman who was murdered in Turkey lives in Cherry Ashton!' said Libby.

'Where's that when it's at 'ome?' asked Flo.

'I thought it was a man who was murdered,' said Hetty.

'There were two,' said Ben, 'a man called Alec Wilson, and a woman, Sally Weston.'

'Not married?' said Hetty.

'No, but they were friends.'

Flo snorted. 'Oh, yeah?'

'Nothing like that, Flo. Alec was gay.'

Flo looked deflated.

'I don't see why it matters where she lives,' said Hetty. 'Ain't nothing to do with you, is it?'

Ben and Libby exchanged another look. Libby shrugged and Ben grinned.

The conversation turned to Steeple Martin and its inhabitants, and what had been happening while Libby and Ben had been in Erzugan, and eventually after Flo, Hetty, and Lenny had retired to Hetty's sitting room for a nap and Ben and Libby had done what clearing up Hetty would allow, they escaped down the drive and by common consent turned right to Peter and Harry's cottage.

'Sorry to disturb your afternoon off,' said Ben, 'but we just found out something interesting.'

'From Hetty?' said Peter peering out from the kitchen and waving an interrogative kettle.

'Yes, please,' said Libby, 'and no, from Lenny, of all people.'

While they waited for the kettle to boil, Libby explained. 'It's really strange, because Ben was only asking this morning where everybody lived because he didn't want to be descended upon.'

'Well, Sally Weston's mother is hardly likely to descend,'

said Peter.

'Unless she finds out you went through her daughter's knicker drawer,' said Harry.

'Oh, don't.' Libby made a face.

Peter poured boiling water into a large teapot. 'Have to do it properly for the old trout,' he said. 'No tea bags in mugs for her.'

'Special treatment wherever she goes,' said Harry, sprawling on the sofa, still in his chef's whites.

Libby sank into her favourite sagging chintz-covered chair. 'I don't ask for special treatment,' she said.

'No, petal, of course you don't.' Peter brought a tray in and put it on the coffee table, before sitting beside Harry on the sofa. 'So tell us what ploy you're going to use to go and question this poor woman.'

'I won't! Of course I won't,' said Libby. 'And we never even met Sally.'

'As you said – collateral damage, poor woman,' said Ben, sitting on the arm of her chair and accepting a cup of tea.'

'I wonder if Sally knew Alec before they both went to Turkey,' said Harry, lifting his legs on to Peter's lap. 'If so, perhaps her mother knew him, too.'

'Nobody suggested that,' said Libby, 'and the police will have asked her that already.'

'Funny that Ian didn't mention her the other day,' said Ben.

'Perhaps he didn't know.'

'But it would have been someone from Canterbury who went out to break the news, and you know how they all pick up on things,' said Ben.

'I suppose it is odd, but he wasn't that concerned with Sally Weston, more with Alec Wilson.'

'Your Commander Johnny may have had one of his own blokes go and tell her,' said Harry, 'and just not bothered to tell Ian.'

'If that's the case,' said Libby, 'why? Ian could be useful. He's on the ground.'

'But the case has nothing to do with her.'

'It has nothing to do with any of us,' said Peter. 'Now, drink up your tea, children, and tell me what gossip was exchanged over lunch.'

But the day's gossip faded into obscurity at the news they received the next day.

Libby's phone rang as she was preparing Ben's breakfast.

'Libby,' Peter's voice sounded ragged. 'Harry's being questioned by the police. Justin Newcombe was found dead in a London hotel bedroom yesterday.'

Chapter Fifteen

'We're coming round.'

'No, Lib, not yet. They're still here. I'll send you a text when they've gone.'

Libby ended the call and turned to Ben.

'Why would they question Harry, for God's sake?' he said, when Libby had told him. 'Harry hardly knew him.'

'But Harry was the one he called.' Libby frowned. 'After all, we assumed that Justin was still in Erzugan when he phoned, but he could have been in London, couldn't he?'

'He must have called other people,' said Ben. 'If he was in London he must have been going to meet someone.'

'Yes – his killer. Which means the killer is in England, not Turkey.'

Libby's phone beeped. *The police have gone. Come on.*

Peter opened the door and gestured them inside. Harry was slumped on the sofa looking worse than he had for at least a year.

'What happened?' Libby sat beside him and took his hand.

'It was that phone call,' said Harry.

'We thought so,' said Libby. 'Did he call from London?'

'No he was still in Turkey.'

'But he must have called other people.'

'Yes.' Harry seem to rouse himself and sat up straight. 'Yes. They told me that. But they seem to be assuming that because of the murders over there ...'

'They've jumped to the conclusion that it must be one of the people who were in the village at the time.' Libby shook her head. 'What about Neal? He would have called him – they knew each other much better than we did.'

'I don't know. I expect they're talking to him, too.'

'Who were they?' asked Ben. 'I mean, were they from Smith's outfit, or were they local?'

'They were plain clothes and they both showed their badges, but I didn't see where they were from.' Harry glanced up at his partner. 'They talked to Pete, too.'

'Well, at least you've got a rock solid alibi,' said Libby. 'He was found yesterday, right? And you were in the caff all day. Then we can vouch for you being at home after that.'

'Oh, yes. They had to accept that, but they didn't act as though it let me off the hook.'

'They said they would need to talk to both of us again,' said Peter, looking more angry than scared. 'Honestly! I'm beginning to wish we'd never been on that bloody holiday.'

'Holidays don't seem to be that relaxing for us, do they?' said Libby. 'Perhaps we should just stay at home.'

'Anyone want coffee?' said Harry, suddenly standing up. 'We haven't had any breakfast.'

'Neither have we,' said Libby. 'I abandoned it when we got Pete's call. Could I have tea?'

'Yes, petal. I'll dig out the bloody teapot again.'

'I wonder if he was coming over to visit Sally Weston's mother?' said Peter. 'That would make sense, wouldn't it?'

'Yes!' Libby clapped her hands. 'Of course. I bet that's what it was. I wish we could talk to her.'

'If he was going to see her the police will already be on to it,' said Ben. 'You'd better ring Fran or she'll complain she's not been kept up to speed.

'Only not now,' said Harry emerging from the kitchen with the teapot and a cafetière. 'I'm making bacon sandwiches for everyone.'

'I'm going down to Nethergate,' said Libby, as she and Ben walked home. 'I'll send Fran a text to say I'm coming. But there's so much to tell her ...'

But Libby's text was answered by a phone call.

'I won't be here.'

'Oh.' Libby felt ridiculously affronted.

Fran laughed. 'It's all right – I'm only going to the hairdresser's. I'll be back later, by lunchtime, at least.'

'Oh, right,' said Libby, relieved. 'Only I've got so much to tell you.'

Next she sent a text to Jane Baker of the *Nethergate Mercury*, Susannah's sister-in-law. Jane replied that she was in her office and Libby was welcome to pop in. Satisfied, Libby waved Ben off to the Manor and his estate office, tidied herself and the kitchen, and set off for Nethergate.

The *Mercury*'s offices were at the top of the town in a converted mansion which had once belonged to a nouveau riche Victorian grocer. Jane came out to reception to meet Libby and led her into the board room.

'Quieter in here,' she said. 'Now, what did you want to know?'

'Do I only come and see when I want to know something?' asked Libby.

'Mostly,' said Jane, with a grin. 'But at work – definitely. Is this about the woman whose daughter died in Turkey?'

Libby's eyes widened. 'Yes.'

'I thought so. The same village you were in, wasn't it? Erzu-something?'

'How do you know that?'

'We saw Susannah over the weekend. She said you were telling her about it and I put two and two together and made five, like any good journalist.'

'Oh, right.' Libby stared at the polished board table for a moment. 'Well, you see, there's been a bit of a development. This is definitely not for publication, but someone else from that village has died.'

'Bit of an epidemic, then?'

'No. He died in London.'

'Wow!' Jane was now impressed and alert. 'Was he one of your fellow holidaymakers?'

'No, that's the point. He was a resident. We were wondering if he came over to see Sally Weston's mother.'

'That's the woman in Cherry Ashton?'

107

'Yes.'

'And I suppose you want to see her?'

'Actually,' Libby looked up at Jane at last, 'no, I don't. I didn't ever meet Sally, and Fran and I were persuaded by a British policeman to help with a search of her villa. Very unorthodox, and I bet he never told his boss. So I don't want to meet her. As Harry said, I've been through Sally's knicker drawer.'

'So what do you want from me?'

'I just wanted to know what she was like. Did you interview her?'

'No. She didn't want to talk to us, and someone who was with her at the time gave us the normal very distressed angle. We accepted it. I know your friend Campbell McLean went out there on spec, but he got the door slammed in his face.'

Campbell McLean worked for the local independent television station, and had been both a help and a hindrance to Libby in the past.

'Serves him right,' said Libby. 'I bet he would have asked her "And how does that make you feel?" I always want the other person to say "Well, how do you think it makes me feel, you idiot?". They never do.'

Jane laughed. 'Perhaps they edit it out.'

Libby sighed. 'Or cut the whole interview. It's so insensitive.'

Jane looked uncomfortable. 'That's what we're paid to do.'

'I know.' Libby patted Jane's arm. 'And you're not too insensitive.'

'Fran thought I was when I first met her.'

'Well, we know better now.' Libby stood up. 'There's nothing you can tell me about – what's the woman's name, by the way?'

Jane also stood. 'Hang on, I'll have to look it up. Wasn't it in the paper?'

'Yes, but we only know about it because Lenny – you remember Lenny – told us about it. We hadn't seen it.'

'Right. Won't be a moment.'

Libby wandered back into reception, where Jane joined her.

'Here. I ran off a copy for you.'

Libby tucked the piece of paper in her basket. 'Thanks, Jane. And don't forget – nothing about Justin. You don't know anything.'

'I didn't even know his name until then,' said Jane. 'I assume that's the newest victim? I'm also assuming that he was murdered. He didn't come to London and the shock of it gave him a heart attack?'

'No, he was murdered. If there's anything else to tell you, I will.' Libby gave her a quick kiss on the cheek. 'Love to Terry and Imogen.'

Libby drove down to Harbour Street and parked right at the end near The Sloop and The Blue Anchor café.

'Boo!' said a voice behind her.

'Fran! You're back already.'

'Well spotted. Which is more than you did five minutes ago. I was actually at my front door when you went past.'

'I was looking for a parking space,' said Libby. 'Busy, isn't it?'

'It's summer – what do you expect? With so many people rediscovering traditional bucket-and-spade holidays, there's nowhere as traditional as Nethergate.'

'Shall we have lunch at the Blue Anchor?' said Libby. 'As we're here?'

'Why not.' Fran led the way to one of tables under Mavis's canvas gazebo next to the environmentally unfriendly heater, provided for her regular smokers, mainly George and Bert, respectively captains of the pleasure boats *Dolphin* and *Sparkler*. Both boats were out today, one chugging round the island in the middle of the bay, the other visiting the small bays along the coast, in much the same way that Captain Joe took the *Paradise* out from Erzugan.

Mavis herself came out to take their orders, and shortly afterwards the current "girl", short of skirt and long of hair, brought their drinks and Libby launched into her story.

'Well,' said Fran when she'd finished, 'it brings up more

questions than it answers. Like who knew Justin was coming to England, who was he coming to see and why. It has to be to do with the murders.'

'Yes, we figured that,' said Libby. 'Could it have been to see Sally Weston's mum?'

'Then he would have come down here – perhaps to Canterbury – rather than London, wouldn't he?'

'Oh, I don't know. I just can't believe Harry was the only person he called in England.'

'No.' Fran stared out to sea. 'The police will be talking to everyone, won't they?'

'Only the people who were in Erzugan at the time of the murders, probably.'

'No, surely not. He could have been murdered by anyone he knew in England.'

'Or even – I mean, he was gay. Do you suppose he picked someone up?'

'What – between the airport and the hotel?' Fran shook her head. 'He'd only arrived in the morning.'

'Do you suppose we could ask Ian?' said Libby, after a moment. 'He did come and see us about it, after all.'

'I think we ought to wait and see,' said Fran. 'I doubt very much if we'll be involved any more.'

'I hope not, for Harry's sake. He looked absolutely crushed this morning.'

'Were they really thinking of him as a suspect?' asked Fran.

'He thought so. They were plain clothes and he didn't know if they came from Canterbury or the Met. Neither did Pete. They questioned him, too.'

Fran sighed. 'Maybe Ian will tell us. Will he come over on Wednesday evening, do you think?'

'I hope so. Are you coming up?'

'I'm in the show, so yes, I'll be there.' Fran turned to her friend with a grin. 'Can you contain your soul in patience until then?'

'I'll have to.' Libby sat up straight and looked determined. 'As I said, I hope we won't be involved any more for Harry's sake.'

'And why don't I believe you?' said Fran.

Libby drove home in pensive mood. At the turning for Steeple Mount and Cherry Ashton she very nearly changed direction, but reluctantly decided against it and continued to Steeple Martin without noticing how she got there.

Ben was still at the Manor and she had nothing to do. Except, of course, the painting still sitting on its easel in the conservatory. She gazed at it gloomily for a moment, then continued into the garden with a book. Which she didn't even open. Sidney came and sat on her lap affectionately digging his claws into her legs as he got himself settled. Barely had he done so, when the phone rang. Not her mobile, but the landline. Cursing, and being cursed by Sidney, she stood up and went back into the house just as the ringing stopped and her recorded voice cut in.

Then a new voice.

'Mrs Sarjeant, I hope you don't mind me phoning you, but I wondered if we could have a chat? My name's Carol Oxford. I'm Sally Weston's mother.'

Chapter Sixteen

Libby snatched up the phone.

'Mrs Oxford? I'm so sorry, I didn't get to the phone in time.'

'Oh ...' Carol Oxford sounded confused. 'That's you, is it?'

'Yes, it is, I'm sorry. How can I help you?'

'Well,' said Carol after a pause, 'I don't quite know how to say this, but last week I heard from Martha in Erzugan.' She stopped.

'Yes?' said Libby encouragingly.

'She happened to mention that you'd been out there when Sally – er –' The voice faltered.

'Yes, we were on holiday. But I'm afraid I never met Sally.'

'No, so Martha said. But she said you were the people who found Alec Wilson's body?'

'Yes?' said Libby again.

'And she wondered if I knew you, because you lived in this area.'

'Oh, I see.' Light began to dawn.

'And I did. Well, not personally, of course, but I'd heard about you and your friend, especially when you were involved with that business over here.'

'At Cherry Ashton, yes.'

'Oh, you know that?'

'It was in the local paper, Mrs Oxford.'

'Oh, so it was. Well, I just wondered ...' the words petered out.

Here it comes, thought Libby.

'Your friend ...'

'Fran Wolfe.'

'Yes. She's – um –'

'Psychic.'

'Is she really?'

'She is, although very reluctantly.'

'Oh. I don't suppose …'

'Would you like us to come and talk to you?'

'Would you?' Relief shone out of every word.

'I'm sure we can, but you must understand the police might not be very pleased.'

'The police? Why? I've had the police here twice already, wanting to know of the connection between Sally and poor Alec, but they haven't been back. Sally's body has been brought home for her funeral next Thursday.' The wobble came again.

'You hadn't heard about Justin Newcombe then?'

'Justin …? Who? Oh, yes, he was a friend out there too, wasn't he? What about him?'

Libby took a deep breath. This was going to sound so brutal.

'He was murdered here in London over the weekend.'

'What?' It was almost whispered.

'I believe the police here and in Turkey are linking the murders.' Libby paused. 'I suppose he didn't contact you after Sally died?'

'No, I didn't know him. I never actually went out there myself, although now I wish I had. Sally used to come home once or twice a year and we were in regular touch on all the social media sites, you know …'

'Yes, I know.'

'So do you think you could come and see me? Or I could come and meet you somewhere if you liked?'

'We'll come to you,' said Libby. 'When would be convenient for you? I'll call Fran and try and set it up.'

Carol said any time would suit her, and how about tomorrow morning? Libby agreed, rang off, and immediately called Fran.

'Oh, dear. She'll want me to start trying to get through to her daughter,' said Fran.

'I don't think so. I think she just wants to talk. Tomorrow morning, then?'

'Yes, all right. About eleven? We might have lunch in that pub.'

'The Ashton Arms? We could, but it doesn't have particularly happy memories.'

'Don't be silly, Libby. There's no one left now who could hurt us.'

'I know.' Libby sighed. 'I'll ring Mrs Oxford.'

On Tuesday morning at five to eleven Libby parked in the car park of the Ashton Arms. Fran's little Smart car pulled up alongside.

'Where does she live?' asked Fran, as they both emerged.

'Not up there, thank goodness,' said Libby, nodding towards the tunnel-like lane that led to the abandoned barn that had featured in a previous adventure. 'Just round the corner here.'

They walked the few yards to the little development of newish properties where Carol lived. Suddenly Fran stopped dead.

'What?' said Libby, coming to a halt beside her.

'I don't know why I didn't link it up before,' said Fran. 'The two names, Weston and Cherry Ashton. Remember?'

'Of course I remember Cherry Ashton, but –' she stopped. 'Oh my Lord! Colonel Weston!'

'Of course, it could be a coincidence.' Fran frowned. 'I wonder when Sally went out to Turkey?'

'You think she went out to escape the fallout?'

'Was he her father, do you think?'

'Then Carol was his wife? We never heard about a wife. And if she is, why stay here?' Libby looked across to Carol Oxford's house.

The last time they had been to Cherry Ashton they had made the acquaintance of Colonel Hugh Weston, who was now safely behind bars.

'It can't be,' said Fran. 'It's just too much of a coincidence.'

'I am very suspicious of coincidences,' said Libby darkly.

'Come along, we might as well get it over with. And don't go asking questions about Colonel Weston.'

The front door was dark blue. 'Oxford blue,' commented

Libby. It positively gleamed with cleanliness, but the woman who opened it looked grey and defeated.

'Mrs Oxford?' Libby held out her hand. 'I'm Libby Sarjeant and this is Fran Wolfe.'

Carol Oxford shook hands and waved them into the house.

'Please call me Carol,' she said, and led them into a neat and rather colourless sitting room. 'Would you like tea or coffee?'

'Not for me, thank you,' said Fran. 'What did you want to talk to us about?'

Straight to the point, thought Libby. That's to stop me putting my foot in it.

'Well,' Carol began nervously, looking from one to the other. 'Sally, of course.'

'We never met her,' said Fran gently, 'although we did go to her house.'

'You did?' Carol looked surprised.

'I'm sure this sounds unethical, but when the first English policeman arrived, he had no back up, and he wanted find details of her family in England and asked us to help. We didn't find anything, and he took charge of her computer.'

'And her phone was missing,' put in Libby.

'You didn't find *anything*?'

'We found a box of old photographs, but we assumed any recent ones would be on her phone or computer,' said Fran.

Carol nodded. 'Yes, they would be. But,' she turned to Fran. 'Didn't you pick up anything about her? About her … death?'

'No, Carol, I didn't. But why did you think I might?'

'Er – I knew about – well, I knew …' She stopped.

Libby took a deep breath. 'Carol, I've got to ask. Did you hear about us in connection with the White Lodge case?'

'Yes – I told you.' Carol looked away.

'And Sally's surname is Weston,' said Fran.

Carol's face crumpled. 'I knew you'd realise,' she said, and began to cry.

Libby looked at Fran helplessly. Fran jerked her head and mouthed 'tea', then went over to crouch beside the weeping woman.

Libby found the kitchen – not hard in such a small house, filled the kettle and began looking through cupboards. She found mugs and teabags in a tin, and had located milk in the fridge just as the kettle boiled. The kitchen was as neat as the sitting room and equally as colourless.

'I didn't find any sugar,' she said as carried the mugs into the sitting room. Fran had found some coasters for the coffee table.

'I don't take it.' Carol sniffed into a tissue. 'I'm sorry.'

Doesn't have many visitors, thought Libby.

'Tell us your story, Carol.' Fran handed her a mug. 'And why you think we can help.'

Carol sighed. 'Sally was Hugh's daughter.'

Fran and Libby exchanged looks, but said nothing.

'And I wondered if she was killed because of … of … that other business.'

'As far as we can tell she wasn't,' said Fran. 'The police think it was linked to the murder of the other person out there, Alec Wilson. You didn't know him?'

'She'd mentioned him – and that other one, Justin. And Martha. She seemed to be specially close to Martha.'

'Martha – and Justin – said she was particularly close to Alec,' said Libby. 'You didn't get that impression?'

'No.' Carol shook her head.

'Forgive me,' said Fran, 'but if Sally was Weston's daughter, and you're her mother –'

'Yes, I was married to him.' Carol's face was stony.

'But you're living here. Isn't that difficult?'

Carol sighed again. 'This isn't my house, it's Sally's.' She put her mug back on the table. 'Hugh and I had been divorced for years and I moved away and eventually remarried. At that point, Hugh gave Sally this house.' She waved a vague hand. 'He had money in this development.'

'Sold by Riley's, I bet,' said Libby.

Carol gave a wan smile. 'Of course. He had money there, too. But you know that. You were the ones who solved that case.'

117

'No, the police did that,' said Fran. 'So Sally came and lived here?"

'She furnished it and came here once or twice, but after the case she decided to let it – she was already living in Turkey. She didn't want ...'

'No, of course not,' said Fran. 'So why did you come down here? It said in the paper that you were from Cherry Ashton.'

'I was, at one time, but I came down to see if there was anything here that would help the investigation, and that's when I thought of you. You see, it seems too much of a coincidence.'

'Do you think it could be a revenge killing?' asked Libby. 'One of the victims' families, perhaps?'

'Well, yes. You knew one of the victims, didn't you?'

'No.' Fran shook her head. 'Luckily, we didn't. But if someone had wanted revenge after all this time – it seems unlikely, doesn't it?'

'Suppose someone went out there on holiday and recognised her, though?' suggested Libby.

'But nobody knew of her connection with the Colonel at the time of the case,' said Fran. She turned to Carol. 'She wasn't living here then, was she?'

'No, this house was let. I think he gave it to her to put her under obligation.'

'Yes, he was definitely manipulative, wasn't he?' said Libby. 'So you've found no clues here to what might have happened?'

'She hasn't lived here since ... well, since. There's nothing of hers here. She either got rid of things or took them to Turkey.'

'So this is a dead end,' said Libby. 'I really don't think Sally's death is anything to do with – with anything that happened here in Cherry Ashton. It's far more likely, as the police think, that it's linked to her friend Alec Wilson.'

'So it's to do with something over there? But what about this person who was murdered in England?'

'That's the problem,' said Fran. 'If the murderer of Sally and Alec needed to keep Justin silent, he or she is now in England.'

Carol looked frightened.

'Maybe not,' said Libby. 'He or she could have got straight back on a plane and gone back again. I expect the police will be checking all the flights, won't they?'

'So it's much more likely that the reason is out there?' Carol was grasping at straws.

'Much more likely,' Fran reassured her.

'But … you asked me if he – Justin – had been in touch with me.' Carol looked from Fran to Libby and back again.

'We wondered who he came to see in England. Why he was here. You see,' said Fran, 'he called a friend of ours the other day, and the police found that call on Justin's phone, so they questioned Harry – our friend – because they thought Justin was coming to see him.'

'And he might have murdered Justin?' said Carol. 'And did he?'

Libby laughed. 'No, and luckily he has a cast iron alibi. But they are looking for anyone Justin talked to.'

'Well, it couldn't have been me. He wouldn't have had my mobile number, and no one has the landline number of this house, only Sally.'

'And her phone's missing,' said Fran.

'Had you heard from Sally recently? Did she say anything particular had happened?' asked Libby.

Carol shook her head. 'I wrote to her a few months ago, but she never replied. She tended to keep in touch through social media. I haven't even got a letter –' Carol broke off, her voice suspended.

'The police will return her effects to you,' said Fran. 'Now, is there anything we can do for you?'

Carol wiped her eyes and shook her head again. 'No, I'll be fine. My husband didn't want me to come on my own. I think I'll go back home tonight.'

'That's sensible,' said Libby. 'And you've got my number. Don't hesitate to call if we can help with anything.'

'Actually –' Carol stood up. 'I wonder if you'd do me a huge favour? I know you didn't know Sally, but would you take the key to this house? If the police want to see over it or anything, it would be easier to get the key from you.'

'Of course,' said Libby. 'We don't mind, do we Fran?'

Chapter Seventeen

'I don't think I fancy eating at the Ashton Arms now,' said Libby, as they walked back to their cars.

'Nor do I. Shall we go home, or do you want to go somewhere else?' said Fran.

'George,' they said together.

Fran led the way to The Red Lion in Heronsbourne, where they parked in Pedlar's Row.

The bar was almost empty, and George was, as he often was, found at the bar reading a newspaper.

'Ladies!' he said as they came in. 'Pleasure to see you.'

Libby hoisted herself on to a bar stool. 'Nice to see you, too, George. How's the posh coffee machine?'

'Doing well, thanks, Libby. Coffee?'

'Yes, please.'

'I'll have one, too,' said Fran, 'and have you got anything on for lunch?'

'My missus's meat pies. How does that sound?'

'Brilliant. I'll have one of those, thank you.'

'So – you off investigating again?' asked George as he served coffee.

'Now, why would you think that?' said Fran with a smile.

'Because you usually are. Especially if you come over here.'

'Fair enough,' said Libby. 'And yes – in a way.'

'Not really,' said Fran. 'There were two murders while we were on holiday, and someone connected with one of them lives near here. We've just paid a courtesy visit.'

'Murders on holiday, eh?' George shook his head. 'Can't trust you anywhere, can we? Nobody'd believe it if you put it on telly.'

'Not sure I believe it myself,' said Libby.

'So where does this person live? Here in Heronsbourne?'

'No, actually, she used to live in Cherry Ashton. Doesn't any more, though.' Libby sipped coffee and licked froth off her upper lip.

'So why was you over there, then?'

'Her mother came down to collect things.' Fran also sipped coffee, although more delicately.

'Ah.' George surveyed them both shrewdly. 'Wouldn't be nothing to do that White Lodge business?'

'No,' said Fran firmly. 'This was a young woman who used to live there and moved to Turkey.'

'Ah,' said George again, looking disappointed. 'What happened to the White Lodge then? And that there barn?'

'It was put up for sale,' said Libby, 'but as far as we know, it hasn't sold. The only people interested were a development company, and the Lodge and the barn are both listed, so you can't pull them down.'

'Best thing to happen to them, in my view,' said George. 'Nothing but unhappiness in them buildings.'

'Well, not our business,' said Fran. 'We just came in for lunch.'

'Point taken,' said George cheerfully. 'I'll go and see how them pies are coming on.'

'Did we put him off enough?' Libby asked, when they were settled at a table.

'I think so,' said Fran. 'Not that it really matters, but I suppose the police would want as little gossip as possible.'

'I wonder who it was Justin was coming to see? Or even if he was coming to see someone. We don't even know that.'

'Well, someone knew he was in the country, unless it really *was* some kind of mugging. I think both Ian and Smith are going to keep an eye on us because we could lead them to possible suspects.'

'But *what* possible suspects? We only knew the people who were staying in the hotel, and they didn't know Alec or Sally.'

'Yes, they did. It was Greta who told us about Sally.'

'They didn't know Alec, though.'

'They all said they didn't. Suppose they did?'

'Betty and Walter didn't, I'm sure of it,' said Libby. 'And Walter didn't move enough to murder anyone.'

'We haven't heard back from any of them, have we?' said Fran. 'do you think the police will have been in touch with them?'

'I expect so.'

'Even though Alec had no connection with Jimmy's hotel?'

'But it was a visitor to the hotel who first identified his body, and we were on the boat that found him. That's enough of a connection in the minds of the police.' Libby looked up as George brought over their steaming pies.

'Missus says hello.' he said, placing their plates carefully in front of them. 'Tuck in.'

'Well,' said Fran, when he'd gone, 'we'd better let Ian know about Carol, whatever happens. Now I'm going to concentrate on this pie. God bless my waistline.'

To Libby's surprise, when she arrived home there were three emails in her inbox, from Martha, Greta, and Neal, all of them concerning Justin Newcombe's murder. Greta's and Neal's both contained telephone numbers, with requests to send hers if she would prefer it. Martha's was simply a request for information, as she had only been informed because her number was in Justin's phone.

Libby called Greta and sent Neal an email with her own number.

'How did you hear about it?' asked Libby when Greta answered.

'Martha called me because the police had told her. She said she was going to contact you.'

'She has. Everything seems to be a terrible muddle. Did she tell you about the Turkish policeman who's now investigating?'

'Yes, but I'm not sure what he's doing. I thought that Johnny Smith's people were investigating?'

'They are – but they're not on home soil. And the Turkish policeman may well be a bit suspicious.' Libby didn't want to go into the theories of Alec's witness protection status, nor tell Greta anything about Sally Weston's mother.

'Will you let me know if you hear anything else?' asked Greta. 'It's very worrying, all this.'

'Yes, of course,' said Libby, mentally crossing her fingers. She would if she could, of course.

She had barely ended the conversation with Greta when the phone began ringing.

'Libby? Is that you? It's Neal here – Neal Parnham.'

'Hello, Neal. How are you?'

'I'm fine, thank you, but what's all this about Justin? Do you know anything?'

'Only that he was found on Sunday in a London hotel. How did you find out?'

'Oh, the police. He had my number in his phone. They apparently wondered if he'd arranged to meet me.'

'Yes, they thought the same about Harry,' Libby felt safe in replying.

'*Harry*?'

'Oh, yes. They turned up to question him on Monday morning. Quite nasty with it, too.'

'Fuck!' Libby was quite surprised as swearing didn't seem to fit Neal's rather quiet personality.

'Did they come and see you?' she asked.

'No, they just phoned. I got the impression they were going through all the British numbers in his phone.'

'Whatever did they do before mobile phones,' said Libby.

'So why did they go and see Harry?'

'Justin called him on Friday night to tell him about the Turkish policeman.'

'What Turkish policeman?'

'I told you in the group email I sent. I sent it to you, Greta and Tom, and Betty, and Harry emailed Justin.'

'Oh, I didn't realise it was – er – serious. And you said Commander Smith had turned up, too? Here?'

'Yes, on my doorstep, but it seems as if Smith's team are working on one theory and the Turkish policeman on another.

They don't appear to like each other very much. But none of them like the crowd at the Istanbul Palace.'

'Oh, them. I didn't go there more than once.'

'What did you think of them?'

Neal was silent for a moment. 'I didn't think much of them at all,' he said eventually. 'They seemed very cliquey.'

'Did you go with Alec?'

'Yes. He was very good about taking me to places ...' His voice trailed off.

'And he introduced you to people like Justin and Sally.'

'And Martha. He even introduced me to the owner of that hotel and his awful wife.'

'Geoff and Christine Croker.'

'Is that who they are? I can't remember. I thought they seemed as if they should be on the Costa del Sol, not Erzugan.'

'Fran and I thought that, too. We thought they were all lotus-eaters in that place.'

'They were what?'

'Lotus-eaters. From Homer's *Odyssey*. The island where the sailors were given lotus to eat and forgot all about going home and stopped caring about their homes and families.'

'Ah.'

Libby decided Neal now thought she'd been showing off. 'It's quite a common expression,' she explained. 'Means people who run away from obligations and hide.'

'Like criminals in Spain.'

'Well, that's what you meant about the Costa del Sol, isn't it?'

'Exactly. So are the police looking into those people?'

'I believe so,' said Libby cautiously.

There was a short silence.

'Who's looking into the boat?' Neal said suddenly. 'The Turkish police or the English?'

'His boat? I don't know – the Turkish, I think. It was in its normal place the day he was found, wasn't it?'

'I think so. I can't remember. Don't forget I didn't know anything about it until the Jandarma came to talk to you in the evening.'

'Of course. I'd forgotten about that. Someone said it was still beached.'

'But if someone had used the boat the night before they would have been careful to beach it again, wouldn't they?'

'But wouldn't it have been damp? Or would it have dried out by the time they had a look at it?'

'I don't know,' said Neal. 'It's very hot out there, isn't it? It could have dried. Someone must be looking into it.'

'I expect they are. Infuriating, isn't it, that we can't just pop over and see what they're doing.'

'Couldn't we?' said Neal hopefully.

'No. Both police forces would find that very suspicious. Anyway,' added Libby cruelly, 'your two best friends out there ...'

'Are dead. I know. That's why I want to know.' Neal sighed. 'Honestly, I feel as if it's my fault.'

'Why on earth do you feel that? You said that while we were out there.'

'It all happened after I got there and made friends with them.'

'Unless it was you that killed them, I can't see the connection,' said Libby, wondering, all the same.

'But perhaps it was something I said? You know, something I didn't realise ...'

'Like talking about something in the past that struck a chord?' Libby saw a glimmering of light.

'Exactly! I can't think what it could be at the moment, but I could have done, couldn't I? In general conversation.'

'Think back,' said Libby. 'Who was there when you were in company with Alec? Was Justin always there?'

'Ye-es,' said Neal slowly. 'Sometimes we ate at Martha's, sometimes at The Red Bar, and there were always several people around. Justin and Alec, Sally sometimes, a couple of others who I don't remember very well.'

'So a lot of conversations could have been overheard?'

'Oh, yes.'

'But if that was it, wouldn't you have been the victim? If someone thought you knew something you shouldn't?"

'Oh.' Neal sounded miserable. 'I suppose so. Oh, God!'

'What?'

'If that *is* the case, someone might be after me!'

The thought had occurred to Libby, too. 'It's unlikely, though,' she said. 'If all three deaths are connected, the reason is surely more likely to be out in Erzugan than here.'

'I suppose so.' Neal sounded reluctant to agree. 'Do you know any more about the investigation?'

'Not really. Just that we've been questioned again by the police, as I told you.' Libby paused 'Neal, I don't suppose Alec or Justin ever said they knew one another in this country before they went to Turkey?'

'No.' Neal now sounded surprised. 'That's a thought though, isn't it? I wonder ...'

'Nor Sally?'

'I didn't talk to Sally much. She wasn't always around.'

'Only –' Libby hesitated. 'Only Fran and I met her mother this morning.'

'Her *mother*?'

'Yes. Turns out she used to live near us. We didn't know her, though.'

'I suppose they all would have had relations here,' said Neal. 'I just hadn't thought about it. How did you find out?'

'It was in our local paper. It does make you wonder about Alec's long-lost mother, doesn't it?'

'Poor woman. I don't suppose she even knows.' Neal sighed. 'Oh, well, unless the police come knocking on my door I don't suppose I'll hear any more about it.'

'Are you on Facebook?' asked Libby.

'Yes, why?'

'If you join Martha's page, and Jimmy's, we're all keeping in touch on those.'

'Great idea. Thanks, Libby. And I'll send you a friend request, if I may.'

'Of course,' said Libby. 'I'll check it out later. Nice to talk to you, Neal.'

'If only it wasn't for such an awful reason. Bye, Libby.'

And that's that, thought Libby, switching off her phone. Now we just have to wait until someone sees fit to tell us what's going on.

And then someone did.

Chapter Eighteen

'Is that Libby Sarjeant?'

'Yes – who's calling?' asked Libby, suspecting a cold caller of some sort.

'Geoff Croker here – from the Istanbul Palace in Erzugan. I don't know whether you remember?'

Libby's heart gave an uncomfortable thump. 'Yes, I remember. Why are you calling?'

'I was wondering if you could tell me why my friends and I are being harassed by the British police.'

There was no doubt of the aggression in Geoff Croker's voice.

'Are you? What about?'

'Mrs Sarjeant, you and your friend were seen in the company of that commander from the Met, and we know he consulted you about the murders. So why are we all being investigated?'

Libby sighed. 'Look, Mr Croker. Mrs Wolfe and I were being questioned because we were the people who found the first body. I have no idea why you are being investigated. The police aren't still there, are they?'

'I'm sure you know that they are.'

'I'd heard that it was being investigated by the Turkish police now,' said Libby disingenuously.

'And where did you hear that?'

'On one of the social media pages,' said Libby glibly.

'Oh.' There was a short silence. 'So you don't know?'

'Look,' said Libby, suddenly exasperated. 'How can I know what's going on over there? I'm in England, for heaven's sake, and I only went to Erzugan once, I'm not even a regular visitor.' She wondered if the Crokers knew about Justin and decided not to ask. 'And how did you get my number, by the way?'

'You can find anything on the internet.'

'I didn't think my telephone number was on there,' said Libby frostily.

Croker grunted.

'Why are you bothered about being investigated by the police anyway? Unless you've got something to hide, of course.'

'What do you mean by that?' Croker's voice now was more shocked than aggressive.

'What I said. They've been investigating us, too. Proper in depth police checks to see if we've got any connection to any – either – of the victims. So it stands to reason they'd investigate friends from their own home village.'

'They weren't friends of ours.'

Libby just stopped herself in time from saying 'So we'd heard'. 'Well, I'm sorry I can't help you,' she said instead. 'What are the Jandarma doing now?'

'We've got some inspector or something from Antalya and his sidekick. He's at least up front.'

'How do you mean?'

'Asks us all where we were on the night in question, that sort of thing.'

'Sensible,' said Libby. 'Have they found out anything about the boat?'

'The boat?' Croker snapped.

'Yes. Whether Alec Wilson's own boat was used to take him out to sea.'

'No idea. If you talk to the police any more, tell 'em to lay off.' And the call was abruptly ended.

'Now that was interesting,' Libby said to Sidney, as she replaced the handset into its cradle. Sidney, sitting on the third step of the staircase, chirruped. The front door opened and Ben grinned at her.

'What was interesting?'

130

'Guess who just rang?'

'I've no idea.' He went through the sitting room into the kitchen. 'Are you ready for a drink?'

'It's a bit early, isn't it? I haven't started dinner yet.'

'Well, let's have one anyway, and you can tell me all about your day.'

Armed with a glass of red wine, Libby recounted the day's events and conversations.

'And what's so interesting is that Croker actually bothered to track me down and call me,' she concluded. 'Does he really think that I have any influence?'

'It must have got around about you helping Smith search the houses,' said Ben, 'but, yes, it is significant. I think you ought to tell Ian.'

'Not Smith? It's his team on the ground out there.'

'You don't really want to speak to Smith, do you? Ian can pass it on.'

'OK.' Libby sighed. 'Fran was going to tell him about Carol Oxford. He'll be moaning at us again.'

Ian called back in response to Libby's message just as she and Ben were sitting down to a hastily constructed meal.

'Can you tell me all that again, please?' he said. 'I've just got Fran's message about Cherry Ashton – and now this. Can't you keep out of it?'

'Hey! Neither of those things were our fault. Carol phoned me out of the blue, and so did Geoff Croker. And that worried me, because he's in Erzugan, yet he tracked down my home telephone number. When I asked, he said you could find anything on the internet.'

'There are searchable online directories, Lib.'

'Yes, but he'd have to know where I lived, wouldn't he? And how to spell my name.'

'Hmm. So tell me exactly what he said.'

Libby gave her plate a despairing glance. 'Ian – I've just started my dinner.'

'Well, carry on eating. You can talk at the same time.'

Libby sighed, and between mouthfuls once again related the

131

whole of the day's events.

'I think I'd better pass all this on to Smith,' said Ian when she'd finished. 'This is coming uncomfortably close to home.'

'I just don't see how Croker got hold of me, and why he should think I had anything to do with the investigation.' Libby swallowed a mouthful of sausage.

'He told you that himself,' said Ian. 'And there is obviously a reason that he and his cohorts are uncomfortable with being investigated.'

Libby was thinking. 'You know you said Wilson was in a witness protection scheme? Well, suppose he was a criminal himself and there was a falling out of thieves?'

'You said there was no love lost between Wilson and Croker.'

'We've been told not, but suppose –'

'Stop supposing, Libby. Leave it the police.'

'OK. But what about the boat? Croker seemed interested – or nervous – when I asked about the boat.'

'I'm sure Smith will be looking into that as well. Now go back to your dinner, and I'll see you on Wednesday.'

'He's going to pass it on,' Libby told Ben, resuming her meal. 'He does think it's significant, like you said.'

'And what did he say when you suggested Wilson might have been a criminal himself?'

'Told me to stop supposing.'

'What were you thinking, then?'

'Oh, I don't know, but we've already decided that most of the ex-pats are escaping from something. Suppose he's escaping from a criminal past and that's why he was flagged up on the police system, nothing to do with witness protection?'

'It's possible,' said Ben, pushing his empty plate away. 'And what about the boat?'

'I find it odd that the boat hasn't been mentioned more. And it meant something to Geoff Croker, I'm sure of it.'

'Not necessarily Wilson's boat,' said Ben. 'It could be some other boat.'

'Academic, anyway,' said Libby. 'I don't know why I'm

bothering about it.'

Ben laughed. 'If you didn't, I'd be worried.'

Ian called back a little later that evening.

'I passed the information on. Apparently, it was Smith's people who called on Sally Weston's mother at her home somewhere up north to tell her and it's the Met who are dealing with Newcombe's death, so I'm completely out of the picture. I didn't speak to Smith myself and I can't say the sergeant who dealt with me was helpful. So I'm afraid that's that, Libby.'

'So it is.' Libby heaved a sigh. 'I wish I knew what had really happened, but I suppose we won't, now.'

'Don't go poking around. There's obviously something sensitive about the case, so keep out of it.'

'All right, all right. I'll be good. Are you still coming for a drink on Wednesday?'

Ian laughed. 'Of course. Wouldn't miss it for the world.'

Libby sent a round robin email to her fellow visitors to Erzugan and Martha to tell them what had been happening, and tried to tell herself to stop thinking about the case. It didn't work.

On Tuesday morning, just as Libby was setting out to do some essential shopping in the village the landline rang.

'Libby? It's Carol Oxford.'

'Oh, hello,' said Libby, surprised.

'I just thought I'd let you know I was going back to Norfolk today. I've told the police you have the key to the house and you're looking after it.'

Am I? thought Libby. Aloud, she said 'The local police?'

'I had the card of the sergeant who came to see me at home. I called him.'

'Perhaps you ought to tell the local police as well,' said Libby. 'The people who came to see you were from the Met, weren't they?'

'No, they were from our local police in Norfolk, but I suppose they don't need to know.'

'Tell you what, give me the name and number of the

policeman you called, and then if the police here have any questions, they can call him.'

'Right. Wait a minute ...' Libby heard a scrabbling noise. 'Here we are.' Carol read out the name and number. 'Have you heard anything else since yesterday?'

'No,' said Libby, 'except that there's no reason to talk to any of us visitors again. So I won't learn anything else, I'm afraid.'

When Carol rang off, Libby tucked the piece of paper inside her purse and set off down Allhallow's Lane. When exactly she decided to go and search Sally Weston's house she couldn't quite pinpoint, but certainly by the time she reached the 'eight--til-late', Ahmed and Ali's mini supermarket, she'd decided.

'I don't suppose you've got any of those thin medical gloves, have you?' she asked Ali, who had appeared to serve her.

'Course we have.' Ali led the way to the right section. 'Have to buy them a hundred at a time though.' He looked at her quizzically. 'Avoiding fingerprints?'

As this was exactly what she was doing, Libby gasped. 'Of course not!' She grabbed the box, put it in her basket and hurried off towards the tinned food section to hide her red face.

When she emerged a few minutes later, she pulled out her mobile phone and called Fran.

'I'm going to have a look round Sally's house,' she told her. 'Want to come?'

'What for?' asked Fran dubiously.

'I've just got a feeling about it.'

'That's my line. Anyway, Sally hadn't lived there for years and she was killed because of Alec Wilson's murder, nothing to do with her life here.'

'We don't know that.'

'Oh, I think we do. You're just being nosy.'

'All right, I am. But we've got the key and I've got the name of the policeman Carol told about us, so it's all quite legal.'

Fran sighed. 'I suppose I will. You'll only get into trouble if I don't come with you. When?'

'This afternoon? I'll meet you there. I'm not going to park in the pub car park though. There must be a parking space behind the house.'

'OK. Two o'clock? I want lunch first.'

Deciding not to tell Ben where she was going, Libby went home, made herself a sandwich and reviewed everything she knew about the murders from the discovery of Alec Wilson's body onwards. As she'd gone over everything so many times, this was not particularly fruitful, but served to put her in the right frame of mind for a probably negative search of Sally Weston's house.

She found a space with parking bays behind the row of houses containing Sally Weston's. Approaching the front door, she met Fran coming the other way.

'I parked at the pub,' said Fran. 'It seemed easier.'

'Right,' said Libby. 'Let's go in.'

Chapter Nineteen

'What are we looking for?' asked Fran.

'I've no idea,' said Libby. 'I just thought we ought to see.'

'We went through her house in Erzugan and didn't find anything, and that's where she actually lived,' said Fran.

'But she might have stored things in the loft here,' said Libby.

'Libby!' said an exasperated Fran. 'That was years ago – before she went to Turkey and before she ever set eyes on Alec Wilson.'

'I've just got a feeling,' said Libby stubbornly, and made for the stairs.

Luckily, the loft hatch was easily reachable and equally luckily, there was a pull down ladder. Libby cautiously went up and found a light switch.

'Not much up here,' she called down to Fran. 'Just a couple of boxes.' She sat on the floor of the loft and opened the first box.

Ten minutes later, having discarded several years of bank statements and birthday cards, she tried the second, which appeared to contain old clothes. Suddenly, there was a furious knocking at the front door.

'Hello?' Libby heard Fran say.

'Who are you? What are you doing in this house?' asked an angry female voice. Libby clambered over the edge of the loft and cautiously descended the ladder.

'... for Sally's mother, Carol,' Fran was saying as she reached the ground floor. On the doorstep stood a small woman with greying red hair and a pointed nose, squaring up to Fran aggressively.

'I always kept an eye on it for her,' said the woman. 'What did she want to go and ask someone else for?'

'This was Carol, not Sally,' said Libby. 'She went back to Norfolk this morning.'

'I know that. I saw her go.'

'Oh, do you know Carol?' asked Fran.

'Course I do. Known her for years, both of 'em. Even that old bastard up there.' The woman jerked her head in the direction of Ashton Court.

'So did we,' said Libby.

That stopped the woman in her tracks. 'You did?'

'Yes. So why don't you come in and have a sit down. We're here perfectly legally, you know.'

Looking mollified, the woman stepped over the threshold and edged towards the sitting room. 'Sally asked me to look in now and again. She never came back, you see, after that old business.'

'You must have lived here a long time,' said Libby, sitting down and motioning the woman to do the same.

'Years. Lived up the road in one of them cottages, but when these nice new ones was built, I moved. I used to clean for Carol years ago.'

'Didn't she come and see you yesterday, or the day before?'

'I come and see her. She wouldn't know I lived almost next door. She was upset though.'

'She would be. Sorry, what's your name? I'm Libby Sarjeant and this is my friend, Fran Wolfe.'

'Agnes Stewart. Now I know you.' Agnes peered at them both through watery blue eyes. 'You're them women who got the old bastard arrested.'

Fran sighed. 'Yes, we are.'

'So you trying to find out who killed young Sally?'

'No, that's up to the Turkish police,' said Libby, improvising rapidly, 'but they want to know if there was any connection with any of the people over there before she left England.'

'Oh. Ah.' Agnes looked at her feet. 'Well, I wouldn't know.

I knew Carol, and Sally when she was a girl. And the two friends who come over regular to lunch.'

'Carol's friends?'

'Old schoolfriends, they was. All come from here or roundabouts. But then Carol moved away. Don't know what happened to the others.'

'Well, if we hear what happened to Sally we'll be sure to let you know,' said Fran, 'and in the meantime, we'll come and tell you if we're coming to the house again, shall we?'

'No need.' Agnes gave them a sweet smile. 'I know who you are now.' She stood up and made for the door. 'Sorry about Sally. She was a lovely kid. And that Gerald she was friends with. Always thought they'd end up together, but they didn't.'

'Was he her boyfriend?' asked Libby.

'Not sure. He was the son of one of Carol's friends I was telling you about. He was lovely, too.' She shrugged. 'But there. Haven't seen any of them for ten years – more.'

'So how is any of that relevant to Sally's murder?' Fran asked as they closed the door on Agnes. 'It all happened years ago. Carol's old schoolfriends are nothing to do with this.'

'No, I know,' said Libby with a sigh. 'It was interesting though. I'll go back up and close the loft.'

Before she did so, Libby had another quick look through the first box she'd opened, flicking through the birthday cards she'd discarded earlier, and sure enough came to a card signed 'Jean, Bob, and Gerald'. It was a child's card, so certainly not relevant to the enquiry, as Fran had already said. She sighed again and tucked it back into the box.

'I think we ought to tell Carol we've been here. I'm pretty sure Agnes will tell her otherwise,' said Fran as Libby reappeared in the living room.

'I suppose so,' said Libby. 'Shall we call from here?'

'That would be a bit cheeky,' said Fran.

'Oh, all right. Good job I've got her number in here,' said Libby, pulling her mobile out of her pocket.

'Hello?' Carol sounded breathless as she answered the phone.

'Carol, it's Libby. Oh, sorry, you're not still on the road, are you?'

'No – I've just this minute walked through the door. What's the matter?'

'Nothing. Fran and I came over to check the house was secure and met your friend Agnes, so we thought we'd tell you we'd been because I expect she will.'

'Yes, she would. But why did you want to check? I only left this morning.'

Libby stared at Fran in panic. 'Well, actually,' she began.

'Someone was seen looking round,' Fran whispered.

'Someone was seen looking round,' said Libby with relief. 'You know we told you about our policeman friend? Or did we? Anyway, we told him about us having the key, just in case, you know, and he relayed the information that someone was seen.'

'Really?' Carol sounded puzzled. 'When was this?'

'Lunchtime,' said Libby promptly. 'So we thought we'd pop over. Agnes hadn't seen anybody.'

'Good. Well, it's a relief to know someone's looking out for the property. They're so vulnerable standing empty, especially in such a rural area.'

'Agnes will be keeping an eye out, she said. She was telling us she's known you and Carol for years. She told us about your lunch parties.'

'Lunch parties? Oh!' Carol laughed. 'I used to have a couple of old schoolfriends over regularly when I lived up at the Court and Agnes always insisted on coming to help. In the holidays they brought their children and Agnes used to look after them.'

'She mentioned a Gerald,' said Libby. 'Was he one of them?'

'Jean's son, yes.' Carol sighed. 'Sadly, she died and we completely lost touch with Gerald.'

'Sad when that happens,' said Libby. 'Well, we just thought we'd keep you informed.'

'That's very good of you,' said Carol. 'Now I'm dying for a cup of tea.'

'You were fishing,' accused Fran, as Libby put her phone

away.

'No I wasn't.'

'Yes, you were. There was no reason at all to mention what Agnes told us. I keep telling you, none of Sally's past life is relevant.'

'I can't help feeling that it is,' said Libby, 'and no, I'm not stealing your thunder, I just have a feeling. I think it's because of Justin Newcombe's murder. That happened in this country, and unless the murderer did that flit back and forth thing, which I'm sure the police will have checked by now, the murderer is here.'

'But is the root of the problem here?'

'I don't know. But look – something connects Justin, Sally, and Alec. They were all British and now they're all dead.'

'And they were all residents of the same Turkish village. It makes much more sense that the motive is out there.'

'Oh, all right. Come on then. You didn't find anything down here?'

'No. Where did you put your gloves?'

'Oh, hell! I left them in the loft. I took them off when I first heard Agnes.'

'Off you go then. Don't want to leave evidence of our poking about.'

Libby drove home once again without really noticing where she was going. She couldn't explain why she had been so sure there was some connection with Sally to the motive for the murders, and just hoped Fran's psychic moments hadn't rubbed off on her. She decided there was no point in telling Ian about their visit until she could mention it casually tomorrow night.

In the event, she didn't have to wait until Wednesday evening. Ian called an hour after she got home to ask if he could see her.

'Business or pleasure?' she asked warily.

'Business, I'm afraid,' said Ian. 'I'll see you in half an hour.'

Half an hour. Libby rushed her preparations for dinner and shoved everything in the oven. Ben appeared through the back door just as she did so.

'What's up?' he asked. 'You look harassed.'

Libby explained and made for the stairs to tidy herself up, but too late. The doorbell rang.

Ian smiled at her.

'This is Inspector Michael James from the Met,' he said indicating the tall, gloomy-looking man behind him. 'He's just got a few questions for you.'

'What about?' said Ben appearing at Libby's shoulder.

'The death of Justin Newcombe, Mr ...?' said the tall man.

'This is Ben Wilde, Inspector,' said Ian. 'He was also in Erzugan at the time of the murders.'

'Do come in,' said Libby, and led the way into the sitting room. Sidney left it.

'How can we help you?' she asked when they were all settled. 'We've already told DCI Connell and Commander Smith everything we know.'

Inspector James sighed a gloomy sigh. 'I know, Mrs Sarjeant. But something's come up, you see.'

'Er – can I ask if you're investigating the murders in Turkey? Or the one over here?' Ben asked. 'Only there seem to be several overlapping investigations going on, and we'd like to know who we're talking to.'

Inspector James looked at Ian and gave him a slight nod.

'It's been decided that the investigations should be conducted together,' said Ian, 'and I and my force have been co-opted to help this end.'

'This end?' said Libby. 'Why here? Because Sally Weston had a house here? But she didn't live in it.'

'No,' said Ian. 'Because Justin Newcombe had a return train ticket in his pocket to Canterbury.'

Chapter Twenty

Libby gaped.

'Canterbury?' said Ben. 'Why?'

'That's what we want to find out, sir,' said Inspector James. 'Now you and Mrs Sarjeant have both said you only met Mr Newcombe while you were on holiday in ...'

'Erzugan,' supplied Libby. 'Yes.'

'And you'd never met him before? In this country?'

Libby sighed in exasperation. 'No! We'd never met any of them. It was the first time any of us had even been there.'

'Except Guy,' said Ben.

'Mr Wolfe,' explained Ian. 'He went there a couple of times some years ago with his daughter.'

'So he could have known all the victims?' said Inspector James.

Libby felt a cold ball form in her stomach.

'He could have, but he didn't,' said Ian firmly. Inspector James stared at him for a few minutes, then turned to Libby and Ben. 'We have to find out why he was coming to this area, and it turns out that you all live around here. And that Newcombe actually called –' he paused to look down at his notebook, 'Mr Harry Price on the Friday before he died.'

'But we've been through all this,' said Libby, turning to Ian. 'Can't you just pass over all the interviews or whatever?'

'We have,' said Ian.

'Has Commander Smith?' asked Ben.

Ian and Inspector James looked each other.

'Not entirely,' said Ian.

'You wouldn't have expected him to, would you,' said Libby. 'Sneaky b –'

'Libby!' Ben broke in sharply.

Inspector James' gloomy face shifted into what could almost be a smile.

'It's difficult when you don't know key parts of the investigation,' he said, 'which is why we are having to go back to the beginning.'

'Are you part of Commander Smith's team?' asked Libby.

'Not exactly.' James sighed deeply. 'Very difficult.'

'So you've got to ignore the murders in Turkey and concentrate on Justin Newcombe?' said Ben.

'In a way,' said Ian. 'But we can't ignore the events in Turkey because it's obviously where the motive for this killing exists.'

'And nobody from the village flew into London and straight out again, I suppose?' said Libby.

Ian and James both smiled at this.

'It's been checked,' said James.

'So the murderer is definitely in this country?' said Ben. 'But it could be anybody – somebody none of us would have heard of.'

'It could,' said Ian reasonably, 'but we've got to start somewhere, and the people who had recently visited and were there at the time of the murders would seem to be logical.'

'What about Justin's family?' asked Libby. 'Surely they'd be the first people to speak to?'

'Both his parents are dead, and his only sister lives in Australia,' said Inspector James. 'And no correspondence with anyone in the UK was found in his apartment in Turkey.'

'No emails?' said Ben.

'And before you ask, no phone calls to this country except from the one to Harry,' said Ian. 'Believe me, everything has been checked and double-checked, both this end and in Turkey.'

'What about the Turkish policeman who's turned up over there?' asked Libby. 'We were told he wasn't exactly welcome.'

'Who told you?' asked James.

'Martha, I think. One of the restaurant owners. She's British,

144

married to a Turkish man, Ismet.'

'You're in touch with her, then?'

'We all email each other. The visitors and Martha, and Jimmy talks to us on his Facebook page.'

'Social media.' Inspector James glared at his feet.

'Don't give anything away, will you?' said Ian.

'Of course not. I can be discreet, you know,' said Libby.

Ben and Ian laughed, and Inspector James looked puzzled.

'Nosiest woman in the world,' said Ben, draping an affectionate arm round his beloved's shoulders.

'Why did he want to come to Canterbury?' Libby ignored them and pursued her own thoughts. 'Unless – perhaps he came from round here? I suppose you've looked into that, haven't you?'

'His last known address in this country was in London,' said Ian, 'and that is definitely verified.'

'Because he was in trouble here before he left?' said Libby.

Inspector James frowned at her. 'How do you know that?'

'That old dodge,' said Libby. 'I didn't, but I do now.'

Ian sent her a warning look. Inspector James sighed.

'Yes, he was involved in some – shall we say – creative accounting. He wasn't prosecuted, but he had to sell up to pay the money back, then he just cleared out. I don't know what he was living on out there.'

'More creative accounting, I shouldn't wonder,' said Libby.

'What makes you say that?' asked James.

'There were several ex-pats out there who we thought probably had pasts. It would make sense if he worked for them, wouldn't it?'

'He'd have to get to know the workings of the Turkish tax and legal system pretty quickly and thoroughly,' said Ian.

'It's an angle to follow,' said James. 'I wonder if Smith's team will give us any leads?'

'They'll be pursuing their own agenda,' said Ben. 'I bet the Turkish policeman is looking into the ex-pats thoroughly.'

'He is. So are the British,' said Libby.

'How do you know?' asked two policemen together.

'Geoff Croker phoned me.'

Libby described Geoff Croker's angry phone call and how he refused to reveal how he'd got her phone number.

'I'll pass this on,' said Inspector James, 'but I don't know if it will help us in finding Newcombe's killer.'

'Justin could have upset someone if he really was into tax fraud – or something similar,' said Ben.

'Meanwhile, we have to look into his reasons for coming to England,' said Ian. 'His passport shows that he's not been back here for at least eight years.'

'Has he been anywhere else?' asked Libby.

Inspector James looked startled. 'I don't know. We'll check.'

'Why, Lib?' asked Ian.

'I've got a theory.' Libby pressed her lips together stubbornly.

'Well, share it, then,' said Ben.

Libby shook her head. 'I can't.'

'Does it explain why he was coming to Canterbury?' asked Inspector James.

'No.' Libby's face fell. 'But it's a nice theory. To do with Alec Wilson.'

Both policemen looked at her suspiciously.

'Not our business, Lib,' said Ben hastily.

Ian stood up. 'Would you excuse us for a moment?' He motioned Inspector James out of the front door, leaving it ajar. Libby looked at Ben.

'What's this all about?' she whispered.

'We're just about to find out.' Ben nodded towards the door, where the two men were coming back.

'Now, Lib,' said Ian, after they had re-seated themselves, 'strictly off the record – I've told Inspector James to forget it unless it's relevant – what's the theory?'

Libby looked nervously at the London policeman. 'It concerns something I don't think I'm supposed to know.'

'I guessed that,' said Ian. 'But I think you had your guess confirmed by Commander Smith, didn't you?'

146

'More-or-less,' said Libby.

'What guess?' said Inspector James.

'I – we – thought it was possible that Alec Wilson was a false name and that he could be in the witness protection scheme. We don't know if it was that, or whether he was a plant, or a criminal, but we know if anything happened to him it would be flagged up and reported to the Met.' She took a deep breath. 'I wondered if Justin and Alec were working together on something that got Alec killed and then Justin was killed to cover it up. After all, Smith thinks Sally Weston's murder was to stop her talking about Alec. Why not Justin's?'

'What sort of thing would they be working on?' asked James.

'Some sort of smuggling operation? Justin could be – oh, I don't know – sorting out the finances?'

The two policemen looked at each other.

'It's a possibility,' said Ian. 'So what's that got to do with him going somewhere other than England?'

'Well,' Libby looked from one policeman to the other, 'if it was smuggling, he could have been going to where the stuff was going or coming from.'

'It's a bit far-fetched,' said Inspector James, 'but we'll check his passport. As long as it hasn't been handed over to Commander Smith.'

'Why should it be? He was killed here.' said Ben. 'Smith's looking into the other two murders.'

'He'll want all information. And if there was anything at all in Libby's theory, he'd have tied it up as tight as he could.'

Libby nodded, but kept quiet.

'So there's nothing you can tell us about Newcombe, then?' Inspector James stood up. 'Or why he came here?'

'But he didn't come here, did he?' said Ben.

'He was on his way to Canterbury, though.' Libby was frowning. 'I suppose …'

'Now what?' said Ian. 'More theories?'

Libby looked up and smiled brightly. 'No, no. Of course not.'

Ian regarded her suspiciously for a moment. 'Well, it you hear anything else, be sure to let us know.'

'Who? You or Inspector James?'

'Talk to DCI Connell,' said Inspector James. 'He'll forward anything relevant to me.'

'So what new theory were you forming?' asked Ben as they watched the long black car disappear down the lane.

'What makes you say that?' Libby turned and went back inside.

'Because you were. Ian and I both knew it.'

Libby went to check on the progress of the dinner. 'I was just wondering whether Carol's old friends had anything to do with it all. You know, the ones Agnes told us about.'

'Why would they have anything to do with it? That was years in the past before either the business at White Lodge or Sally's departure to Turkey. Come on, Lib! That's pretty tenuous, even for you.'

'I was just thinking about – oh, what was his name? – the boy Sally had been so friendly with. Gerald, that's it.'

'What about him? That must have been – what? Thirty years ago?'

'We don't know. All Carol said was that his mother had died and she'd lost touch with him.'

Ben opened a bottle of red wine. 'And you've now decided he went to Turkey and became either Alec Wilson or Justin Newcombe.'

'Or even Neal Parnham,' said Libby.

Chapter Twenty-one

'Neal Parnham?' Ben stopped in the act of pouring wine.

'Well, it all started after he went out there, didn't it?'

'But that was simply a coincidence,' said Ben.

'What if it wasn't?' said Libby.

'Oh, for ...' Ben broke off and poured the wine. 'Look, now you've got Neal Parnham going out there and causing three deaths because he's someone Sally Weston knew when she was a child. Where on earth is the sense in that?'

Libby shook her head. 'I don't know. I was just thinking that Gerald had disappeared and supposing he turned up in Erzugan and these people all knew him.'

'But there's no connection between any of them before they met in Erzugan. None whatsoever. Come on, Libby, this is pure fantasy.'

Libby sighed. 'I suppose it is. I just can't help thinking there's something somewhere that connects everything. And you have to admit, Justin having a ticket for Canterbury brings it rather close to home.'

'I think Inspector James still suspects Harry,' said Ben, going back into the sitting room.

'Simply because Justin called him? But that was because Harry'd emailed him and given him his phone number.'

'It does look suspicious, you must admit,' said Ben. 'And it probably all comes from being nosy.'

'What do you mean?' Libby was indignant.

'We were trying to find out what was going on, if you remember. If you and Fran hadn't asked Harry to email, none of this would have happened.'

Libby was stricken. She sat down suddenly on the sofa.

'Oh, God, it wouldn't.'

Ben sat down beside her and gave her a squeeze. 'Now don't start blaming yourself. The police suspect Harry simply because of the phone call. It wasn't your fault that someone killed Justin.'

'No.' Libby stared at the empty fireplace. 'Perhaps we need a council of war.'

'Who with?' Ben was wary.

'The other guests are too far away, so just us, I suppose. I'll let the others know, of course, Greta and Tom and Betty.'

'And Neal.'

'Must I?' said Libby.

'Just because you've decided to be suspicious of him doesn't mean he's guilty of anything.'

'Doesn't mean he's innocent either. I mean, any of them could be guilty, I suppose. We don't know any of them that well, do we? Are we jumping to conclusions?'

'Yes, of course we are. Or you are. But if you want to talk to everybody, you have to include everybody.'

'All right,' said Libby with a sigh. 'I'll email them all after we've discussed it.'

'Can't it wait until tomorrow night after rehearsal? We'll all be there then.'

'So will Patti and Anne and more importantly, Ian,' said Libby. 'I'll call Fran after dinner, and you can call Peter.'

'Oh, can I?' Ben grinned at her. 'Thanks.'

Fran was of the opinion that they need do nothing. Harry had no connection to Justin, so was unlikely to be wrongfully charged with murder, and agreed with Ben that the theory of Gerald, whoever he was, had nothing to do with the case. Ben reported that Peter had said the same thing.

'Oh, well,' said Libby, settling back on the sofa with a large scotch to hand, 'that's that, then. Nothing we can do. But I will email all the others just to keep them up to date. The police are bound to ask them all if they have a connection to this part of the world, don't you think?'

'Of course they will, so I should *leave* it to the police. You don't want to forewarn anyone. Ian would be rather annoyed, wouldn't he?'

'Oh, yes, I suppose so.' Libby stared disconsolately into her drink. 'I shall just have to give up, won't I?'

'Yes, please,' said Ben sitting down beside her. 'Leave it to the police. For once.'

Wednesday dawned hazy and hot. Libby wandered into the garden to do something about the plants that had outgrown themselves and were now falling over each other, but soon became too hot to do anything more than sit under the cherry tree. Her mind kept returning to the three murders, trying to find some kind of pattern that linked them all. On second thoughts, she had decided that any one of the visitors could have been the catalyst for them, not just Neal Parnham, but it seemed highly improbable. She and her friends hadn't even met any of the locals before they discovered the body of Alec Wilson, but she really couldn't see Greta and Tom, or Betty and her grumpy Walter, having anything to do with anything illegal. Walter didn't talk to anybody, so was unlikely to have had contact with any of the locals.

Geoff Croker worried her slightly. How exactly *had* he got hold of her phone number? Earlier this morning she'd done a search online for it herself and had been unsuccessful. Of course, if he had some kind of contact in the area he could …

Libby sat up straight, struck as if by a thunderbolt. A contact in this area!

She stood up, dislodging Sidney, who was curled up on her feet, and went back inside to pick up her phone.

'Fran, listen,' she said. 'Suppose Geoff Croker had a contact over here in this area. Suppose that's how he got my number.'

'Eh?'

'Well, if he did, it could be the same contact that Justin had. Couldn't it?'

Fran let out an exasperated sigh. 'Libby, you're letting this get to you. It's not all conspiracy theories, you know. I'm sure Geoff Croker has all sorts of dubious contacts in this country and any one of them could have found out your number for him.'

'But if it was in this area ...'

'Libby! Stop it! I don't suppose Justin's murder has anything to do with you or anyone in this area. He probably had an old friend living in Canterbury. Or he could just have wanted to visit the Cathedral. Stop making mountains out of molehills.'

'But the police have been to see me ...'

'Of course. Routine enquiries. I expect they will have been in touch with all the visitors to Erzugan by now.'

'Have they been in touch with you?'

'Your Inspector James called Guy last night because he was the only one of us who had been there before, but it was only a very brief call. I gather Ian had already told him Guy didn't know anything.'

'Yes,' said Libby, feeling guilty that Ben had told the inspector of Guy's previous visit.

'So stop looking for mysteries. There seem to be three separate police teams on the case now, British and Turkish in Erzugan and British over here. Surely between them they'll get it right?'

'I suppose so,' said Libby. 'I really should forget all about it, shouldn't I?'

'Until something else crops up that sparks your interest, yes,' said Fran, sounding amused.

Libby cleaned the house. The tops of picture frames, light switches, fluff under the beds, limescale in the bathroom. By four o'clock she was exhausted and ran a bath, complete with her only expensive bath lotion. Ben found her in there nearly an hour later.

'You were asleep,' he said.

'Only dozing. I'd have woken up if I'd slipped under the water.' Libby struggled upright. 'Ooh, it's got cold.'

'So why are you in here? Is it something to do with the smell of lemon polish downstairs and the gleaming tiles in the kitchen?'

'Yes. I had a sort of spring clean. Pass me my towel, will you?'

152

'So what brought that on?' Ben handed over the towel and Libby slithered out of the bath.

'To take my mind off the murders,' she said truthfully. 'I needed to stop thinking about it. I phoned Fran because I thought maybe Geoff Croker had a contact in this area and that was why he'd found my number and she told me to stop it. Like you.'

'So you cleaned the house. I must remember to remind you of this when you need to take your mind off things.'

Libby squelched into the bedroom. 'It didn't though, not really. I was still thinking about it. Off on all sorts of tangents.'

'There is, of course, another way,' said Ben approaching with an evil look on his face.

'No, there isn't. I've got to cook and we're rehearsing,' said Libby, retreating to the other side of the bed. 'Stop it, Ben ...'

The rehearsal went as well as it could, and Libby arranged for a few of the cast to visit a costume store in Canterbury to plug the gaps in their own wardrobe. When Susannah professed herself satisfied with the musical efforts of the chorus, Libby sent them all home and she and Ben locked up the theatre. Ben, Libby, and Fran walked down the Manor drive to the high street and turned left towards the pub. To Libby's surprise, Ian was already there, seated at a table with Peter, the Reverend Patti Pearson, and her friend Anne Douglas.

Peter and Ben went to the bar to fetch more drinks and Libby and Fran sat down at the table.

'We've been hearing all about your murders,' said Anne, moving her wheelchair sideways to make room for Libby.

'Really?' Libby raised her eyebrows at Ian. 'Well, you heard about them last week, didn't you?'

'Yes, but there's another one now,' said Patti. 'It's whetted Anne's appetite. The Canterbury connection, you see.'

Ian was looking amused. 'I think Libby's rather puzzled that I should have said anything about it, when I'm always telling her to keep quiet.'

'Well, I was, rather,' said Libby.

'I simply asked Anne if there were any special events going

153

on in Canterbury at the moment. It might have provided our victim with a reason to come over here.'

'And there weren't,' said Anne.

'Ah,' said Libby. Deliberately turning away from Ian, she spoke to Patti.

'How are you? How's the parish?'

'Fine,' said Patti, looking surprised. 'And yours is fine, too. I went to see Bethany earlier.'

Bethany Cole was the vicar of Steeple Martin, and lived in the vicarage on the corner of Allhallow's Lane with her husband John.

'Good.' Libby fidgeted a bit and turned to Fran, who was watching her with as much amusement as Ian.

'You don't know what to talk about, do you?' said Ben with a sigh, placing a frosted glass on the table in front of her. 'Honestly, she can't stop thinking about this case.'

'And making up scenarios,' said Fran, accepting her coffee.

'Come on, then,' said Ian, 'what's the latest?'

Libby felt her cheeks growing hot. 'Don't be patronising,' she snapped.

'I wasn't,' said Ian. 'Go on. You know your theories can often provide results.'

'Not this one,' sighed Libby. 'I just wondered if Geoff Croker had any contacts in this area which was how he got my telephone number, and if so, could it be who Justin was coming to see?' She sighed again. 'See. Far-fetched as all get out.'

'No, it's logical,' said Ian. 'But I have a piece of news.'

'We haven't got a clue what you're talking about,' said Patti, 'but go on. It's still interesting.'

'Inspector James heard from the team in Turkey, who are just about to give up and come home.'

'And?' said five voices.

'The Turkish policeman has uncovered the fact that it was Alec Wilson's own boat that took him out.'

Libby and Fran gasped.

'But why hadn't the British found that out? They must have searched his boat, surely?' said Peter. 'That's one big black

154

mark against them.'

'Yes, I think it's the cause of some tension between our Commander Smith and his troops.'

'I can imagine,' said Ben. 'So has this got them thinking the murderer is definitely local?'

'It's certainly got Smith going back out there. I think he's looking to work more closely with the Turkish force – or that particular policeman, anyway.'

'So the investigation will close down over here?' asked Peter.

'I doubt it,' said Ian. 'Inspector James is still in charge of Justin Newcombe's murder.'

'But it's probably just a coincidence, his coming over here,' said Fran.

'If only we knew whether Alec Wilson was a criminal or in the witness protection scheme,' said Libby. 'At least we might have a clue.'

'You might,' said Ian. 'But it looks to me as if it was neither.'

Chapter Twenty-two

'But Commander Smith said it was,' said Libby, when everyone had registered astonishment.

'He didn't say definitely,' said Fran. 'He just confirmed that Alec was a false name and that the Met were "aware" of him.'

'I've been given a clue,' said Ian turning to Patti. 'You remember the smuggling operation going on near you a few years ago?'

A murmur went round the table. 'How could I forget,' said Patti.

'And you remember that at the time we said there wasn't enough cover from the Border Force to prevent the illegal landings along the coast?'

'I do,' said Libby.

'Well since last summer the Border Force cutters are all over the English Channel because of the increase in immigrants trying to get to Britain.'

'Are you saying,' said Libby, her eyes wide, 'that Alec Wilson was a Border Force officer?'

'It's just possible,' said Ian, 'although of course it wasn't called Border Force then. And I'm not at all sure about this, but the hint has been dropped.'

'By whom, and in relation to what?' asked Libby.

'Now, you know I can't say that,' said Ian, with great good humour, 'but what Inspector James has been led to believe is that Newcombe's arrival in this country has something to do with illegal immigration.'

'In what sense?' asked Peter. 'Was he for it, or agin it?'

'There's no proof of anything, but we believe he was here to make contact with someone.'

'And it wasn't any of us!' said Fran with relief.

'Inspector James doesn't know that,' said Ian with a grin.

'He still thinks it was one of us?' Libby was indignant.

'There's a connection to the Kent coast, as I said, so it makes sense to question visitors to Erzugan from Kent.'

'But we can't be the only ones!' said Libby.

'No, but you're the most recent. And don't forget Sally Weston came from here, too.'

'Not recently,' said Peter.

'Surely she didn't have anything to do with – with – well, whatever it is,' said Libby.

'Not that I know of,' said Ian, 'but it does look suspiciously like all roads leading to Kent.'

'And Guy,' said Fran slowly. 'He went there years ago with Sophie. And now he's been back, and he lives on the coast at Nethergate.'

Silence fell round the table. Anne and Patti were looking horrified, Ben and Peter concerned and Fran and Libby thoughtful.

Ian broke the silence. 'I'm not saying that James is looking specifically at anyone, only that his investigations are pointing to the involvement of someone in the Kentish community.'

'And especially recent visitors,' said Libby bitterly. 'Why, oh why did we go?'

'It was Guy's suggestion,' said Fran. 'That makes it even worse.'

'How are you going to find out who it is, though?' said Libby. 'I mean, we know it isn't any of us, but it could be anybody living in Kent at the moment. Anybody.'

'The Met, Border Force, Commander Smith, and the Turkish police are currently looking for any recent contacts that show up in Newcombe's phone or computer.'

'Would he have been silly enough to keep any contacts in either place?' asked Fran. 'If he was over here to meet someone, he wouldn't have had any details on him I would have thought.'

Ian smiled at her. 'Quite right. I believe they now think there must have been a second, unregistered phone.'

'So the call to Harry is really a red herring?' said Peter.

'To us, it is,' said Ian, 'but not necessarily to Inspector James, or Commander Smith. They may think it's all part of a conspiracy.'

'Oh bloody hell,' said Peter, throwing himself back in his chair. 'Where is this going to end?'

'When we find Newcombe's murderer,' said Ian with a shrug. 'If we can find his contact over here we should be close enough.'

'And how do you do that if you haven't got the right phones or whatever?' asked Libby.

'All the computers in the case will be undergoing forensic examination, you know that,' said Ian. 'Any links between any of the protagonists will be investigated.'

'Including Geoff Croker?'

'I have no idea. Maybe. I told Smith about his call to you.'

'Oh, goody.' The corners of Libby's mouth turned down. 'Now he'll start threatening me.'

'There's not much he can do while he's in Turkey,' said Ben.

'And anyone who's of concern to the police in either country will be carefully watched. He's not likely to slip away,' said Ian.

'Unless he comes by night in an unmarked vessel,' said Libby. 'If that's what the powers that be are thinking that's what's been happening.'

'I think that's what they're afraid of,' said Ian. 'And I've told you far more than I should, as always. Patti, I fear you may have some unwelcome police presence around for a while.'

'They blocked up the tunnel from the inlet, didn't they?' said Patti. The isolated inlet near her village and church of St Aldeberge had been the focus of police attention in the past.

'Oh, yes, but there are many beaches along our coast where small boats can land. It's happened a lot in the past, although now that the Border Force cutters are so omnipresent, it's not happening as frequently. The lifeboats and the coastguard are also more vigilant. There's far less opportunity to land than there was ten years ago.'

'Ten years ago?' Libby fastened on to this. 'That's when Alec went out to Turkey.'

'I wouldn't think there's anything in that,' said Ben.

'Here's Hal,' said Peter, standing up. 'Fill him in while I get him a drink. Anyone else?'

Ian précised his explanations for Harry, with frequent interpolations from Libby, and occasionally from the others. At the end, Harry looked round the table.

'So I'm still not off the hook?'

'Only in Inspector James' mind,' Libby hastily assured him. 'We know you're as innocent as a babe, and so does Ian.'

'And what about Johnny-come-lately? Our precious commander?'

Libby looked uneasily across at Ian. 'We don't know about him.'

'I'm trying to act as a sort of buffer state between you all and the other forces,' said Ian. 'I know you all, and while I see that as an advantage, James and Smith might see it as a hindrance. I'm expecting to be told to butt out any minute.'

'Is there anything we can do?' asked Ben. 'I mean, I know I'm not usually keen on the girls getting involved with investigations, but if Harry and Guy are potentially under suspicion (even though we don't quite know of what) it seems we ought to do something.'

Libby beamed at him.

'I don't know what you *can* do,' said Ian. 'If I'd been taken into Smith's confidence and knew the actual background to this, it would help, as Libby said earlier. Even James is whistling in the dark. All I can say is that it appears that Wilson was on the side of the angels, as far as it goes.'

'And we don't know how far that is,' said Ben.

'No,' said Ian, standing up. 'And while I appreciate that you're all still on edge about this, possibly even more so, now, I still say don't go barging in.' He turned to Libby. 'Especially you, Lib.'

'I wouldn't know where to barge in *to*,' said Libby. 'There's not a hint of anything to go on, is there?'

When Ian left, and Patti and Anne had gone back to Anne's little house in New Barton Lane, they all sat in silence round the table.

'So I'm about to be even more thoroughly investigated,' said Harry eventually. 'Me and Guy.'

'Ian didn't say Guy definitely,' said Libby.

'But he will be,' said Fran. 'As I said earlier, it couldn't look more obvious.'

'OK,' said Ben, leaning forward, elbows on the table, 'so what do we know? Ian said illegal immigration. You've dealt with that before, Lib and Fran. What do you know about it?'

'It wasn't this sort of illegal immigration,' said Libby. 'This looks like small groups of people being brought in on small boats, doesn't it?'

'From Turkey, do you think?' said Peter.

'From Erzugan, I would think,' said Fran. 'It's a tiny, unspoiled bay, miles away from most other civilisation, with the mountains between it and all the main roads. That would make sense of Alec being there.'

'But doing what?' said Harry. 'He was living there as a quiet Englishman, he hadn't any back-up. How would he have stopped anything like that going on?'

They all thought about it for a moment.

'We'd have to start this end,' said Fran. 'Find out what anyone knows about small boats being landed along the coast. Who would we ask?'

'George and Bert,' said Libby. 'They go to all the little bays along the coast in the *Dolphin* and the *Sparkler*, don't they? And they've been at it for years. I bet they'd know.'

'What about the people in Felling?' asked Fran. 'They thought illegals were landing there, didn't they?'

'But it was disproved,' said Libby. 'The river's too narrow – almost unnavigable.'

'But there was a surveillance operation there,' said Fran. 'As we know only too well.'

'So they'd have caught anyone who came that way,' said Ben. 'No, I think your idea of George and Bert is a good one.' He looked round the table. 'Are we all in on this?'

'I can't believe you're saying this,' said Peter, amused. 'You're usually counselling caution.'

'Let's face it,' said Ben, 'over the years I've got inured to these two,' he indicated Libby and Fran, 'getting into trouble, and several times I've even got a bit involved myself. So have we all, if we're honest. Particularly if it affects one of our own. And this time it's two of us.'

'I'll come down to Nethergate tomorrow,' said Libby. 'Will you tell Guy what's going on?'

'I'm hardly likely to keep it to myself, am I?' said Fran, a little tetchily. 'I'll see you in the morning, then. George and Bert usually have their lunch hour around one, so we should catch up with them then.'

They broke up, then, Fran to drive back to Nethergate, Peter and Harry to their little cottage along the high street and Ben and Libby to walk back to Allhallow's Lane.

'Be careful of Fran,' said Ben, as they passed under the overhanging lilac tree on the corner.

'Careful?' repeated Libby.

'She's worried about Guy.'

'Of course she is. If it was you, I'd be worried. I'm worried about Guy, too.'

'There's more to it than that,' said Ben. 'She doesn't know much about his life before they met.'

Libby gasped. 'You can't believe that she thinks he's guilty!'

'No, in her heart of hearts she doesn't, but she herself spelt out the reasons that the authorities might. I think it's a very sensitive subject,' said Ben, 'so tread carefully.'

'I always tread carefully,' said Libby, huffily and erroneously.

Summer had evidently settled in, and Libby drove to Nethergate with the windows down. She aimed to arrive in time to have a chat with Fran before they went to talk to George and

Bert, but when she arrived at Harbour Street, there was nowhere to park, not even right at the end at the back of The Sloop. She turned the car and drove slowly back, across the square and past the ancient Swan Inn, before climbing up to Cliff Terrace, where she parked in front of Peel House, just in time to see Jane Baker descending the front steps.

'Hello! How's the investigation going?' Jane crossed the road to speak to her.

'Investigation?' repeated Libby cautiously.

'The murders in Turkey? And the other one in London?'

'Oh, they aren't anything to do with us,' said Libby. 'The murderer's still in Turkey, they think.'

'What about the woman who lived out at Cherry Ashton?'

'Turns out she was only staying in her daughter's house,' said Libby.

'So Sarjeant and Wolfe are out of the picture?' said Jane, with a knowing look.

'Quite,' said Libby, uncomfortably.

Jane laughed. 'All right, I won't push, but let me know if there's anything remotely publishable.'

Libby escaped gratefully back down to Harbour Street, and to her surprise, spotted Fran already seated at a table with George and Bert outside the Blue Anchor.

'I've got some news for you,' she said, as Libby came up. 'George and Bert actually found a boat full of illegal immigrants ten years ago.'

Chapter Twenty-three

'No! Really?'

Libby stopped dead. George, Bert, and Fran all grinned up at her.

'Yes, really.' Fran pulled out the chair next to her. 'Sit down and we'll tell you all about it.'

Mavis sent the current girl over to take Libby's order, and Fran began the story.

'It was about ten years, ago, wasn't it?' George and Bert nodded. 'And well before the season started, so they went out on a fishing trip.'

'We got a little ole fishin' boat, see,' said Bert. 'Don't use it so much now.'

'Them fish quotas, see,' said George. 'Throwin' it all back. An' we don't want to take the bread out o' they fishermens' mouths.'

Libby knew how the European Union's fishing quotas had almost destroyed the small fishing fleets along the south-east coast of Britain.

'So you were just out for a bit of sport,' she said. 'Where did you go?'

'All along the coast towards Creekmarsh,' Fran said. 'How about that?'

Creekmarsh Place was the home of Lewis Osbourne-Walker, the television presenter for whom Adam and his gardener boss Mog worked. Its grounds led to the bank of an inlet, into which fed the little River Wytch, and was only a few hundred metres from the open sea.

'Bit of a storm blew up, see,' said Bert, 'so we popped inter the creek. And there's this boat, see, driftin' like.'

'So we goes up to see iffen they wants some help. And there's all these girls. Cor.' George shook his head. 'Nearly nekked they was. So us called coastguard.'

'No one was with them?' asked Libby.

'Nah,' said Bert. 'Couldn't speak English, either, any of 'em.'

'So what happened?'

'We give 'em all the blankets and stuff we had on board and waited for coastguard. They wasn't long, an' they took our names. Put someone on board the boat and took 'er in.'

Mavis came to the table with Libby's tea and ham sandwich. Libby smiled her thanks, and Mavis stomped back to her kitchen.

'Heart o' gold, really,' said George, indicating with his cigarette.

'So do you know what happened to the girls on the boat?' asked Libby.

'We both 'ad policeman come and take a statement, and there was a little bit on the telly. Not much. I reckon they wanted to keep it quiet.' Bert sucked on his pipe reflectively.

'We got our blankets back.' said George. 'Dunno what happened after that.'

'You never came across any more?' said Libby.

'Girls, or boats?' Bert threw his head back and guffawed.

'Nah,' said George. 'Customs boats got busier. Border Force now, o'course. An' we don't go out at night. 'Appen there's a few land along there at night. There was them tunnels up at Creekmarsh, wasn't there?'

'Yes. Blocked now, though,' said Fran.

'Like the one at St Aldeberge,' said Libby.

'Oh, ah?' said George, looking interested. 'Smugglin' all over, innit?'

Libby laughed. 'Seems to be.'

She thought back over the adventures she and Fran had been involved in over the years, and yes. There was a lot of smuggling. But the Kent coast, the nearest to the European continent, was a prime target for smugglers, those taking things

166

out, and those bringing things in. And illegal immigration and people trafficking was on the increase. Even two-way trafficking, where illegal immigrants would be smuggled out of Britain via Dover, taken to Italy where they would claim asylum, then get smuggled back into Britain. If they were repatriated, it would only be as far as Italy, as the last place they had claimed asylum. There were huge organised gangs operating these systems and charging their victims large sums of money.

'I was thinking,' she said to Fran as they left George and Bert and wandered back down Harbour Street. 'The nearest village to Creekmarsh is Cherry Ashton.'

'Is that relevant?'

'Well, I wondered if Sally's father had anything to do with smuggling these girls into the country. It sounds like his sort of thing.'

'Sally and her mother had both moved away by that time,' said Fran, 'so you can't link Sally with this. Besides, the fact that that boat was found in the creek was pure accident, I expect. Abandoned by the crew as soon as they found a place to get out safely.'

'Doesn't that strike you as odd?' said Libby, stopping by Lizzie's ice cream booth. 'Want one?'

'Chocolate, please, Lizzie,' said Fran. 'Why is that odd?'

'Eh?' said Lizzie.

'Sorry,' said Libby. 'We were continuing a conversation. I'll have a double vanilla, please.'

'Anyway,' she continued as they went to sit on the sea wall with their cornets, 'Odd because the crew should have been the ones to hand over the girls and get paid. Why did they scarper?'

'Thought they were going to get caught?'

'But by whom?' persisted Libby. 'Why go to all that trouble of bringing the boat over here, presumably all the way from Turkey – how would they have gone? Right through the middle of the Mediterranean, through the Straits of Gibraltar, up the coast of Portugal, northern Spain and France, blimey, it's a journey.'

'Yes,' said Fran thoughtfully, 'it is. And you're right. If you've brought them all that way, why leave without being paid. And without the boat. Someone would have been wanting that back.'

'I bet I know.' Libby waved her ice cream cone. 'The crew were illegal immigrants! Betcha!'

'That makes sense,' said Fran. 'Careful with that ice cream. If the crew volunteered to bring the boat over, they could have planned to get into the country and not go back. If they'd handed over the girls, the contacts over here would have made sure they left again.'

'But the contacts here must have tried to find them – and the girls. And they would have reported back to the people in Turkey.'

'Who were – who? Geoff Croker and his pals?'

'Well, we don't know, do we?' Libby frowned. 'But I bet that was what happened. And the police would have found a translator so they would have known where the boat set out from.'

'And where the girls themselves came from. They could have come from anywhere, via one of those dreadful organisations who organise them.'

'Like the girls from Transnistria.' Libby shuddered. 'Poor things.'

Transnistria was a tiny sliver of a country between Moldova and Ukraine with a bad reputation as far as people trafficking was concerned.

'I suppose ten years ago it would have been easier to get from the bank of the inlet across Creekmarsh's grounds. You couldn't do it now,' said Fran.

'No – all those security patrols,' said Libby. 'I'm glad we saw it before it was fully restored.'

'And while the tunnels were … '

'Still open,' Libby finished for her. 'Yes.'

They sat quietly consuming ice cream for a minute, then turned to one another simultaneously.

'They knew!'

'Must have done.' Libby nodded. 'That Creekmarsh was empty and unprotected.'

'So someone here was organising it,' said Fran.

'That was always the case. It's obviously one of those gangs.'

'But someone knew specifically about Creekmarsh. It's quite hidden away – unless you knew it was here ...'

'And you'd have to know about the inlet, too.' Libby frowned out at the sea. 'Why does it always seem to come back here?' She turned to Fran. 'Hang on – how did Guy hear about Erzugan in the first place?'

'What?' Fran nearly lost her ice cream.

'Well – did someone mention it? Was it in the paper? We know it has never been a package tour destination, so how did he come across it?'

Fran stared, her mouth open. 'Do you know, I never thought of that!' She slid off the wall. 'Come on, let's go and ask him.'

They had to stand outside the shop until they'd finished their ice creams, to Guy's amusement.

'What we want to know,' said Libby, once they'd made it inside.

'Is how did you first hear about Erzugan?' said Fran.

'How ...?' Guy looked bemused. 'What do you mean?'

Fran explained. 'So how did you hear about it?'

Guy frowned and sat down behind his counter. 'I can't remember. It wasn't through a travel agent, because I booked everything direct, as we did this time, although it wasn't as easy then.' He picked up his phone. 'I'll ask Sophie if she remembers.'

Sophie, as so many young people were, was almost surgically attached to her smartphone and answered immediately. Guy asked his question, and listened intently, his face clearing.

'Oh, of course! I'd completely forgotten that. Thanks, Soph. See you soon.' He switched off the phone. 'She remembered.'

'And?' said Libby and Fran together.

'It was Rachinda Sharma.'

'Rachinda!' Again, Fran and Libby spoke together. They had met Rachinda and her sister Rachita at the same time they'd met Sally Weston's father.

'How did she know about it?' asked Libby. 'Those girls were never allowed to go anywhere.'

'She brought some pictures into school, Sophie says, when they were doing some project or other in geography. I remember now, that Sophie had been very surprised, but Rachinda said she'd found them in her father's shop. Sophie said how lovely it looked, so I found out about it and off we went. I was busy indulging Sophie's every whim at the time.'

'We can hardly ask her now,' said Fran.

'Or her father,' agreed Libby. 'But it's rather telling, isn't it?'

'Explain,' said Guy.

'I was wondering why even this murder seems to come back here to Kent, to our very own area,' said Libby, 'and then I realised that you might hold the key. You were the first one to go over there, and if you found out from someone here, it might explain why there were links back here.'

'I think I follow that,' said Guy. 'So you think Rachinda's father might be connected to – what?'

'People trafficking,' said Fran. 'Oh, probably only a small cog in a bigger wheel, but it's very suggestive. I think I'd better tell Ian.'

'But it wouldn't have been Mr Sharma Justin would have been coming to see,' protested Libby. 'Not now.'

'No, but the link to the area is there, isn't it?' Fran pulled out her phone. 'I'll just leave a message.'

Libby left Fran with Guy in the shop and walked back up to Cliff Terrace. So that was the link. Rachinda Sharma's father somehow had connections to Erzugan, so there might be other people in the area who were also part of the trafficking scheme, which could explain why Justin Newcombe was coming to Canterbury.

Despite her seemingly logical reasoning, even Libby realised that this was possibly a leap too far. Yes, Rachinda's father had

170

been mixed up in something criminal, although it remained shadowy, but there was nothing but coincidence here to link him to any of the events that had begun in Erzugan. Photographs shown to Sophie, found in his shop. No, Libby shook her head. She and Fran were now in danger of building whole buildings out of straw, not just the bricks.

She walked past her car on Cliff Terrace and up to the car park called The Tops, built over what had been empty cliffs, where Libby had walked as a child. The view here was less populated than from Jane's Peel House, as there was no building below the car park, only rocks. Nowhere to land anything, thought Libby, peering over the railings not like ... She stood up straight. Not like the inlet at St Aldeberge.

Chapter Twenty-four

Libby remembered they had already spoken about the surveillance operation at Felling that had been part of a recent murder investigation, the one in which she and Fran had first met Patti Pearson, and in which a small inlet beyond the village had actually played an important part. And where, in fact, illegal immigrants had been landed. She thought back. Could those immigrants have been from Turkey? They were brought in by boat, but Libby had always assumed the boats had come from France. She had not been part of the further investigation into the criminals in the case, except for the unpleasant business of giving evidence in a trial. But that was all over, now, and whoever was organising large-scale illegal immigrations would surely have stopped using that particular landing point.

However, she realised, the landings at St Aldeberge were after George and Bert had come across their boatful of girls. So were the destinations constantly changing? She peered down over the cliff again. There were certainly enough places along this coast for concealed landings. The public didn't see most of them, because even if they went out on a boat trip with George or Bert, the *Dolphin* and the *Sparkler* wouldn't venture in close to the rocks. Most people thought of the wild coastline of Devon and Cornwall as smugglers' and wreckers' territory, but Kent and Sussex had their fair share. Just along from here at Nethergate and beyond Creekmarsh were the marshes, from where wool had been smuggled out and silks, tobacco, and brandy smuggled in.

She turned back to Cliff Terrace and her car. Below her now stood The Alexandria, where in a few weeks the Oast Theatre Company would be performing their End Of The Pier Show.

She sighed. She really should be concentrating more on that and less on mysterious murders.

When she got back to Steeple Martin, she called Patti.

'You remember when the police broke up the smuggling that was landing in the inlet at St Aldeberge?'

'How could I forget?' said Patti, a trifle bitterly. Her own congregation had been under suspicion during that investigation.

'I just wondered if that could also be connected to our Turkish murders.'

'I suppose so,' said Patti slowly. 'It was only a couple of years ago, but I don't see ...'

'I'm just trying to pin down a connection between the bloke who was murdered in London and our area,' said Libby. There must have been connections here apart from the St Aldeberge one and before that over at Creekmarsh.'

'Creekmarsh?'

Libby explained about George and Bert and the cargo of Turkish girls.

'And you told me about the other time you found out about the trafficking of girls, didn't you?' said Patti. 'From – where was it?'

'Transnistria,' said Libby. 'It's a wicked traffic. But I'm just wondering if the links to this area are still here, and some of those girls were shipped from our little village in Turkey.'

'It begins to look like it, doesn't it?' said Patti. 'It can't be entirely coincidental that your Sally came from here.'

'Actually, I think it's more to do with her family, not her so much,' said Libby. 'She'd moved away from Cherry Ashton long before she went to Turkey. Her house here was let.'

'Well, it sounds very complicated to me,' said Patti, 'but it does seem that there is a history of people trafficking along our part of the coast, so it's quite conceivable that if it's a regular occurrence some of it should come from Turkey.'

'By sea,' said Libby, 'that's the thing. Most of them come overland from wherever they're initially picked up, some are landed along the Italian coastline, for instance, and then taken to Calais. But this way the traffickers aren't relying on anyone else along the way. They get the girls – or men – onto the boat in Turkey, then off it goes all through the Med, right round Portugal to France and bingo. Mind you, they could land anywhere along the south coast, so I don't know why they come right round to the Channel, where the Border Force boats are constantly patrolling.'

'Perhaps because there *is* already a network in place here?' said Patti.

'Maybe,' said Libby. 'And before you say it, I know it isn't any of my business, but I can't help wondering what's been going on.'

'Of course you can't. You've been involved in so many investigations now it's second nature. And especially as this one touches on things you've dealt with in the past.'

'I haven't actually dealt with them,' said Libby. 'They rather thrust themselves on to me.'

Patti laughed. 'Well, you're dealing with this one, and it certainly thrust itself on to you, although finding a body isn't exactly funny.'

'You nearly found one in your church,' said Libby.

'Yes, but it wasn't me, and anyway at the time we thought it was a natural death, didn't we?'

'Yes, and look where that ended up.' Libby sighed. 'Oh, well, I'd better get on with doing something else, I suppose.'

'You could paint. Don't forget you promised to do one especially for me, and Fran's Guy always wants more.'

'I know, and I've got the show to do, too, although that isn't that much effort. The team at The Alexandria know what we want by now, so I don't have to worry so much. I'll keep you posted, Patti. Thanks for listening.'

'That's what vicars do,' said Patti. 'See you soon.'

Libby wandered into the conservatory and wondered what she ought to paint for Patti. Not the St Aldeberge inlet, with its two isolated houses, one either side on the cliffs, both still standing empty, that was for sure. What else did Patti like? Her lovely friend Anne, of course, but Libby didn't think a portrait of Anne would go down too well hung on the vicarage wall. The Pink Geranium and the pub, then? Libby brightened. Of course! That was where Patti spent the happiest time of her week with Anne. She would make a start now.

After setting up the easel with a piece of fresh stretched watercolour paper, she frowned. However well she knew her own high street, she'd never really looked at it properly. She could do pictures of Nethergate from her various viewpoints from memory because she painted them in real life so often, but she'd never painted anything in Steeple Martin. She scowled afresh at the easel. And the inhabitants of her own village would be sure to come peering and commenting if she took up a position on the corner of Maltby Close with her easel and she'd never get anything done. So a quick pencil sketch, then, and a photograph for the detail. She unearthed her sketchbook and found her camera, luckily able to download pictures to the computer. She didn't have a smartphone with all its photographic capabilities, which was a shame at moments like this. Armed with the tools of her trade, she set off down Allhallow's Lane.

At the corner, she met Bethany Cole, the vicar.

'Shopping?' said Bethany, eyeing the basket.

'Sketching,' said Libby, 'but don't spread it about. I'm going to take a photograph and do a lightning sketch before anyone notices.'

'Why?' Beth was obviously amused.

'Everyone will want to come and look. And they think I'm mad enough already.'

'Why do you need to do it, though? You know the village so well.'

'I want to do The Pink Geranium and the pub, and I never really look at them from over the road.'

'Is it for the pub, then? Or Harry?'

'No, actually, it's for Patti,' said Libby. 'She wanted a picture, and I thought as this was where she spent her days off ...'

'With Anne.' Bethany nodded. 'Good idea. This is where

she's happiest. If ever the dear bish decides to move me on, I should recommend Patti to take over here.'

'Wouldn't that be difficult with Anne living here? They can spend their time together here because it's away from Patti's parish, but if she was here ...'

'Yes,' Bethany mused. 'You're right. I hadn't thought of that. God, I wish the bloody clergy would stop being so hypocritical.'

'I think it's the laity who are worse,' said Libby. 'After all, who was it who defeated the first synod vote for women bishops?'

Bethany sighed. 'I know. Well, I'll let you get on with your sketch. Unless you'd like a bulldog to guard you?'

'Really? Would you?' Libby beamed. 'No one would dare push past the vicar, would they?'

She and Bethany took up positions on the corner of Maltby Close, where Flo lived with Lenny, and at the end of which stood Bethany's church. Libby wrestled the sketchpad out of her basket and began – awkwardly – to sketch the view she wanted. Bethany stood just to her right said and tried to look as though she was deep in conversation without saying a word. After a moment, Libby gave up and took out the camera.

'It's no good,' she said with a sigh. 'I can't do quick sketches any more.'

Bethany laughed. 'I can't do sketches, quick or otherwise. Here, give me the basket.'

Libby took a selection of pictures she thought might be good enough and put the camera away.

'Thanks, Beth. At least I've got something to start on. Are you on your way to the church?'

'I wasn't, no. I was going to the farm shop, but as I'm here, I'll pop down. I think I've got flower ladies or someone in there.'

'Good luck, then, and thanks for being a bulldog.'

Libby went slowly back to number 17, thinking as she went. Patti's picture had temporarily driven the murders out of her mind, but now they surfaced again. Although there was nothing to be done, she still felt as if she needed to know what had been going on. She would send a little updating email to Jimmy's former guests, and see what they had to say. Not that she could tell them much, but at least she was keeping in touch.

By the time Ben came home, she'd made a start on Patti's painting, sent emails, and started cooking. She brought him up to date with George's and Bert's surprising revelations and her own tenuously made connection with the events at the St Aldeberge inlet.

'All very plausible,' said Ben, 'but I expect the police will be looking in to all of that. But I said talking to George and Bert was a good idea, didn't I?'

'You did. Do you think we ought to tell Ian about that?'

'I'm sure he knows. If they are thinking trafficking, then any reports that have come in over the last few years will have surfaced already.'

'Yes, I suppose so. I just want to know why Justin was coming here.'

'We'll probably never know, and it could be nothing to do with this case after all.'

'I know, but even the police think it is.' Libby went back into the kitchen. 'Dinner's nearly ready.'

Greta, Betty, and Neal all emailed during the evening, but none of them had anything enlightening to say. Libby replied to them all, trying to remember just what she was allowed to say, and went to bed.

Friday, Saturday, and Sunday passed uneventfully. Ben and Libby drove down to Nethergate for Ben, as stage manager, to have a conference with the team at The Alexandria, and on Sunday they went to lunch at The Manor with Hetty. Fran and Guy paid a duty visit to Fran's daughter Chrissie, her husband Bruce, cat Cassandra, and daughter Montana, and after closing The Pink Geranium on Sunday afternoon, Peter and Harry went up to London to visit friends.

And on Monday, the anonymous letters started.

Chapter Twenty-five

'Ian? What are you doing calling at this time in the morning?' Libby clutched her dressing gown round her and cranked open her eyes. 'Oh, God, what's happened? Who is it?'

'Relax, nobody's hurt. At least I hope not. Have you had any post this morning?'

'Post? No. It never comes this early.' Libby tucked the phone into her neck and filled the kettle. 'Why?'

'We've had a rather interesting communication. I don't want to talk about it on the phone, so Maiden and I will come over in an hour or so. And don't open any envelopes if they arrive.'

'But ...' began Libby, but Ian had gone. She made tea and was just about to carry a cup up to Ben when he appeared behind her.

'Who was that?'

Libby told him.

'That sounds ominous,' said Ben. 'He's not thinking about bombs, is he?'

'I hope not. I think they'd stake out the postman if they thought that,' said Libby, emptying cat food into Sidney's bowl. 'I rather thought fingerprints.'

'Oh, yes, it could be.' Ben sipped thoughtfully. 'I wonder what this "communication" is.'

'We'll find out in an hour or so,' said Libby. 'Will you be here?'

'Of course. I'm not really needed in the office, and Hetty can always call me if anything urgent crops up.'

The postman hadn't arrived by the time Ian and DS Maiden arrived on the doorstep, the sergeant as brightly blue-eyed and startlingly red-haired as ever.

'This arrived through the post this morning addressed to the Canterbury Police Station.' Ian drew a plastic envelope from his briefcase. 'It found its way to me, unsurprisingly.'

Printed on what appeared to be an ordinary sheet of copier paper was a message.

Warn Libby Sarjeant to stop interfering in the Turkish murders or she will get hurt.

Libby raised astonished eyes to Ben. 'What ...?'

'There are no clues as to where it came from. It was postmarked Central London, there are no fingerprints on either the envelope or the paper, and as usual these days, both the envelope and the stamp are self-adhesive. However, it does show signs of panic.'

'It does?' Ben was frowning at the message.

'Yes, I see,' said Libby. 'This will have exactly the opposite effect – it will make not only the police look even harder into the murders, but me, too.'

'No!' said three voices at once.

'Oh,' said Libby.

'And you think Libby might get one?' asked Ben.

'It's possible, if whoever sent it could find her address,' said Ian.

'Is it that Geoff Croker? He found my phone number,' said Libby.

'I doubt it,' said Ian. 'He wouldn't make that sort of mistake. A bit of a career criminal, was Geoff Croker.'

'Oh, you've looked, then?'

'Smith's team did. Most of the people living in your idyllic village had some sort of past. Croker was one of those with fingers in a lot of pies.'

'So who is it? And why me?'

'Because you've been asking questions, as usual,' said Ben. 'And now you'll have to stop.'

'To be fair, Ben,' said Ian, 'both Smith, James, and I have asked Libby and Fran for information and help, so it isn't their fault. Although they have gone beyond the call of duty.'

'As usual,' said Ben. 'So what do we do?'

'Nothing,' said Ian. 'And I mean it, Libby. However vague this threat is, and I believe it is vague, and definitely not the work of a habitual criminal, it is a threat. Somewhere along the line we've uncovered a link, and this person, murderer or whoever it is, attributes it to you, so don't do any more digging. Now,' he leant back in his chair and nodded to Sergeant Maiden, who got out his notebook, 'who knows you've been looking into this?'

Libby looked at Ben. 'Well, not exactly looking into it, but the people from Jimmy's hotel know what's been going on. Not all of it, obviously, just the fact that I'd been questioned, and about Justin, of course. I've heard from all of them by email.'

Sergeant Maiden took their names.

'Although,' Libby continued, 'I'm pretty sure you've got them, because they've been asked if they knew Justin was coming here. Carol Oxford knows a bit, but she didn't know anybody out there except her daughter. You know Geoff Croker rang me, oh, and Martha from the restaurant –'

'She isn't relevant,' said Ian. 'I only want people who live here. In England.'

'So that's Greta and Tom Willingham, Betty and Walter Roberts, and Neal Parnham,' said Maiden.

'Yes, but honestly –' began Libby.

'It needn't be one of them, but you've been in touch with them,' said Ian. 'One of them may think you're too close.'

'But Greta and Tom and Betty and Walter didn't know Justin, or Alec Wilson, and Neal had only just met them. None of them have a reason –'

Ian cut her off again. 'The two couples were both regular visitors, weren't they?'

'Well, yes, but …'

'So they could have known the residents.'

'I think they knew Sally, didn't they?' Libby turned to Ben. 'They were the first people to mention her. Then we heard more about her from Martha – before she was killed, of course.'

'So they did know some of the locals?'

'Yes, but honestly, Ian, if you met them …!'

181

'They are very unlikely villains,' said Ben, 'and Walter Roberts barely stirred from the hotel. He certainly didn't mix with anybody. We took his wife out a couple of times just to get her away from him.'

Ian sighed. 'You ought to know by now that villains of all types come in many guises.'

'But you said this one – or the person who wrote that message – isn't a professional,' said Libby.

'It doesn't look like it, as I said, it looks more like someone in a panic, but even that could be a bluff.'

'Oh, for f –' began Ben.

'I know,' said Libby, 'but the other way to look at it is, if it is a mistake, this person is getting careless. He – or she – might make more mistakes.'

'One of the things we still haven't got is a motive,' said Ian. 'Smith is pretty sure Wilson's murder is something to do with what he was doing out there, which makes sense. Everything had been removed so there are no clues. The Weston woman's computer was retrieved, but there's nothing untoward on there.'

'And he still thinks Sally Weston was murdered to shut her up about Wilson's death?' said Libby.

'Yes.' Ian frowned. 'Although there's something he isn't telling us. I understand it's sensitive, but it's hampering us somewhat.'

'Justin seemed as much in the dark as we were at the time,' said Libby.

'I'm sure he was. Whatever it was Wilson was up to, I don't think Newcombe was involved.'

'But if Wilson was on the side of the angels, was Justin on the other side?' asked Libby.

'To Wilson? I've no idea, but Newcombe does appear to be what you thought he was.'

'So there could be all sorts of motives for his murder,' said Libby. 'A client he'd shafted –'

'Where do you get these terms, Lib?' asked Ben.

'You know what I mean. It could be someone like that whom he'd arranged meet, couldn't it?'

'It could,' said Ian, the corners of his mouth turning down. 'In which case, we'll be lucky to find them.'

'His computer in Turkey?' said Ben. 'He must have had one.'

'It's been sent over here for forensic examination,' said Maiden. 'No results as yet.'

'I bet Commander Smith didn't like letting go of that,' said Libby.

'I don't think he did,' said Ian with a small smile, 'but this is our investigation, even if it does link in with his.'

'So is it trafficking?' asked Libby. 'We know George and Bert in Nethergate picked up a boatload of girls on an abandoned boat about ten years ago.'

'How did you know that?' asked Ian, looking startled.

'Fran asked them if they knew where small boats might come in with smuggled goods. And then there were illegals being brought in over at St Aldeberge, weren't there?'

Ian's brows drew together. 'You're not to go looking into this, Libby.'

'No, but I knew about all of that already, didn't I? And the workers that were trafficked to work on the farms? Fran and I have been involved in all of those cases.'

Ian sighed. 'Yes, all right. There appears to have been regular trafficking from Turkey, and as far as we can find out, Wilson was supposed to be keeping an eye on the trade. Fairly unsuccessfully, it seems.'

'There, see!' said Libby triumphantly. 'We were right. So they were taking people out of the bay and bringing them all the way here by boat?'

'That isn't certain,' said Ian cautiously. 'It would be very unusual if that was the case. Normally they would be landed in Italy and brought overland.'

'That's what I thought. But they were being landed here?'

'Possibly,' said Ian. 'You were right, it has been done here in the past, but the Border Force cutters haven't intercepted any recently, so it may well be that the trade has dried up. Or this area of it, anyway.'

'Are there other illegal immigrants being brought in? Like those poor people in Calais?' asked Libby.

'I would think so. It avoids the major ports, but we don't know where they embark.'

'If it isn't Turkey itself, you mean?' said Ben.

'Exactly,' said Ian and stood up. 'So don't go poking around any more, Libby. And if you get anything that looks as if it might be one of these –' he held up the message, 'don't open it, and call us.'

'So will you take any notice?' asked Ben, when Ian and DS Maiden had left.

'Yes.' Libby pulled a face. 'I've got into trouble without having warnings in the past, haven't I? So I think I ought to take notice. Fran and I can still speculate, though.'

'So long as that's all you do,' said Ben. 'Now I'd better go and see if there's any work to do in the office.'

The post arrived without any warning messages, so Libby called Fran and brought her up to date.

'That's worrying,' said Fran.

'Ian thinks it's merely alerted the police and me and made them more determined to find the killer. It does sort of feel as if the killer is in this country, though, doesn't it?'

'And could be anybody … although I'm sure it's to do with Erzugan.'

'Really?' Libby's metaphorical ears pricked up. 'Is this a moment?'

'I don't know. I just feel it is.' Fran sounded doubtful. 'And I'm still not sure about Commander Smith.'

'Eh?'

'You remember when we went to Wilson's house with him?'

'And you thought there was something wrong with him.'

'Yes. There was some connection there, I'm sure. I don't know what it was, but there was just this feeling.'

'In that case I'm surprised that he took us with him. If he wasn't supposed to be there.'

'Camouflage, I said.' Fran paused. 'And theoretically, he wasn't supposed to be in either of those houses, was he?'

'The Jandarma had okayed it,' said Libby.

'But it wasn't really an official investigation. That came a bit later.'

'What are you thinking, then?' asked Libby, after the silence had lasted a fraction too long.

'I'm just wondering,' said Fran. 'It's all these daft links to this area of Kent, whether it's Sally coming from Cherry Ashton, Justin with a ticket to Canterbury, illegal immigrants and people trafficking along our coast...'

'Yes, they are a bit daft,' said Libby. 'And we've spent a good deal of time looking into them and making bricks with straw, which we usually do. So?'

'Suppose the beginning really is here? And Alec Wilson actually came from here in the first place?'

Chapter Twenty-six

Libby was silent for a moment.

'OK, suppose he was from here. What difference does that make?'

'Commander Smith told us Alec Wilson was a false name. We subsequently found out that he wasn't in the witness protection scheme, but was some kind of undercover person. However, he doesn't seem to have done much, does he?'

'I still don't see where this is all leading,' said Libby. 'You're making me more confused than ever.'

'I just wondered,' said Fran, 'if Alec Wilson – or whoever he was – came from this area of Kent and had a link to, say, people trafficking here, he could have been sent over there to, I don't know, track it from the other end.'

Libby frowned out of the window. 'So you're saying he was a criminal after all?'

'I don't know. I just thought if he had lived or worked in the area, under a different name, of course, it would make sense of all these links back here.'

'Even if it's true, there's no way we could find out,' said Libby, 'and I might remind you that, having received official threats, I am now forbidden to do any investigating at all.'

'Yes ...' said Fran vaguely.

'And so are you,' warned Libby.

'I know, I know. Oh, well, we'll just have to go back to being ordinary people, won't we?'

'I've always been ordinary,' said Libby. 'And now, are you coming to rehearsal tonight? Only a couple of weeks to go now.'

'Yes, I'll come. Have you managed to sort out a rota for the five weeks?'

The End Of The Pier Show had a revolving cast, to allow for holidays and other commitments during the summer. Some people, like Libby herself, were permanent, but others would appear as soloists or ensemble members for one week and be replaced the following week, possibly coming back in a week later. It gave the cast a break, and meant that if audience members went to the show two weeks running, which, amazingly, some of them did, they wouldn't see exactly the same show.

After her conversation with Fran, Libby felt unsettled. She wanted to do something, but didn't know what she *could* do. She went into the conservatory and peered at Patti's painting, went into the garden and stared up at the cherry tree, then went back into the house and picked up the keys to the theatre and her basket. A wardrobe review seemed the best thing to take her mind off other things.

Ben found her two hours later surrounded by dress rails and piles of costumes.

'That lot have all got to be cleaned,' she told him. 'I shall have to drive them over to Nethergate.'

'You can leave them at The Alexandria when you pick them up that way,' said Ben. 'What brought this on?'

'I need something to do, said Libby.

Ben looked amused. 'Because you can't do any more investigating?'

Libby looked up and grinned. 'Yes. It's so frustrating.'

'I can see it would be.'

'Besides, whoever it was writing that letter obviously doesn't know where I live, or he would have sent *me* a message, not the police. That was a mad thing to do.'

'You've still been threatened,' said Ben. 'Just stay out of trouble.'

Libby loaded costumes into the estate Range Rover and set off for the dry cleaners in Nethergate. At least it was giving her something to do.

When that task was accomplished, she wondered what she

could do next. The day stretched before her with nothing to occupy her until dinner time and the rehearsal. She looked at her watch. It was lunchtime now, so perhaps Fran was free?

Fran was making sandwiches in her kitchen to take to Guy in the shop.

'You take these to Guy, then, and I'll make some more for us,' she said. 'Go on. I'll put the kettle on.'

Guy, surprised to see her, asked after her painting.

'Er – well, I'm doing a commission just now,' she said, fidgeting a bit.

Guy narrowed his eyes. 'To avoid doing commissions for me? High season any minute now. There'll be a demand.'

Libby sighed. 'I'll get on with them, I promise.'

'They don't take you long, unless you're doing a new view,' said Guy. 'You need something to take your mind off investigating.'

'Did Fran tell you what happened this morning?'

'Yes, and let's face it, we've all been telling you not to go nosing around for years.'

'Ian said that he and Commander Smith had actually asked us to help,' said Libby indignantly.

'He's also telling you to back off,' said Guy with a grin. 'Off you go. Don't eat all the ham.'

Fran and Libby tried to keep off the subject of the murders over their sandwich lunch, but by the time they'd finished the sandwiches and Libby was picking at the lettuce garnish, it was inevitable that the subject should once more raise its head.

'You know what nobody seems to be taking into account?' said Libby. 'Alec Wilson's mother.'

'I was thinking about that earlier,' said Fran. 'When I was wondering whether he came from round here.'

'The only thing is, what would his long-lost mother have to do with the trafficking, or whatever it was?'

'Nothing, maybe,' said Fran. 'Suppose that was the reason he was killed. His mother.'

'It seems a long shot, but I suppose it's possible. The trouble is, without his real name there's no way of finding out who she is.'

'Commander Smith would know. He'll have found out about her by now.'

'I suppose he will. And have questioned her,' said Libby. 'And it obviously doesn't have anything to do with Justin Newcombe's death, or he would have told Ian and Inspector James.'

'Perhaps he has,' said Fran, 'and Ian hasn't seen the need to tell us.'

'So we're stymied,' said Libby.

'No, we're just not investigating,' said Fran. 'We're going to be normal for a while. Until something else comes up.'

The subject of Alex Wilson's mother occupied Libby's thoughts on the drive back to Steeple Martin. She remembered Justin's and Martha's conviction that he would have told Sally about her – was that what had got Sally killed? Was Alec's real mother somehow the clue to the whole case and his false identity and role in possible trafficking operations a complete red herring?

Try as she might, she couldn't quite see how, and by the time she had delivered the Range Rover back to the Manor she had resolved to forget all about it and concentrate on her neglected painting and the summer show.

Patti's painting came together surprisingly quickly, if in a slightly more naïve style than Libby's normal one, and it was with great satisfaction that she wrapped it up and took it to rehearsal on Wednesday to hand over later in the pub. Over the last couple of days she'd even completed a smaller painting for Guy and worked on some improvements for the summer show.

Patti was delighted with her painting, as was Anne, and when Harry joined them in the pub, he complained.

'I want one,' he said. 'You could do one of the caff and the cottage.'

'They're too far apart,' said Libby, 'and divided by the Manor gateposts. I'll do you one of the caff, though. It was nice doing something different.'

'And it's kept her out of mischief for the last couple of

days,' said Ben. 'I've never known her paint so quickly.'

'I enjoyed it,' said Libby with a shrug. 'Do you think Ian will come in this evening?'

Ben looked at his watch. 'Not now, it's too late. He can't have anything to tell us.'

'Or ask us,' said Libby.

'So no progress in the case,' said Peter, standing up. 'Who's for a last pint?'

On Thursday morning, Libby posted on Martha's Facebook page that as far as she knew progress was being made on the case both in Turkey and in England. It wasn't quite a lie, she told herself, because progress had been made, just not with any great conclusions.

By the afternoon, she had received emails from Greta and Betty, both hoping for more information. She replied as vaguely as possible. It was after dinner that the landline began to ring.

'Libby? It's Carol Oxford.'

'Oh, hello, Carol,' said Libby in surprise. 'How are you?' She suddenly realised it was Thursday – the day of Sally's funeral.

'Not too good,' said Carol in a wobbly voice. 'You know.'

'I know,' said Libby. 'I'm so sorry.'

'Well, it's over now,' said Carol, 'but what I wanted to ask you was would you let the police into Sally's house?'

'The police?'

'I received a request today, of all days –' Carol's voice quivered with indignation 'via our local police on behalf of – oh, I don't know, the force who's looking into the murders I suppose. I gave my permission. Could you ring them?'

'Of course. Do you have a number?'

Carol read out the number of the Canterbury police station.

'Oh. Do you know who I've got to ask for?'

'A DCI Connell or a DS Maiden,' said Carol. 'Thank you, Libby. And you can let them keep the keys after that. I don't know what they hope to find.'

Neither do I, thought Libby. There's nothing there. Aloud, she said 'Yes, I'll give them the keys. I'll try and keep you informed – if there's anything to tell.'

'Thank you.' Carol's voice was going again. 'I never want to see the place again.'

'I bet she doesn't,' Libby said to Ben when she relayed the conversation. 'Poor woman. First her horrible ex-husband and now her daughter. Don't some people have dreadful luck.'

'Makes you count your blessings, doesn't it,' said Ben, giving her a hug. 'And now you've got a legitimate excuse to ring Ian for once.'

'In the morning,' said Libby. 'Too late now.'

Ben gave her an old fashioned look. 'Punishing him?'

'No!' Libby was indignant. 'Just being considerate.'

But it wasn't ten minutes later that her mobile rang. She and Ben exchanged glances. 'Ian,' they said together.

'Libby. Have you heard from Mrs Oxford?'

'Yes, Ian. I was going to call you in the morning.'

'The morning?'

'Yes. I thought it was too late to bother you this evening. And I must say, it was particularly insensitive to go bothering the poor woman on the day of her daughter's funeral.'

'Her daughter's – oh, shit.'

'That's not like you,' said Libby, grinning at Ben.

'I never would have asked,' said Ian. 'The local force should have used a bit of intelligence.'

'Well, I'm perfectly prepared to meet you at the house with the keys. After all, I was asked to look after it.'

'Meet me?'

'How else are you going to get the keys?'

'I was going to send Maiden to fetch them.'

'Oh, no you don't,' said Libby. 'I'm legitimately allowed to be there, so I'm going to be. What time?'

There was a short silence on the other end of the line.

'Ten thirty?' said Ian eventually in a resigned tone.

'I'll be there,' said Libby triumphantly, and rang off.

Ben roared with laughter. 'Poor Ian.'

'I don't for a minute expect I'll be allowed in, but I'm going to do my best,' said Libby. 'And now I'm going to ring Fran.'

Fran, equally surprised, agreed that she probably shouldn't try to accompany Libby, but would expect her to tell her everything as soon as she'd finished in Cherry Ashton.

'I wonder what Ian's looking for?' Libby said, as she resumed her seat on the sofa beside Ben and accepted a whisky. 'He's only supposed to be helping Inspector James with the investigation into Justin Newcombe's death.'

'Perhaps Smith or James have discovered a link to all three murders at last,' said Ben, 'and as Ian's on the spot he's been asked to look into it.'

'Suppose so,' said Libby. 'It's all very odd though, isn't it?'

Chapter Twenty-seven

Ian and DS Maiden were already waiting on the doorstep when Libby walked from the Ashton Arms car park at twenty-five past ten.

'I'm not late,' said Libby. 'It's not half past yet.'

'All right, don't get on the defensive,' said Ian. 'Just give us the keys.'

'Very polite, I'm sure.' Libby raised her eyebrows. 'And no, I won't. Mrs Oxford wants to know why you want to search the house. Sally didn't live here, you know.'

Ian made a sound of exasperation and DS Maiden grinned.

'We know that. But we might find something ...'

'You won't,' said Libby, then caught herself up. 'Mrs Oxford searched the place. Sally took all her belongings to Turkey and furnished this place to let.'

'There's nothing?'

'What are you hoping to find?' asked Libby. 'Is there now a link between the three murders? Only as far as I knew, you were assisting Inspector James in Justin Newcombe's murder.'

Ian sighed. 'If you must know, I'm now on the official investigation into all three, as it seems to be coming back to my patch. And yes, we're looking for anything that links the three victims.'

'Apart from them all living in Erzugan,' said Libby, taking the keys out of her pocket and stepping forward to open the door. 'Don't worry, I won't touch anything. But if you're looking for fingerprints, I have been here before.'

'I know.' Ian glared at her. 'And now, you can tell me what you found.'

Libby stared, open-mouthed. 'Nothing,' she said at last.

'Really nothing?'

'Except for the boxes in the attic.'

Ian jerked his head at Maiden who leapt up the stairs and could be heard pulling down the lift hatch.

'One is full of old clothes and the other old papers, birthday cards – that sort of thing.' Libby frowned.

'All right, what is it?' Ian leant back against the door jamb with his arms folded.

'It's a theory that Ben and Fran both told me was ridiculous.' Libby hesitated. 'When we were here last a neighbour called Agnes was telling us how she'd known the Westons for years and used to help out with Carol Oxford's lunch parties and look after the children. Sally, that is, and another little boy called Gerald.'

'And?'

'I just wondered if Gerald ...?'

'Could be Alec Wilson?' Ian smiled. 'An attractive theory, but a bit far-fetched.'

Libby sighed. 'Yes. There is a birthday card signed from Jean, Bob, and Gerald, so it looks as if that was his mother's name – hardly long-lost.'

Ian regarded her for a moment, then called up the stairs.

'Can you bring the box of papers down, Dave?' He turned back to Libby. 'And now, Mrs Sarjeant, you'd better hand over the keys. I'm sure Mrs Oxford told you to do that. And if there's anything I feel you should know, I'll call you.'

Libby sighed and handed over the keys. 'OK, I'll go quietly. I'll see you before next Wednesday?'

Ian smiled slightly. 'Maybe.'

Libby drove disconsolately back to Steeple Martin. That was it, then. The last legitimate link to the case had been closed off, and now she had nothing to do with it. All the theorising in the world was not going to help here, either, so she might just as well go home and resume work on the painting she'd abandoned to work on Patti's picture. Or she could, of course, make a start on The Pink Geranium painting she'd more-or-less promised Harry.

A sense of duty persuaded her to carry on with the painting for Guy, and she had a sudden inspiration to do two small rather impressionistic views of Nethergate to see if they would also sell. This took her up to Saturday, when she and Ben had been invited to dinner at Coastguard Cottage. Fran had also invited Susannah and Emlyn and Jane and Terry, leaving Jane's mother in charge of Robbie and Imogen.

'I'm glad the weather's held,' said Fran, opening the door.

'Why?' Libby went past her into the living room, where Guy was busy opening bottles. 'I mean, apart from the obvious that's it's nicer to have good weather rather than bad.'

'Come and see,' said Fran, leading the way through the kitchen and out to her back yard, set against the cliffs.

'Wow!'

Under a stylish gazebo sat a brand new outdoor dining set. Eight places were set, and Balzac sat up from one of the chairs and silently meowed a welcome.

'I got the idea from all our outdoor dining in Turkey,' said Fran. 'I know we don't get that many opportunities to eat outside in this country, but we also bought this.' She indicated a smart black firepit in the corner. 'We're so enclosed here I think that'll keep us warm.'

'It's fantastic, Fran!' Libby gave her friend a hug. 'What a lovely idea.'

Guy joined them, handing glasses to Ben and Libby. 'Fizz to christen the new outdoor room.'

When the other guests arrived, they were equally impressed. Fran produced her usual competent dinner, finishing with Libby's favourite Eton Mess, and Guy offered coffee and brandy.

'That was lovely,' said Libby, leaning back in her chair and gazing into the glowing embers of the firepit. 'I feel quite transported back to Turkey.'

'Any more news on your murders?' asked Jane.

A small silence fell, then Libby pushed her chair back and stood up.

'Oh, Guy – I forgot. I've got pictures. I'll pop out and get

197

them from the car.'

Ben looked at her suspiciously and also stood up.

'I'll get them,' he said. 'Sit down.'

'What did I say?' asked Jane.

'We aren't talking about the murders, Jane,' said Fran. 'We really don't want to think about them any more. We aren't involved.'

'I'm sorry.'

In the darkness she couldn't tell, but Libby was sure colour had crept into Jane's cheeks. 'You weren't to know,' she said. 'I overreacted.

Ben reappeared with Libby's wrapped paintings. 'I'll leave them in the sitting room, shall I?'

'No, let's have a look now,' said Fran, 'I expect the others would like to see them.'

The paintings were duly exclaimed over, and Guy approved the impressionistic experiments.

'Libby, I'm truly sorry,' said Jane, under cover of the general conversation. 'I didn't mean to upset you. It's just …'

'I know, I'm usually off like a dog after a rabbit. But that's why this is so frustrating. There's absolutely nothing we can do and nothing we can find out, so I've been resolutely putting it out of my mind. Hence the paintings. Had to take my mind of it somehow.'

'So I can't ask you any questions?'

'I haven't got any answers,' said Libby, with a grimace.

'What about that woman's mother? Didn't you go and see her?'

'Carol Oxford? Yes, but she didn't know anything. Actually she gave me the keys to the house until I had to hand them over to the police.'

'The police? Why?'

'It wasn't Mrs Oxford's house. It belonged to her daughter and was let out. Although it currently isn't. And,' said Libby, and paused.

'And what?' prompted Jane.

'Did you know who Carol Oxford was? And her daughter?'

'No.' Jane looked bewildered. 'Should I have done?'

'Colonel Weston's ex-wife and daughter.'

'Colonel – oh, my God!'

'Exactly.' Libby nodded and looked for a bottle to top up her wineglass. 'Nothing to do with the Turkish business, but what a coincidence, eh?'

Jane was frowning into the darkness. 'Are you sure?'

'Yes. Ian Connell's on the case now, and it was him I handed the keys over to. He'd have turned up any sort of connection by now.'

'Oh, yes, I suppose he would.' Jane's expression cleared. 'It was just that – well, I thought I remembered something, that's all.'

'All Weston's dirty doings came under the microscope at the time of his arrest,' said Libby. 'It would have come out.'

'What would, though?' asked Jane.

'What would?' Libby realised belatedly that Jane knew nothing about the suspected trafficking, and explained, as briefly as she could.

'Ah, I see. And of course because of the whole immigrant situation it's all blown up in their faces, is that the theory?'

'I honestly don't know, Jane. All I know is that we've been putting together a whole heap of buildings with straw. If you've heard anything about trafficking over the last few years – to this coast, particularly – you ought to let Ian know.'

'I'd let you know first,' said Jane. She grinned and patted Libby's arm. 'Pass the bottle.'

When the other guests had gone, Ben and Libby, who were staying the night, retreated to the sitting room with Fran and Guy.

'What were you and Jane talking about?' asked Fran.

'She apologised again. So did I. I completely overreacted. I've been trying so hard to put it all out of my mind.'

'I didn't help by recreating a Turkish restaurant, did I?' said Fran with a smile.

'That didn't occur to me,' said Libby. 'At least you didn't do the food.'

'I don't think I could,' said Fran. 'Plain English, that's me.'

'Not so much of the plain,' said Guy, coming to sit beside his wife. 'That's accusing me of bad taste.' He looked across at Libby. 'The paintings really are rather good, Lib. I love the new style.'

Libby felt herself go pink with pleasure. 'Thank you, Guy. It happened because I was doing something quickly for Patti. I didn't know I could paint like that.'

'Well you can knock out as many as you like. I guarantee they'll sell.'

'I might even stop painting the view from your window,' said Libby, turning to look at it.

'That window,' said Fran. 'It has a lot to answer for.'

They all nodded solemnly. The window of Coastguard Cottage had figured largely in the second adventure they'd all had together.

'Risking returning to the most avoided subject of the day,' said Ben, 'I wonder if there's been any more progress in the case?'

Libby sighed. 'We're not likely to know, now, are we?'

Unusually, Libby and Ben weren't going to Hetty for the traditional roast that Sunday, as she had been invited to Flo's cottage instead. So Sunday was free.

'You're welcome to hang about here,' said Fran at breakfast.

'No, I think we'll do something different,' said Ben. 'We could go out for the day.'

Libby looked dubious. 'I remember what happened last time we went out for the day on a Sunday.'

'Nothing like that's going to happen this time,' said Ben. 'You aren't in the middle of an investigation, are you?'

'No,' said Libby.

Ben shook his head. 'Look, Lib. It isn't the end of the world, even though it was for the victims. You're behaving like a child deprived of its favourite toy. Come on, snap out of it.'

'Ben's right, Lib,' said Guy. 'I'll tell you what – there's a great exhibition of Eric Ravilious paintings at the Dulwich

Gallery in London. Why don't you go up and see that?'

'Who's Ravilious?' asked Ben.

'He was largely responsible for the revival of English watercolour painting,' said Guy. 'Libby's forerunner, if you like.'

Libby looked interested. 'Nothing like as good as Ravilious, but I love his work. I know it's lovely to have it exhibited in London, but shouldn't it be at the Towner in Eastbourne? That's his home county, after all?'

'A wider audience, I expect,' said Ben. 'It's a great idea, Guy. Come on, Lib. We can get the train to Victoria and back to West Dulwich from there.'

'You know Dulwich?' said Fran. 'I lived not far from there.'

'So did I, once,' said Ben. 'Come on, Lib. Would you like to come with us, Fran? I know Guy won't because of the shop.'

'No, I'll stay with Guy,' said Fran. 'You two have a day out on your own.'

Persuaded, and even quite excited, Libby was ready in time for Ben to drive to Nethergate station for the next London train. For a change, there were no 'works on the line' involving tedious bus journeys through the Kent countryside, and they reached Victoria just before midday.

'Pity our train doesn't stop at West Dulwich,' said Libby as they struggled through the crowds towards the platform for the suburban line. 'We actually pass the gallery and the school, don't we?'

But Ben wasn't listening.

'I know I must be dreaming or hallucinating,' he said, 'but look over there. Next to the barrier we've just come through.'

Libby's mouth fell open. 'Walter Roberts!'

Chapter Twenty-eight

'No, Lib!' Ben caught hold of Libby's arm as she surged back the way they had come.

'Why not?' Libby turned an indignant face to her beloved. 'What's he doing here? They live up north.'

'He's entitled to be in London, you know. Perhaps they're visiting. Going to the theatre?'

'He's getting on our train.' Libby peered through the crowd. 'That means he's going to Canterbury, at least.'

Ben tried to peer too. 'And he's alone.'

'And he doesn't look like Walter.' Libby was frowning. 'I suppose it is him?'

'You mean his clothes? Well, this is London, not Erzugan,' said Ben.

'But he looked smart. Different.'

'I suppose I shouldn't suggest it, but perhaps he has a –'

'Lady friend?' interposed Libby. 'All the way down here?'

'Well, whatever the answer is, we are not going back on that train just to find out.' Ben turned her towards the platform where the West Dulwich train waited.

'No, I know.' Libby sighed and allowed herself to be led away.

On the train, she sent a text to Fran. *Walter Roberts spotted at Victoria getting the Canterbury train.*

Did you speak to him?

No. Ben wouldn't let me.

Sensible.

Libby sighed again and put the phone away.

The gallery, one of the most beautiful, in Libby's opinion, was attached to Dulwich College, the famous independent school for boys.

'Do you know,' whispered Libby, as they entered, 'I don't even know where you went to school.'

Ben shot her an amused look. 'Not here,' he said.

'Oh?'

'Canterbury. And no – proper state grammar schoolboy, me. What about you?'

'London. Girls' grammar school. Actually we used to play the James Allen School at netball and hockey.'

'James Allen?'

'The sister school of Dulwich,' explained Libby. 'Now, come on, let's look at these pictures.'

Two hours later, they emerged, blinking into the sunshine.

'Tea?' suggested Ben.

'Let's get back to Victoria,' said Libby. 'We can pick something up there.'

'A pre-packed sandwich?' Ben sighed. 'We didn't have any lunch, you know.'

'I'll treat you to a curry tonight,' said Libby. 'We can go to that one in Nethergate when we pick up the car.'

'The Golden Spice? Why not? We haven't been since it's been under new management.' Ben cheered up. 'Come on then, there's a train in five minutes.'

The ubiquitous sandwich duly picked up at Victoria station, they boarded the next train back to Canterbury and Libby checked her phone.

'Well?' asked Ben.

'Nothing. Eat your sandwich.'

Despite the slideshow of Ravilious images scrolling through her mind, Libby couldn't help returning to the puzzle of Walter Roberts and why he should be in Kent.

'I suppose,' she said suddenly to Ben, 'he might have been going somewhere else in Kent. He could have been changing at Chatham or Rochester. Or Sittingbourne.'

'Or just getting off at Bromley South,' said Ben. 'If we're talking about Walter Roberts, that is.'

'But if he's got connections in Kent, why didn't Betty tell

us?'

'I don't know, Lib. Perhaps she didn't think it was relevant.'

'Or perhaps she doesn't know,' said Libby.

'You're making mysteries out of molehills again,' said Ben. 'Stop it.'

Libby sighed and turned to look out of the window at the familiar countryside speeding past.

The Golden Spice had only just opened its doors when they arrived. It had been redecorated in a much more European way, and the menu was slightly different, with fewer choices, which Libby appreciated as she always had trouble making up her mind. It also had a long glass window into the kitchen area.

'Do you suppose any of them are still here from before?' she whispered to Ben.

'Any what?'

Libby jerked her head towards the kitchen.

'I shouldn't think so.' Ben leant back in his chair. 'This place has got to be on its best behaviour after the last owners. Stop seeing monsters under the beds.'

'Hmm.' Libby smiled sweetly up at the young man who arrived to take their orders and scared him into dropping his notebook.

'Do you think,' she said some time later, wiping her plate clean with a last remnant of naan, 'we ought to pop in and see Fran and Guy before we go home?'

'No, I don't,' said Ben firmly. 'Leave them in peace. You only want to talk about the murders and Walter Roberts, and I don't want my day spoiled. Neither will Guy, even if Fran doesn't mind.'

'Oh, all right.' Libby sat back and sighed happily. 'That was gorgeous. I wish we had a curry shop in Steeple Martin.'

'We can always order a takeaway from here,' said Ben.

'But it would be cold by the time it arrived.'

'They have insulated boxes,' said Ben. 'Do you want anything else, or shall we get the bill?'

It was only just getting dark when they drove back to Steeple Martin. The lights were on in Peter and Harry's cottage, but

Ben said 'No' just as Libby opened her mouth. She grinned.

'It was a lovely day, wasn't it?' she said when they were seated on the creaky cane sofa with a nightcap. 'Even Walter didn't really spoil it.'

'It was. It's not often we get a whole day to ourselves,' said Ben, stretching his legs out and dislodging Sidney from his lap. 'And just think – you've now got something to look forward to tomorrow.'

'Have I?'

Ben grinned. 'Walter. You can spend all day trying to find out about him, can't you?'

Ben set off for the timber yard on the estate early in the morning and Libby called Fran.

'Morning. I expected to hear from you yesterday.'

'Ben wouldn't let me,' said Libby.

Fran laughed. 'I'm not surprised. So tell me all about your day.'

Libby extolled the virtues of the gallery and the exhibition, The Golden Spice, and finally the surprise of seeing Walter Roberts.

'Ben wouldn't let me speak to him, as I told you. But what's he doing down here?'

'He's probably gone back, now,' said Fran. 'Where was it they lived? Leicester?'

'No, that was Greta and Tom. The Roberts are somewhere near Manchester. Should I email Betty?'

'And say what?'

'That we saw Walter at Victoria.'

'And what do you expect her to say to that?'

'Oh, you know. "Oh, yes, he was down seeing Great-Aunt Maud in Faversham" or something.'

'And if she does, you'll leave it alone, will you?'

Libby was silent.

'Come on, Libby. Tell me why it matters.'

'I've thought about it,' said Libby. 'Betty told us they'd been going for several years, didn't she? And Walter tended to stay back at the hotel on his own. She went out with other people – the woman she mentioned who she's still in touch with and us – so she couldn't know exactly what he got up to when she wasn't there.'

'What about Jimmy? He'd have seen him going out.'

'Not necessarily. He could have gone out the back way.'

'OK – to do what?'

'Meet Geoff Croker. Or one of his mates. To check on the operation.'

'So you've cast him as the Mr Big in the British end of the trafficking operation?'

Libby chewed her lip.

Fran sighed. 'Do you want to tell Ian about it?'

'Oh, hell,' said Libby, 'when you put it like that it does seem a bit pathetic. No, I won't. I won't even email Betty.'

'Oh, I don't know,' said Fran slowly, 'I think that could be a good idea.'

'You do?'

'Just to say what you said before. Bright and chatty.'

'All right,' said Libby. 'And if I get the Great-Aunt Maud answer I promise I'll give up.'

After some thought, Libby decided to send a group email to the hotel guests, to tell them that all investigations seemed to have ground to a halt, and add a 'by the way – saw Walter at Victoria on Sunday' almost as an afterthought. Satisfied with this, and inspired by the Ravilious paintings from the day before, she went into the conservatory and started stretching paper for more paintings. Leaving three boards aside with drying paper, she went to the easel and set up the picture of The Pink Geranium.

So absorbed was she, that Ben was actually standing beside her before she realised he'd come in.

'What's the time?' she asked, rubbing a painty finger over her nose.

'Half past one. How long have you been at it?'

'All morning, really, apart from stretching the paper.' She nodded at the three boards lying on a bench.

'You didn't do that for the little pictures,' said Ben.

'No, I didn't use much water in those, so it didn't matter. You stretch the paper if you know you're going to be using masses of water, so it doesn't split and tear.' Libby rubbed her nose again. 'Did you want lunch or something?'

Ben laughed. 'Not if you don't want to stop. Is there any soup?'

'Yes, there's that leek and potato I made on Saturday in the fridge. I'll have some, too.'

Ben heated up the soup and brought bowls out to the conservatory, where they perched on stools at the bench.

'What did Fran have to say?' he asked.

'Not a lot. She said to email Betty, though.'

Libby explained her Great-Aunt Maud theory.

'And have you had a reply?'

Libby looked surprised. 'I haven't checked. I haven't even thought about it.'

'Do it after lunch,' said Ben. 'I'll fetch some bread.'

After finishing the soup, Libby went into the sitting room and opened the laptop.

'Only one from Greta,' she called through to Ben.

'What does she say?'

'Just thanks for letting them know, and what a coincidence to see Walter. Did he look as grumpy as he always did on holiday.' Libby looked up. 'Did he?'

'He didn't look grumpy. Expressionless, really. And he was wearing a hat.'

'So he was. A little pork pie one, wasn't it? I wonder why?'

'Fashion statement? He was certainly looking very English country gentleman.'

'Oh, well, no use speculating. It's probably got nothing to do with the murders or Erzugan anyway.'

'You've changed your tune,' said Ben, surprised.

'None of the rest of you want to find out, so I might just as well give up. I said that last week.'

'You did. But then you talked to Jane, and after that you saw Walter. I don't want you to get bored and grumpy again.'

'I didn't!' said Libby. 'I started painting again.'

'You did. But I'm sure you'll be worrying away at our mystery underneath, whatever you say or do on the surface.'

Libby stared gloomily at the computer screen. 'I suppose I will. I just don't seem to be able to help myself. And it's so frustrating ...'

'I know. Look, I'll wash these bowls up and leave you to get on with The Pink Geranium. We've got a rehearsal tonight, so that will take your mind off everything else. We've only got another two weeks before we open.'

Two weeks sounded a long time in the professional theatre, but in the Oast Company, where rehearsals only took place three times a week and there was a five-week run to contemplate, it was a bit nail-biting. Libby went back to her painting with something else to worry about.

In fact, the rehearsal went very well, all the soloists knew their songs, the set pieces worked and the chorus numbers were duly rousing. After a quick drink at the pub, Libby and Ben went home happily.

The light was flashing on the answerphone.

'Libby, it's Greta here. I've just had Betty on the phone. Walter's disappeared.'

Chapter Twenty-nine

'What time did she call?' said Ben.

Libby listened again to the message. 'Twenty past nine.' She looked at her watch. 'An hour ago. Should I ring?'

'She could well be expecting you to,' said Ben. 'I'd give it a go.'

Greta answered on the second ring.

'Oh, Libby, I'm so glad you've called. Betty's in a terrible state.'

'Why did she ring you, though?' asked Libby.

'She said she's been worried about Walter since they came back from Erzugan. She knew you'd been keeping us up to date with the investigation but she didn't have your number, so she called me.'

'Why has she been worried about Walter? What's he been doing?'

'I don't really know. But apparently he left the house yesterday morning and hasn't been seen since.'

'Has she reported it to the police?'

'I didn't ask her. Oh, I should have, shouldn't I?'

Libby looked at Ben, who was frowning.

'She must, if she hasn't already. Do you think I should call her?'

Greta sighed. 'I don't know. It's a bit late for an old lady, isn't it?'

'She's not that old, Greta, and she won't be sleeping if she's that worried. Give me her number.'

'Oh, wait a minute …' Libby heard scrabbling, then a thump. 'Oh, sorry, dropped the phone. Here you are.' Greta read out the number. 'Will you let me know what happens?'

'Tomorrow,' said Libby. 'Thank you for telling me, Greta.' She ended the call and turned to Ben. 'So, do we tell Betty we've seen Walter?'

'I wouldn't. If I were you, I'd tell Ian we've seen Walter and tell him about Betty's phone call. Let him take it from there.'

'I will, but I've got to call Betty. What shall I say?'

'Just tell her to report it to her local police. then Ian will have a point of contact.'

'Do you think it's anything to do with the murders?'

'Betty obviously thinks it is, or she wouldn't have been trying to get in touch with you.'

Libby sighed. 'OK, Ian or Betty first?'

'You'll have to leave a message on Ian's work number at this time of night,' said Ben, 'so you might as well call Betty first. Then you might have more to tell Ian.'

'I need a drink first,' said Libby, carrying the phone into the sitting room and perching on the edge of the cane sofa.

'Scotch?' asked Ben, heading kitchenwards.

Libby nodded and punched in Betty's number. Like Greta, she answered on the second ring.

'Betty, it's Libby Sarjeant.'

'Oh, Libby!' Betty sounded as though she might burst into tears. 'He's gone!'

'Yes, Greta told me. Have you reported it to the police?'

'No.' Betty hesitated. 'I – he – I don't think he'd like that.'

'I don't think it really matters what he thinks right now, does it? You need to report it, Betty. You want him found, don't you?'

'Ye-es.'

'You don't sound sure.'

'Of course I do, but –' she stopped.

'Go on, "but" what?'

'He's been so peculiar since we came back from holiday,' Betty said in a rush. 'And when I told him what you were saying about the investigations, he was – well, he was most – um –'

'Derogatory?' suggested Libby. 'I can imagine. Has he ever

212

behaved like this before? When you've come back from Erzugan before, for instance.'

'No, never. The funny thing is,' Betty was speaking more slowly now, 'I always wondered why he wanted to keep going back. You saw what he was like when we were out there. Every year I suggested we tried somewhere else where he might like the food better and enjoy it more, but he always said he didn't want to have to get used to a new place. And he never came out with me. You saw.'

'We did,' said Libby. 'And he's been what, since you came back? Erratic?'

'A bit. Crankier than usual. And one day he just upped and went off for the day without a word, but he came back the same evening. I thought that was what he would do this time.'

'Did he say where he'd been?' Libby took her whisky glass from Ben and sipped.

'No. I asked him of course, and he bit my head off.'

Libby took a deep breath. 'Look Betty, you obviously weren't happy with him and he treated you badly –'

'No, no! He never hit me!'

'But he treated you badly,' insisted Libby. 'Just report him missing to the police and then enjoy the peace and quiet for a bit.'

'Oh.' Betty sounded doubtful, but less like bursting into tears. 'All right. Now?'

'If you can find the number of your local police station, yes now. I wouldn't call 999 just yet.'

Assured that Betty would indeed call the police, Libby ended the call, took a healthy swallow of scotch and pressed the speed dial button for Ian's work number. As expected, it went straight to voicemail. She told him as succinctly as she could the story of Walter, ended the call and switched off the phone.

'Well, what about that?' she said.

'Tell me what Betty said again?' Ben settled opposite her on the armchair.

'Didn't you hear what I told Ian?'

'Yes, but I wanted to ask some questions.'

'What, then?'

'Which day did he disappear before?'

Libby stared. 'Oh, bloody hell! Could it have been that Sunday?'

'Sounds like a possibility, doesn't it?' Ben gave her a crooked smile. 'Sounds as though you weren't fantasising as much as Fran thought earlier.'

'About Walter being involved with the trafficking? Well, I don't know. And I've just realised – I already *did* tell Betty about seeing Walter. I added it to the group email I sent. Why didn't she say?'

'Perhaps that was why she was trying to call you in the first place?'

'Surely she'd have mentioned it?'

'Then perhaps she hasn't seen the email? She might not check the computer as often as you do.'

'I suppose so.' Libby sighed. 'Nothing more we can do, anyway.'

But the following morning it appeared that Ben was right. Betty called at five past seven.

'Why didn't you tell me last night you'd seen Walter?' Her voice was shrill.

Libby, struggling to unglue her eyelids, tried to answer.

'You knew he was alive!'

'Betty, calm down.' Libby cleared her throat and mimed 'tea' at Ben. 'It's only just gone seven, you know.'

'Well, at least I gave you time to get up,' said Betty, with the unconscious superiority of the habitual early riser. 'But why didn't you tell me?'

'I did,' said Libby, only just refraining from adding 'you idiot'. 'I emailed you on Monday afternoon.'

There was a short silence.

'I've only just seen it,' said Betty reluctantly.

'Ben and I thought that was why you wanted to speak to me last night,' said Libby, only slightly bending the truth.

'Oh.' More silence.

'Did you report it to the police?'

'Er, n – no.'

'Do it now, Betty. And tell them he was sighted on Sunday midday at Victoria station in London.'

'How did he get there so quickly?'

'I don't know. When did he leave? You said Sunday morning.'

'Well – actually I don't know. He wasn't there when I woke up on Sunday morning.'

'So, during the night? Wouldn't you have noticed?'

Betty cleared her throat. 'We didn't – er – share a room.'

'Ah.' Libby slid out of bed, blessing the day she had invested in an upstairs phone. 'Well, I'd do it now, Betty. Really.'

Betty sighed. 'All right. I'll look up the number.'

'OK.' Libby paused, considering. 'Look Betty, you must be prepared for them to ask about the – well, the murders.'

'Yes.' Betty's voice trembled.

'That's why you've been putting it off, isn't it?'

'Yes.'

'They'll find out anyway,' said Libby gently. 'Have you anyone you can go to? Or who can come to you? Your daughter?'

'Yes. I'll call her after I've called the police.'

'If you don't want to do it, ask her to call me. You've got my number now.'

'All right.' Betty paused. 'Um – thank you, Libby. I'm sorry.'

Libby staggered down the stairs and Ben held out a mug of tea.

'So that's that,' she said after she'd filled him in on the conversation. 'Now we just wait for Ian to get in touch.'

They didn't have to wait long.

'Why didn't you tell me on Sunday?' were DCI Connell's first words.

'That I'd seen one of our fellow guests at Victoria? What would you have said to that? Until I heard from Betty I didn't know it would be relevant to anything.'

215

Ian sighed. 'I suppose not. Now tell me again what Mrs Roberts said.'

Libby told him, adding in the information she'd just received. 'And I still don't know if she's reported it to her local station. She's somewhere in Manchester – I haven't a clue where.'

'We have,' said Ian. 'Everyone was spoken to earlier in the investigation, if you remember.'

'Well, good luck. It's got to be relevant now, hasn't it?'

'Possibly.' Ian was non-committal. 'Where exactly in the station did you see him?'

'By the barrier to the platform we'd just left.'

'So the Canterbury train?'

'And Nethergate.'

'The train divides,' said Ian. 'He could have been going anywhere.'

'Do you think he was the one who killed Justin? Betty said he disappeared for a day before, and she didn't know where.'

'It's possible. Thank you for the information, Libby. I think under the circumstances you ought to be taking extra care of where you go and who with.'

'What?' Libby looked across at Ben, alarmed. 'Why? Why would anyone want to hurt me?'

Ben's expression changed.

'If Walter Roberts thinks you know anything at all about the operation in Turkey and he's in any way involved, you could be. I know this isn't your fault, but just take care. Is Ben there?'

Libby handed over the phone to Ben, who wandered into the conservatory listening intently.

'He's right, Lib.' Ben came back and sat down at the kitchen table. 'I don't think you should stay here on your own during the day, either.'

'What –?' Libby gaped. 'I'm not going to be turned out of my own house! And how would Walter Roberts find me, anyway?'

'How did Geoff Croker get your telephone number? Whoever's involved, it's a criminal gang and they have almost

216

as many resources as the police. I think you should come up to the Manor with me. We can come back here at night.'

Libby thought for a moment. 'Couldn't I go to Fran's?'

'Roberts could look her up, too.'

'But Harbour Street's much busier than Allhallow's Lane, and Guy's almost next door.'

Ben looked doubtful.

'Please, Ben. What would I do in the Manor all day?'

'All right. Give her a ring now and see what she says. I'll ring Guy.'

Libby's conversation lasted much longer than Ben's, but when they were both concluded, Libby went up to shower and dress while Ben made breakfast, after which, they went their separate ways.

'Do you think Sidney will be safe?' Libby said before she pulled away.

'He'll just run,' said Ben. 'If anyone tried to get in.' He bent to give her a kiss through the window. 'Off you go.'

Libby was nervous on the drive to Nethergate. She was convinced that every car that came up behind her was following her, but eventually she was driving thankfully down the hill towards Harbour Street. She had to park in The Sloop car park, as every space on Harbour Street was taken, which somewhat spoiled the view from Coastguard Cottage. Fran had been hoping for yellow lines and restricted parking for years.

Fran was waiting on the doorstep. 'Ian just called. Come in and I'll tell you.'

Chapter Thirty

'Was he warning you, too?' Libby stepped inside and peered round, as if expecting hidden figures in the corner.

'In a way.' Fran closed the door. 'He approved of us being together, anyway.'

'Does he really think we're in danger?' Libby's eyes were wide. 'I mean, I know we've run in to the odd bit of trouble in the past, but not been hunted down.'

'Sit down, Lib, do.' Fran pushed her onto the deep window seat. 'Tea?'

'No, I don't want anything, thank you. What did Ian say?'

'Betty apparently did finally report to the police, just about at the time Ian got in touch with them, so he's actually talked to her. And the local force are sending people round to have a look.'

'Oh, poor Betty! Perhaps her daughter will take her back with her?'

'I would hope so,' said Fran, perching on the edge of her favourite armchair. 'But the important thing is they've got confirmation of our friend Geoff Croker's involvement in the trafficking operation.'

'Wow! So who got that? Our Johnny?'

'His team, I gather. And now they're looking for connections between him and Walter.'

Libby stared into the empty fireplace. 'Suppose Walter hasn't got anything to do with it? He could just be a nasty old man who just does what he wants and couldn't care less about his wife.'

'Until the other day, that's exactly what I would have said. But it all seems to piling up, doesn't it? The suspicious circumstances?'

'Letting Betty go off on her own while they were on holiday, refusing to anywhere else, being seen down here …'

'It's all a bit tenuous, but obviously the police think it's worth looking into,' said Fran. 'And especially the day he went missing. Ian said they're trying to work out exactly when that was. Betty seemed confused.'

'I'm not surprised. I feel so sorry for her.'

'But she's been incredibly dumb, hasn't she? If she really hasn't known what's going on?'

'We-ell, yes …'

'Let's face it, she left it quite a long time before she said anything, and even then it was you she wanted to talk to, not the police.'

'And she didn't even do that until this morning. And she was furious about me seeing Walter at Victoria.'

'I'm not saying she's involved, but it's a bit suspicious, surely?'

Libby stared at her. 'God, yes. I didn't even think.'

Fran grinned. 'No. But then, Betty seemed such a nice person compared to Walter, didn't she?'

'She was nice. And she introduced us to Mahmud. And he told us about Geoff Croker.'

'And she knew all about them, didn't she?'

'Oh, bother.' Libby stared gloomily out of the window. 'Have we let anything out, do you think?'

'I haven't spoken to her, or even emailed. You're the only one who's done that,' said Fran.

'Well, thanks for that.' Libby sighed and stood up. 'I wonder what Ian will get out of her?'

'Nothing, if she's smart,' said Fran. 'Even if she knew about the operation, she wouldn't have been involved in the actual running of it, so she won't have any of the details.'

'Except that she must have known why they kept going back, even though she said she didn't.' Libby stretched. 'I got up too early. Can we have tea?'

Fran led the way into the kitchen. 'I'm not sure what Ian

thinks could happen to us. I don't see Walter as a killer, whatever else he is.'

'You don't think he's Justin Newcombe's killer?'

'I know he went missing for a day at roughly the same time, but – I don't know, it seems wrong.'

'Perhaps he met up with the killer and told him all about the other murders?'

'But why?' Fran asked. 'Why would the killer want to kill Justin? And why would Walter tell him?'

'We're speculating that Walter was the English contact for the trafficking organisation, aren't we?' said Libby. 'And Justin was the money man?'

'I doubt very much if he was,' said Fran. 'I suspect that he was merely peripherally involved. Croker's accountant, maybe. He just wasn't the type. Also, being gay, Croker wouldn't have trusted him.'

'Hmm.' Libby scowled at the mug Fran set in front of her. 'Why was he here, then?'

'Justin? No idea. He could have been a messenger of some sort. Perhaps to speak to Walter. Perhaps that's why Walter went missing, to pick up a message from Justin.'

'He could have killed him to silence him, if Justin knew all about the operation.'

'Only if Justin was threatening to blow the whole thing.'

'Oh, it's useless, isn't it?' Libby sighed, and went out to the back yard, where Balzac slept curled up in the big plant pot. 'And I still don't see why anyone would want to harm either of us.'

'Because we've been asking questions.'

'But how would they know?'

'You've been keeping all our fellow guests – and Martha – up to date with the progress of the police investigation as far as we know it. They all know. And Carol Oxford knows, don't forget.'

'Who's she going to tell? That's nothing whatsoever to do with the killings.'

'But the police have talked to her. Word could have got out.'

'Even so, she has nothing to do with anything.'

'She's the mother of one of the victims,' said Fran.

'Oh, so she is.' Libby pulled out one the dining chairs and sat down. 'But nothing to do with the trafficking – her or Sally.'

'And I wonder what her job was when she was in this country?'

Libby frowned. 'Come to that, what was Alec Wilson's job before he had his name changed?'

They both contemplated the dining table seriously.

'And actually, what difference does it make?' said Libby eventually.

'None, I suppose. I think Ian's being over-cautious about us. I expect he'll have told Smith about Walter, won't he?'

'Bound to have,' said Libby. 'It would have helped if he'd been a bit more up front at the beginning, wouldn't it?'

'Only if he knew about the whole operation,' said Fran. 'I can't see how it would have saved Justin Newcombe.'

'But if they'd found the murderer quicker, he wouldn't have killed Justin.'

'The murderer was in Turkey –' began Libby.

'And came back to England. That's what the thinking is now, isn't it?'

'If it turns out to be Walter, yes.'

'It has to be, surely? If he was over there checking up on the operation and wasn't happy?'

'Maybe, but a, we haven't got confirmation that it's a trafficking operation and b, why was Sally killed? She's not involved.'

'Aha!' said Libby. 'How do we know that? You just said we don't know why she really went to Turkey. I said she wasn't involved and you queried it.'

'Yes,' said Fran with a sigh. 'Round and round in circles as usual.'

Although neither of them would admit it, Libby and Fran got very bored that day. Fran pottered around doing household chores for the rest of the morning while Libby prowled the bookshelves, then they both went to relieve Guy in the gallery/shop at lunchtime. Business wasn't as brisk as it would be in a couple of weeks' time when the schools broke up, so there was very little to occupy them. After lunch, they went to The Alexandria to see how bookings were going for the summer show, then climbed up to Cliff Terrace to see if Jane was in. She wasn't.

They wandered along to The Tops, which had once been open fields on the cliff tops, but was now a car park with a view. They sat on a bench and looked out at the bay, Dragon Island in the middle and the lighthouse on the point.

'What would you normally be doing on an ordinary day?' asked Libby. 'When we're not investigating.'

'Housework, reading, helping Guy.' Fran squinted at the sequins sparkling on the sea. 'I don't know, really. What about you?'

'Not much housework, painting, fiddling about on the computer. How do we fill our days, for goodness' sake? I think I ought to go back to work.'

'Your painting's your work. And you do a lot for the theatre.'

'S'pose so. But aren't you bored?'

'Sometimes, a bit. You remember just after I got married? When we came back from honeymoon? I was bored then.'

'That was a culture shock, though. You'd spent years scraping a living in a horrible flat in London, and all of a sudden you had a lovely cottage, a lovely husband and no money worries.'

Fran nodded. 'It always feels disloyal to Guy to say I'm bored.' She turned to look at Libby. 'I think that's why we get involved in these things. We haven't got enough to keep us occupied. I think you're right. We ought to go back to work.'

'We can't go back to the pro theatre though. Nobody would have us,' said Libby.

They looked at each other for a long moment.

'Do you remember ...' said Fran.

'What Harry said ...' began Libby.

'We couldn't,' said Fran.

'We could,' said Libby.

'There's legislation,' said Fran. 'You have to be licenced now.'

'Not for informal investigations.'

'I don't know why we're even thinking about it,' said Fran with a deep sigh. 'We already investigate things. People have asked us in the past.'

Libby nodded. 'Gemma and the Green Man murder.'

'Alice and the murder in the church.'

'And even Patti with the reliquary in the monastery,' concluded Libby. 'We just don't get paid for it.'

'We don't need to be paid,' said Fran.

'I might,' said Libby.

'Let's just accept that people might want us to look into things informally, especially if the police aren't interested,' said Fran. 'Carry on as usual, in fact.'

'Oh, all right,' said Libby with a shrug. 'But no one asked us to look into this one, did they?'

'Carol Oxford did,' said Fran.

'So she did.' Libby looked thoughtfully out to sea. 'Do you think we ought to speak to her again?'

'I don't see why.'

'We could ask her if she or Sally knew Betty and Walter Roberts.'

'Why on earth should they have done? The Roberts come from Manchester.'

'But Walter might have been down here on – um – on – well, on trafficking operations.'

'He'd keep out of sight, then, wouldn't he? Anyway, ten years ago he might not have been involved. If he is now, of course.'

'Oh, all right.' Libby stood up. 'Want an ice cream?'

Fran looked surprised. 'Yes, that would be nice.'

'Only in that lovely ice cream parlour, not Lizzie's. So we can have a proper knickerbocker glory or something.'

The ice cream parlour had been kept completely and authentically retro and served ice cream sundaes in traditional dishes, and coffee and hot chocolate in glass mugs complete with chrome holders. Libby had something called 'Nethergate Sunrise' and a hot chocolate, and felt quite sick.

'I shouldn't have had that,' said Libby, eyeing the empty dish. 'I'm never going to get thin.'

Fran laughed. 'Ben wouldn't like you if you were thin.'

'Wouldn't he?' asked Libby wistfully. 'I've always wanted to be thin.'

'It wouldn't suit you,' said Fran. 'Come on, what are we going to do next?'

'Oh, Lord,' groaned Libby. 'I don't know. What's the time?'

'Half past three. Too early to cook dinner.'

'And I don't want afternoon tea after this. Shall we just go back to yours and read or something?'

'We could do some research on the laptop.'

'On what, though?' Libby pushed her chair back and stood up.

'Trafficking operations?' suggested Fran. 'How long they've been going on?'

'We've done all that before,' said Libby. 'I can't think of anything we haven't done.'

They walked slowly back towards Harbour Street. Where the square joined it in front of The Swan Inn, Libby suddenly stopped.

'Now, I'm not being paranoid, but look.'

A hundred yards away, leaning on the sea wall almost in front of Guy's shop, was Walter Roberts.

Chapter Thirty-one

'He's found us,' whispered Fran, digging out her phone.

'Who are you calling?' Libby whispered back, digging out her own phone.

'Guy, to tell him not to come out of the shop.'

'I'll call Ian.'

Ian's instructions were succinct. 'Stay where you are, but out of sight if you can, and take note if he moves off. Do not follow him. Someone will be with you in about five minutes.'

Guy's were more querulous, intimating that no one was going to frighten him into hiding in his own home.

'Be sensible, darling,' said Fran. Libby raised her eyebrows. She'd never heard Fran call anyone darling before. 'Ian wants us to stay put and not be seen. That includes you.'

'Oh, so you called him first, did you?'

Fran sighed. 'No. Libby called Ian. I called you.'

'All right.' Guy was mollified. 'I can see him. I might go upstairs and watch from there.'

'You know,' said Fran, as she put away her phone. 'I think this is actually a coincidence.'

'What? Walter Roberts appearing right in front of your home?' said Libby. 'Don't be daft.'

'No, really. He must know he will have been reported missing to the police now, and why risk being out in the open anywhere near where either of us live? If he really did know where we were and wanted to harm us, he would have come at night and not wanted to be seen.'

Libby grudgingly acknowledged this might be the truth, and perched on the edge of one of the benches The Swan provided for its customers. Walter Roberts was still leaning on the sea wall.

Suddenly he stood up straight and turned towards the other end of Harbour Street.

'He's seen someone,' said Libby.

A figure had emerged from behind The Blue Anchor and The Sloop. Libby squinted to see.

'Mrs Sarjeant?' A voice behind her made her jump and stifle a squeal.

'Mr Maiden! What are you doing here? You're supposed to be in Canterbury.'

DS Maiden grinned. 'Today I'm in Nethergate, and a good job, too. I'm just going to stroll up and have a word with our gentleman there. Constable Drew will wait until I call him.'

Libby belatedly noticed a large uniformed constable trying to make himself inconspicuous against the wall of The Swan.

'What do we do?' asked Fran.

'Go inside the pub,' said Maiden. 'Don't come out until I give you the word. We don't want him to see you.'

Fran gave Libby an I-told-you-so look, and they went inside the pub. The customers had already noticed the police presence and were eager to know what was going on, but Libby and Fran politely declined to explain.

'That's them women who do the murders,' said somebody at the bar. Libby and Fran exchanged scowls.

'You investigatin' then?' called someone else.

Libby turned a furious face on him. 'Do you want to mess up a police operation?' she hissed. 'No? Then keep quiet.'

'Sorry, I'm sure,' said the drinker, shrugging and turning back to his pint.

Fran was peering out of the window. 'The other person's vanished. Maiden's talking to Walter, who looks as though he's going to do a runner.'

But before Walter could do more than take a hesitant step away from DS Maiden, Constable Drew had materialised by his side, laying a gentle hand on his arm, and the trio began a slow stately progress down Harbour Street. As he passed The Swan, Maiden turned his head slightly and gave the ghost of a wink through the window. Libby and Fran watched as the three men got into an unremarkable black car parked, illegally, on the other side of the square. When it had gone, Libby's phone beeped with an incoming text.

'You can come out now.'

'From Ian,' said Libby. 'Maiden must have told him.'

'Well of course he did. Shall we go back to mine, now? We'll have to wait for him to call, I suppose.'

The two women emerged cautiously.

'Whoever that other person is, they'll still be around,' said Libby nervously.

'And Walter won't have told anyone about him.'

'Or her,' said Libby. 'I couldn't see. It had trousers on, I'm sure.'

Guy was waiting for them at the door of the gallery.

'What happened?'

The followed him inside and told him.

'I think Fran's right,' he said when they'd finished. 'I don't think he'd have risked being right outside our house if he knew where we were. Not in daylight.'

'No, that makes sense I suppose,' said Libby. 'So who could he have come to meet? Here, of all places?'

'Well,' said Fran slowly, 'I was thinking about that. He's obviously using public transport, so it makes sense to go to populated places where he won't stand out and which are easy to get to. So, say he was going to meet someone from somewhere else along this coast, it would be practically impossible to get there without a car. And we know he was travelling on this line from Victoria on Sunday.'

'We think he was,' said Guy.

'Making an educated guess,' said Libby. 'Do you think this proves he's got something to do with the trafficking?'

'If it is trafficking,' said Fran. 'It'll be fascinating to hear what he says, won't it?'

'If Ian will tell us,' agreed Libby. 'Do you think I could go home now? Has the threat been removed?'

As if in answer her phone rang.

'All right, Libby, you can stand down now,' said Ian. 'And thanks for doing what you were asked to do for once.'

Libby spluttered. Ian laughed. 'I'll call you both later.'

Libby drove home feeling safer. The threat from Walter Roberts – if there had been a threat – had been removed, although if there was a threat from anyone else it remained. However, it seemed likely that now Walter had been asked to help with enquiries (into what, Libby wondered) nobody would risk coming anywhere near her or Fran.

'I really must replace Romeo,' Libby said later to Ben.

Romeo the Renault had finally failed his MOT and would have cost far more than he was worth to put right, so Libby had regretfully sent him off to the automobile graveyard and relied on sharing Ben's Range Rover.

'What brought this on?' Ben handed her a glass of wine.

'Whenever I go anywhere these days it means you haven't got a car. And it's very inconvenient.'

'Well, yes.' Ben looked amused. 'But you haven't heard me complain, have you?'

'No, of course not. But I'd like one of my own again.' Libby looked up at him. 'Will you come with me to buy one?'

'Don't you trust yourself?'

'I'm very good with most things, but I think you probably know more about cars than I do.'

'Thanks.' Ben came to sit beside her on the creaky sofa. 'And while we're about it, why don't we buy a new sofa?'

'We?'

'Don't I live here now?'

Libby looked away, remembering her ambivalence about moving into Steeple Farm, technically owned by Peter's mother Millie, but restored by Ben. Ben had been the one to compromise, moving into number 17 Allhallow's Lane and acceding to Libby's desire *not* to get married.

'Yes, of course,' she muttered.

'Then why don't we consign this one to the conservatory and buy a new one? We could even get a sofa-bed for when your hordes descend.'

Libby looked up at him and smiled. 'You do have good ideas,' she said. 'And you're very tolerant of my horde.'

Ben's own children lived at the other end of the country and relations with them were rather strained, although Libby had never understood why. Ben was one of the nicest and kindest men she'd ever met. Far kinder and nicer than she was herself, she reflected.

'So, when shall we go?' the nice kind man was asking now. 'Tomorrow?'

'Yes, please. Can you just buy one on the spot? And drive it away?'

'Unless you want to order it, I suppose so,' said Ben. 'Provided you can get the insurance cover and all that sort of thing. Take your old cover note with you and we can probably do it all online. Providing we can find one you like.'

'Oh, I will,' said Libby confidently. 'And it's about time. Romeo was getting too well-known round here.'

Ben frowned at her. 'Does this mean you'll be back on the investigation trail?'

Libby tried to look innocent. 'Not now. Ian's got hold of Walter, so we'll know the whole story any minute now, won't we?'

'But in the future, you will.'

'Not if I can help it.' Libby looked away.

'Unless someone asks you.'

'Well ...'

Ben laughed. 'And then you won't be able to resist it. And someone will, I guarantee it.'

Libby turned back and smiled with relief. 'Maybe. But I will try not to get into trouble.'

The next morning, Libby and Ben set off for Canterbury. Libby had all her important documents in her latest basket.

'Ian didn't phone last night,' said Libby.

'Did you expect him to?'

'He said he would.' Libby sighed. 'I don't suppose we come into the picture at all now, though.'

However, Libby's mobile rang halfway through a

salesman's encomium on one of the cars that Libby had taken a fancy to. Seeing that it was Ian, she excused herself and took the call.

'I'm in the middle of buying a car!" she hissed.

'You're what?' Ian sounded startled.

'Buying a car. I'm in the showroom with a salesman in mid-flow.'

'All right. Call me when you've finished. Where are you?'

'In Canterbury.'

'Do you want to come to the station?'

'Not particularly. Ben and I are visiting all the showrooms this morning. Can't it wait?'

Ian sighed. 'Just give me a call between visits, all right?'

Libby ended the call and went sheepishly back to the men.

'Ian,' she said to Ben. 'Do go on,' to the salesman with a bright smile.

Two showrooms later she was the proud possessor of a small silver car which she couldn't pick up until the following day. Giving it a final pat, she followed Ben out to this car and called Ian.

'Well? Did you buy one?'

'Yes. Now, what did you want me for?'

'I wanted to tell you what Walter Roberts has told us. It's interesting.'

'Oh.' Libby climbed in beside Ben. 'He wants to tell us what Walter Roberts has said.'

'Shall we go to the station?' asked Ben.

'I heard that,' said Ian. 'Yes please. I'll see you then.'

Ten minutes later, with the luxury of parking in the police station car park, they were ushered into Ian's office, where Libby had only been once or twice before.

'Coffee?' offered their host.

'Yes, please,' said Ben.

'No, thanks,' said Libby.

'Now,' said Ian when Ben had been served. 'Walter Roberts.'

'Did he know where we were?' asked Libby.

'No, he had no idea.'

'That's what I thought,' said Ben.

'And Fran,' said Libby. 'And I suppose it made sense.'

'Well, he didn't. Not that he was very pleased with you, of course. He was quite rude about you, in fact.'

'I bet,' said Libby with a grin. 'If he was involved in – oh, hang on, we don't know, do we?'

'We do now.' Ian sighed. 'And yes, it was trafficking. Of the most unpleasant kind.'

'Girls?' said Ben.

Ian nodded. 'All of whom had paid to get to England for a better life and were then forced into prostitution.'

'From Erzugan?' asked Libby.

'Not only there, but certainly a lot of it was controlled from there.'

'By?'

'Geoff Croker, of course.'

Chapter Thirty-two

Libby let out a deep breath. 'We were right.'

'Yes.' Ian smiled. 'A lot of leaps of faith as usual, but yes, you were right, although you certainly didn't suspect Walter Roberts, did you?'

'Not until he disappeared, no. Or until we saw him at Victoria, actually. So what did he tell you?'

'Not an awful lot until your Commander Smith arrived – in full battledress, I might add.'

'He came here? Why?'

'He wasn't terribly pleased with us.' Ian smiled reminiscently. 'By the time he arrived, Walter had already admitted some of it, and unfortunately, Smith could no longer pull rank and shut him up. Then, Roberts turned on him. He's a very spiteful old man. I feel sorry for his wife.'

'Poor Betty, yes.' Libby looked up warily. 'She didn't have anything to do with it, did she?'

'I think she almost certainly knew there was something going on,' said Ian, 'but was probably too scared to do anything about it.'

'She was scared when I spoke to her,' said Libby. 'So was it Walter who killed Justin? And was he mixed up in it, too?'

'He says not, and there's certainly no evidence that he was there. As for Newcombe's involvement, we think so far it was peripheral at best.'

'So where did he go?'

'That's what he won't say. Nor where he was between Sunday and yesterday.'

'And what does our Commander Smith have to say about it all?'

'He wasn't too pleased, as I've said. Especially as Walter Roberts said quite definitely that he and the Crokers knew perfectly well who Alec Wilson was and took pains to avoid him.'

'So who was he?' asked Ben.

'He was there to monitor the trafficking that had started going through Erzugan about ten years ago. Apparently, it happens all along the Turkish Mediterranean coast from small bays. Normally they're taken across to Italy and landed somewhere on the heel near Brindisi.'

'Poor Italy,' said Libby. 'And I still don't understand why these people want to come here.'

'That's not a question for us, but for the politicians,' said Ian. 'Anyway, the Erzugan traffic was to try and evade the notice of the authorities who were monitoring the other routes.'

'So they weren't coming direct to England?' said Ben.

'Yes, some of them were.' Ian looked at Libby. 'Like the ones that George and Bert found at the Creekmarsh inlet. That was an early trial, Smith thinks. He had to open up a bit about it after Roberts had let all the cats come tumbling out of the bag.'

'And it carried on?'

'Intermittently. There was a contact in Nethergate apparently, but that was stopped.'

'Rachinda's father!' said Ben and Libby together.

'What about Colonel Weston? Sally's father?' asked Libby.

'No knowledge of that, yet, but I daresay Smith will be looking into that.'

'So does Sally come into any of this?' asked Ben. 'Or was she, as I think someone said before, simply collateral damage?'

Ian frowned. 'I don't know. She wasn't mentioned by either Roberts or Smith, even as a victim.'

'So collateral damage, then,' said Libby. 'Poor Sally.'

'And you still don't know who killed Newcombe?' asked Ben.

'Undoubtedly the person whom he came to meet. Roberts was uncomfortable about it, so he knows something, but his DNA wasn't found at the scene.'

'Heavens!' said Libby. 'So nothing's that much clearer now, is it?'

'There are still a lot of things we need to know. Roberts' contact down here, who he was meeting yesterday and if it was the same person. Smith's team can round up Croker and his chums in Turkey, but they're unlikely to give us any names. We've got people beavering about all over the south-east chasing up other members of the organisation, and identifying places the girls were taken.'

'Aren't our policemen wonderful!' said Libby admiringly.

'Don't be sarcastic, young Lib,' said Ian.

'I wasn't! I genuinely mean it. We don't know the half of what you do.'

'And that's the way it has to stay. Although I must say, you having found Wilson's body in Turkey does look as though it's put us on to the whole trafficking organisation.' Ian sighed. 'But I doubt if we'll ever catch everyone involved. We didn't in the Berini case.'

'But that was more than illegal immigrants,' said Libby. 'And as far as I remember, it wasn't prostitution either.'

'No, it wasn't, but don't forget you nearly ended up in a rather nasty position on that case.'

'It was a very uncomfortable position we did end up in,' said Libby, remembering being thrown onto a boat in the dark.

'So don't get involved again,' said Ben.

'Unless she's asked,' said Ian.

Ben sighed.

'There's one thing I would like you and Fran to do.' Ian opened a drawer in his desk. 'I gather from Mrs Oxford's local force that she's been agitating to be allowed to put the house on the market. She says she wants to cut all ties to the area, and I can't say I blame her.'

'So what do we do?'

'Here are the keys. Apparently, she's asked if you would sort out the details for her. She doesn't want to come down.'

'Ri-ight,' said Libby. 'And?'

'I want you to do just that and see what happens.'

'You think something will?' gasped Libby.

'That's making them sitting ducks!' protested Ben.

'If there is a link to Sally Weston, it's the only way we might ferret it out. There might be nothing.'

'What about her computer?'

'Nothing. And as you know, her mobile was missing. There was nothing personal in her house in Turkey, only ordinary bills and those photographs you told me about. No letters.'

'People don't write letters any more,' said Libby. 'They text, phone, and email. That's why I'm surprised there was nothing on her computer.'

'I would think her phone and computer weren't synced and all her contacts were on her phone,' said Ian. 'That's why it's gone.'

'And Wilson's computer was gone, too.'

'Smith hasn't even traced her mobile phone records. Although it appears that Turkish phone records aren't that easy to get hold of.'

'It all makes my brain hurt,' said Libby. 'I'm glad I don't have to do any of that.'

'All you have to do is put Sally Weston's house on the market. We'll give you authorisation. We don't want to do it, for obvious reasons.'

'OK.' Libby took the keys he held out. 'What did Fran say?'

'She was non-committal,' said Ian with a grin. 'I think she was waiting to see what you would say.'

'She knew I'd say yes.' Libby tucked the keys into her basket. 'Any particular estate agents? Both the ones we've come up against in the past have been closed down.'

'It doesn't matter, but tell us, obviously. And I'd ring Mrs Oxford, if I were you, just to make things quite clear.'

Five minutes later, with one of Ian's cards signifying authority to sell the house in Cherry Ashton tucked alongside the keys, Libby and Ben were back in his car.

'Now you can't moan about this,' said Libby, belting herself in. 'We've been asked to help the police. And it isn't dangerous.'

'You're talking about an international trafficking organisation, for God's sake!' Ben swung the car out of the car park. 'Of course it's bloody dangerous.'

'They'll keep a low profile, though, won't they?' said Libby, a shade doubtfully. 'And will they really want to buy a house just to search it? Because that's all they could do, surely?'

'I have no idea,' said Ben. 'But don't you ever offer to accompany prospective buyers. Either of you. Even with the agent.'

'As if we would,' scoffed Libby, going slightly pink.

'So which agents do we go to?' Libby asked Fran later when she called.

'Any of the local ones,' said Fran, 'but I thought we could pull strings a bit.'

'Eh?'

'Well, I did work –'

'Goodall and Smythe!' Libby shouted down the receiver.

'All right, all right! You practically deafened me. Yes, Goodall and Smythe.'

'But surely this house is far too small for them to bother with? And if anyone's looking, they'll look in the local papers, won't they?'

'Keep up, Lib! You don't look in papers any more, you go online. You put in the location you're searching and up comes every property within your budget, whatever the agent.'

'Oh,' said Libby. 'So all we do is ask them to handle it?'

'I'll ask them and let you know. My contact there is very discreet. I think you met him – he came to our wedding. Richard Smart.'

'Probably,' said Libby. 'There were a lot of people I'd never met before at your wedding.'

'Well, I'll talk to him and let you know what he says.'

'OK. I'll call Carol to let her know what's happening.'

Libby made tea and took the phone out into the garden.

'Carol? It's Libby Sarjeant.'

'Oh, Libby! Is there any news?'

'Not exactly,' said Libby, gazing thoughtfully up into the

239

branches of the cherry tree, 'but our local policeman says you want to sell the house in Cherry Ashton.'

'I do. Did he ask you to handle it for me?'

'He did. I just wanted to check that it was all right with you. And how much of the history you wanted made public.'

'None of it,' said Carol promptly. 'It would certainly put people off, even though nothing actually happened there.'

'Right. We're thinking maybe we should say "probate sale", what do you think? Although probate hasn't been granted yet, has it?'

'Oh, Lord – I didn't think!' Carol's voice went up a notch. 'Why didn't the police tell me that?'

'I don't know,' said Libby, who thought she did. 'We can test the water, though, can't we? Did she actually leave a will?'

'Thankfully, yes, she did. She made it when she went to Turkey. She said if she died abroad it would make life very difficult unless everything was tied up neatly over here.'

'Did she now?' said Libby thoughtfully. 'And have you read it?'

'No, it's with the solicitors. I had to tell him when she – she –'

'Yes, of course. So didn't he tell you what was in it?'

'He just said it was very straightforward and I was the only beneficiary. She hadn't got very much to leave except the house.'

'What about the house in Turkey?'

'Oh, that was rented. I suppose they'll send her belongings home, won't they?'

'I expect so, but we didn't see much when we were there. Only some old photographs.'

'No letters?' Libby could almost hear the frown.

'Not that we could see. Mind you,' she added hastily, 'we weren't actually searching. We were merely there because we could speak and read English.' No need to mention that Johnny Smith was also there.

'Oh, I see.' There was a short silence. 'Only I would have thought she'd have kept my letters ...' Carol's voice wobbled.

'Had you written to her recently?' Libby asked after a decent interval. 'You said you hadn't heard from her.'

'I wrote a couple of months ago – well, March, I think it was. I'd heard from an old friend I hadn't seen for years and I wrote to let her know.'

'That wasn't Jean, was it?'

'Jean?' Carol sounded surprised. 'Who Jean Burton? Good Lord, no! She died ages ago, poor thing. How did you know about her?'

'Both you and Agnes told me about your lunch friends,' said Libby, keeping her fingers crossed that Carol actually *had* mentioned Jean.

'Oh, yes!' Carol uttered a half-hearted laugh. 'Fancy you remembering. In fact, it was our other friend who used to come to those lunches, Valerie. She was trying to get in touch with someone else.'

Chapter Thirty-three

Libby's mind leapt ahead making fantastical connections.

'Libby? Are you still there?' Carol was now sounding querulous.

'Yes, I'm still here,' said Libby, wondering how she could ask the questions she wanted to and deciding she couldn't. 'Well, I expect when they pack up Sally's belongings they'll find the letter, and you've kept all those she sent you, haven't you?'

'Not all of them,' said Carol. 'I never thought I'd have to.'

Libby resolved in future to keep everything her offspring sent her. She cleared her throat. 'Well, keep me posted about the probate. Meanwhile, we'll sound out an estate agent.'

As soon as she ended the call with Carol, she called Fran, whose phone was engaged. She tried the mobile, but it went straight to voicemail, so she tried Ian's office number.

'Connell.'

'Ian, what about probate?'

Sort silence. 'What?'

'Sally Weston's house. It can't be sold until probate has been granted. I just remembered. And Carol Weston – I mean, Oxford – said the solicitor didn't remind her, either.'

There was a longer silence. 'I'll see what I can do.'

'Well, we needn't actually sell it,' said Libby. 'Not if you're using it as bait.'

'No. Thank you for telling me, Libby.'

Libby realised her tea was cold and went inside to make some more. Just as she was pouring boiling water into the teapot, her phone rang.

'Fran.'

'You called when I was speaking to Richard.'

'Yes, because while I was talking to Carol I remembered that she couldn't sell the house until probate had been granted. I've told Ian.'

'Yes, Richard reminded me of that.'

'Oh.' Libby deflated. 'So no go, then?'

'Oh, yes. He said lots of houses are put on the market as "probate sales" with the understanding that prospective purchasers are getting in before the general public. Remember the old house at Mountville Road?'

Fran's family had once owned a large Victorian house in London that had been sold in the same way. Libby wondered whether it was this that had triggered her own memory of probate sales.

'Oh. So is Robert going to help?'

'Richard. Yes. He's coming down tomorrow to measure up and so on. You've got the keys, haven't you?'

'Yes. Shall I meet him there?'

'You'll meet *us* there. I'm picking him up at the station at half past eleven, so we'll be there by about a quarter to twelve.'

'Right. So we can have a really good look round.'

'There won't be much left, will there? Ian will have taken everything of note away when you handed over the keys.'

'Oh, yes. That's a pity. Because …'

'Because what?'

'Well, when I was talking to Carol just now she said she'd written to Sally in March because she'd heard from an old friend she hadn't seen for years.'

'So?'

'She wondered why that letter hadn't been found. And apparently the old friend was the other one who used to go to lunch – you know – the ones Agnes told us about.'

'I don't see …'

'Well, this friend, Valerie, her name was, was looking for someone. And it wasn't Jean – you know, the other friend – because she died ages ago.'

'Libby, slow down. I think I followed all of that, but I don't

244

see what relevance it has. It isn't anything to do with the trafficking operation, is it?'

'No, I suppose not, but –'

'What you were thinking is that Valerie is Alec Wilson's long-lost mum.'

'Er – yes.'

'That really is far-fetched, Lib.'

'Why is the letter not there, then?'

'How do we know it isn't? And why would Sally have kept it? It was just a chatty letter from her mum.'

'Which she didn't answer.'

'I expect she would have done in time. Look, Sally's got nothing to do with all this.'

'Then why is Ian using her house as bait?'

'Because there's a link to her father?'

'Ian said if there is a link to Sally this will show it up.'

'And he didn't mean finding Alec Wilson's mother.'

'No.' Libby sighed. 'Oh, well. I'll meet you at the house tomorrow morning then. Text me if the train's late or anything.'

But the train wasn't late. Libby was leaning on a low fence staring across at the Ashton Arms when Fran's car drew up beside her and a tall, well-built man with greying fair hair climbed out.

'Oof!' he said, holding out a hand. 'Bit of a squash that. You must be Libby.'

Libby took the hand, beaming at him. 'That's me, and you're Richard. Fran says we met at her wedding.'

'I don't think we were actually introduced, but I remember you, of course.'

'Come on then, Lib,' said Fran, coming round the back end of the car. 'Let us in.'

'Wait a moment, Fran. Let me have a proper look.' Richard stepped back into the road and studied the terrace of houses. The he wandered off to the back of the properties and finally, to the end of the lane, where he peered over the hedge.

'That's it, got the bearings now,' he said. 'In we go.'

Fran and Libby watched as he went from room to room, not

even needing to hold the end of a tape measure as he pointed his laser model at walls and ceilings. Eventually they came back to the bland sitting room.

'Best to market it as a holiday let, don't you think?' asked Richard, sitting down on and dwarfing the equally bland sofa. 'That's what it has been, hasn't it?'

'I don't know about a holiday let,' said Libby, 'but it was always let out. Although it's been empty for a little while, I believe.'

'Pretty enough village,' said Richard. 'But Fran tells me this is more of a fishing expedition?'

Libby looked at Fran. 'In a way. But it just occurred to me, by advertising it for sale, won't we be advertising the fact that it's empty?'

'Is there supposed to be something hidden here?' Richard looked interested.

'We think – or the police think – that someone might think so,' said Fran. 'We've searched and so have the police, so we're pretty sure there's nothing here, but the owner *was* murdered, so the killer might think ... well, you know.'

'And you haven't felt anything here?' Richard was looking at Fran shrewdly, and Libby remembered that here was a man who actually employed Fran for her psychic 'moments'.

'Nothing.' Fran shook her head. 'If Sally Weston had anything to hide, she either took it with her to Turkey or hid it somewhere else. Personally, I don't think there is anything.'

Libby looked at Fran, then back to Richard. 'So you see, this is a bit pointless.'

'I don't think so.' Richard leant back in the sofa. 'If your policeman thinks this is worth it, it must be. They don't invest in this sort of operation unless they've got good reason.'

'What do you mean, this sort of operation?' said Libby.

Richard raised his eyebrows. 'You don't imagine Goodall and Smythe would do this without some kind of financial recompense? We'll be advertising, using our resources and, of course, if any viewings are required, we'll have to send someone down. There will be discreet police surveillance at

246

those times.'

Libby's mouth was open.

'I don't think we'd thought of that,' said Fran. 'Perhaps we should have used a local agency.'

'It wouldn't have made much difference, and we have a longer reach.' Richard grinned across at the two women. 'We have worked with the police before, you know.'

'Have you?' Libby leant forward. 'When Fran found things?'

'No, and she only once found something – ah – current, as it were. And then the police shut us down, apart from going through all our paperwork on the property.'

'So what?' Libby leant further forward, in danger of falling off the edge of the chair. Richard regarded her with amusement.

'I see why you get involved, as Fran says.'

'You mean I'm nosy.' Libby grinned back. 'Yep, that's me. A nosy old bull in a china shop.'

Richard let out a guffaw of laughter.

'Don't encourage her,' said Fran. 'So what do you think?'

'I'll go back to the office and think up a nice tempting little ad, which I'll run by your policemen.'

'Plural?' said Libby.

'Apparently. Your DCI Connell, DI James from the Met, and a Commander Smith who I'm not sure about. He comes with his own shroud of mystique.'

'Doesn't he just,' said Libby. 'Although his ID said the Met, we think he must be MI5, or MI6 or something.'

'Human trafficking.' Richard nodded and looked solemn. 'Can't see this little house having been used for anything in that line though.'

'Neither can we,' said Fran, 'but as you said, the police would hardly sanction this sort of operation if they didn't think so.'

Richard stood up. 'Now, much as I'd like to buy you a drink at that nice-looking pub over the way, I think I must get back to London.'

'And I've got a car to pick up,' said Libby. 'Thank you so

much for coming, Richard. Do you need to take my keys?'

'No, apparently I'm being sent a set by your Mr Connell.'

'He must have taken copies,' said Libby. 'Sneaky.'

'I think he's allowed to,' said Fran. 'Come on, then, Richard. I'll take you to the station.'

Libby locked up, drove Ben's car back to Steeple Martin, and picked him up from the Manor estate office.

'Richard was telling us how much an operation like this costs the police,' she told Ben, as she buckled herself into the passenger seat. 'I didn't realise.' She reported everything that had happened that morning.

'At least you won't be going out there on your own, then,' said Ben.

'Like the heroine into the cellar,' agreed Libby.

'Eh?'

'You know I've always said how stupid heroines – and heroes, come to that – are in films and books? When they hear a noise in the night in a spooky castle and go off bravely on their own with only a candle. Daft.'

'I expect it makes for better tension and excitement,' said Ben.

'It just annoys me,' said Libby.

'Are we going to start looking at sofas today?' asked Ben, as they drove along Broad Oak Road towards the car showroom.

Libby looked at him sideways. 'Do we have to? I've just given in on the car. I need to think about it.'

'Always resistant to change,' sighed Ben.

Libby subsided guiltily. Over the past few years she had refused to move from 17 Allhallow's Lane into the much larger and more comfortable Steeple Farm, vacillated about marriage, and hung on to an almost threadbare blue cape and an equally battered basket instead of the more suitable handbags foisted on her by her nearest and dearest at Christmas and birthdays. She was, as Ben said, highly resistant to change.

The new car duly collected, Ben opted to go and pay a visit to the architectural practise in which he was now a sleeping partner, while Libby decided to take a drive to get used to the new controls. The car was lighter than both Ben's Range Rover and the old Renault, which indeed took some getting used to, and the range of computer-controlled devices rather took her breath away. Narrow lanes where she would have to go slowly seemed to be the best place to practice, so she turned the car towards Keeper's Cob.

Eventually, she found herself in Dark Lane, where a few years ago she and Fran had been involved in yet another murder case. Gritting her teeth, she carried on until she came to Steeple Cross, which had also figured in an investigation. Shaking her head, she carried on and crossed the main Canterbury Road, arriving in Itching, at which point she stopped the car.

It seemed that everywhere she went in her corner of Kent she was reminded of a murder investigation in which she had been involved, either because she'd stumbled into them, been invited in, or been a suspect. She sighed, and got out of the car. Perhaps it was time she stopped. It was almost inevitably upsetting, sometimes dangerous and often caused annoyance to her friends and family. In this current investigation, for instance, why was she really involved? Yes, Ian had asked her – and Fran – to organise putting the Cherry Ashton house on the market, but apart from that, why was she involved? Simply because they had all been present when Alec Wilson's body was found? And then they'd stated asking questions.

Although, Libby argued with herself, the Jandarma had asked them questions. But then they'd rather pushed themselves in by talking to Martha and finally by being co-opted by Johnny Smith. Which they could have refused. There was always a point in every case where there was the opportunity to back out, and perhaps this was where they'd got to now.

Libby took the keys to Sally Weston's house out of her basket and looked at them. She would hand these back to Ian and tell him enough was enough. Getting back into the little silver bullet, she turned it round and headed back to Canterbury.

Chapter Thirty-four

'I'm giving the keys back to Ian.' Libby called Fran from the police station car park.

'You're what?'

'Giving the keys back. I don't want to be involved any more. He doesn't need us. Well, I suppose he might need you sometimes, but he doesn't need me.'

'What brought this on?' asked Fran.

Libby sighed. 'Oh, it was Ben saying how I'm resistant to change, and then driving through Kent and realising there's nowhere I know that hasn't been touched by murder. And how upsetting it all is.'

Fran was silent.

'Fran? You still there?'

'Yes. Look, I want to think about this.'

'All right, but I'm going in now to give the keys back to Ian, or leave them here for him. I'll see you tonight for rehearsal.'

'It's Wednesday, isn't it? Ian might come to the pub afterwards.'

'That's all right, but not to talk about the case. If he isn't in right now, I'll leave him a message.'

Ian wasn't in, so she left the keys with the desk sergeant and a message on Ian's office phone.

With a slightly lighter heart, she drove back home, parked the silver bullet in Romeo's old place opposite number 17, and set out for the eight-til-late for something for Ben's dinner.

'Oi!'

Libby turned round and saw Harry standing outside The Pink Geranium, arms akimbo.

'What?'

'Why were you walking straight past?'

'I often do.' Libby turned slowly and went back. 'And it's afternoon. You should be closed.'

Harry peered at her. 'Are you all right?'

'Fine, thanks.'

He peered even closer. 'Have you had any lunch?'

'Oh!' said Libby, surprised. 'No, I haven't! I went to meet Fran this morning, then went to pick up the car in Canterbury – no. I haven't.'

'Come on, then. Low blood sugar, that's what you've got.'

He ushered her inside the restaurant and sat her at the large pine table in the left-hand window.

'Soup and a roll? A glass of something?' he suggested.

'Lovely.' Libby sighed and leant back in the chair.

'Coming up, then.' Harry disappeared kitchenwards.

A very short time later, a bowl of steaming hot *Sopa de Chicharo*, Mexican green pea soup, was put before her, together with a chilli muffin and a glass of red wine. Harry sat down opposite her.

'OK, old trout. What's up?'

'Nothing.' Libby took a spoonful of soup. 'Ow.'

'It's hot, dear heart. Take a sup of wine while you're waiting.'

Libby obediently drank some wine and pulled the muffin apart.

'Go on, then. Tell your old mate. What's up?'

'I said – nothing.'

'Bollocks. You don't even *look* like you.'

Libby looked up. 'I'm backing out of the case.'

Harry raised perfectly shaped eyebrows. 'You've said that before.'

Libby repeated what she'd said to Fran earlier.

'Well, you're right, of course. The cases are always upsetting, particularly if they come close to home. But what about the times you've helped people?'

'I haven't really. The police have always got to the bottom of these cases in spite of us.'

'And sometimes because of you. Look at the times you've actually linked things together for the police. Ian's always been grateful, hasn't he?'

'And irritated, mostly. I always said I didn't want to become one of those storybook characters always falling over bodies. And that's what I've become.'

'You haven't fallen over them,' said Harry. 'Well, not literally. Only once.'

'And then it had been so long dead it didn't really count,' said Libby.

'And usually people ask you to look into things because of the experiences you've had.'

'I know, but I don't want to do it any more,' said Libby discovering with surprise that her soup bowl was empty. 'It's upsetting.'

Harry looked at her thoughtfully. 'What's got to you about this particular case? You aren't even personally connected with it.'

'I told you. I just realised that everywhere I go in Kent is tainted by murder. Even here, at home. And Nethergate, and Creekmarsh. And all the villages.'

'I expect everywhere in the country is tainted by murder,' said Harry. 'That's why there are policemen everywhere.'

'But not murder you've been personally involved with,' said Libby.

Harry sighed. 'No, of course not. So you're backing out of this one. Have you told Ian?'

'Yes. I handed the keys to Sally's cottage in at the police station – oh, did you know Fran and I went there this morning?'

She told Harry about Ian's request and the visit from Richard Smart. 'So now I've handed the keys back and left a message on his office phone. I don't want anything to do with it any more.'

'Just this?' asked Harry shrewdly.

She smiled slightly. 'No. I don't want to get involved ever again.'

'I wonder,' said Harry.

253

'Look, unless another murder turns up on my doorstep I don't have to, do I? If anyone asks me to look into something, I don't have to. Because even that can have disastrous results.'

'Yes, it can. But I honestly don't believe you'll be able to back off. Especially if someone comes and asks you – or Fran – for help.'

'Fran can do what she likes,' said Libby.

'That sounded pettish.'

'Wasn't meant to. Fran may well be asked because of her abilities, although she hasn't really used them this time, has she?'

'She saw someone drowning when we were on holiday, before we found the body.'

'But nothing since. No, she can do it if she likes, but I shan't.'

'All right,' said Harry. 'Now, drink up your wine like a good girl and I might even get you another.'

Libby walked home half an hour later feeling rather strange. Not because of unaccustomed wine at two thirty in the afternoon, because to be fair it wasn't all that unaccustomed, but because it felt as though part of her life had been amputated. Almost ever since she'd moved to Steeple Martin with the help of Peter and Harry, who had been the mainstay of the 'Search for Bide-A-Wee' as they'd called it, she had been involved with murder. Her relationship with Ben was rooted in their first mutual encounter with it, her friendship with Fran was a direct result of that first encounter, and many of the people in her life nowadays were there because of the adventures she and Fran had had together over the last few years. There had been marriages – Guy and Fran, of course, and Jane and Terry Baker. Shows – the End Of The Pier show at The Alexandria and Sir Andrew McColl's concert at The Oast Theatre just two of them. No wonder the investigations had become such a big part of her life. Perhaps Harry was right. Perhaps she couldn't back away.

To her own surprise, when she got home and unpacked her shopping, she didn't even check the computer for emails or the landline answerphone for messages. She remembered switching off her mobile in the police station car park and decided to leave it off. Leaving chicken marinating in the fridge, she made tea and took it out into the garden.

'Where have you been?'

Ben burst through the back gate from the Manor woods.

'What?'

'I said – where have you been? I've left messages on both the phones.'

Ben subsided on to the other unstable deckchair and pushed a hand through his short grey curls.

'Oh, Ben, I'm sorry!' Libby's hand flew to her mouth. 'I didn't even think!'

Ben sighed. 'I know you didn't. But you're in the middle of an investigation and I can't get hold of you. What the hell was I supposed to think?'

'That's just it,' said Libby. 'I'm not.'

'Not? Not what?'

'In the middle of an investigation. I've backed out. Told Ian. And Fran.'

'And Harry?'

'Yes. Only because he found me in the middle of the high street and fed me.'

Ben grunted. He had always been slightly jealous of Libby's close friendship with Harry, in spite of the fact that it was anything but sexual.

'What has Ian said?'

'I don't know. The phone's been off, as you discovered.'

'Ah. Don't want to be talked out of it?'

'I doubt if Ian would do that. He's always been all for me to back off, hasn't he?'

'Not always. He's asked for help often enough.'

'You'd rather I wasn't involved any more, though, wouldn't you?'

Ben looked up in surprise. 'What? Not ever?'

Libby nodded.

Ben looked away. 'This needs thinking about.'

'That's what Fran said.' Libby stood up, looking mournful.

255

'I'll get you some tea.'

'Why are you looking like that?'

'Because it seems that everyone sees me as a little round bundle of nosiness and very little else. It's very disillusioning.'

She went into the kitchen and peered into the teapot. Ben came up behind her.

'We don't see you like that.' He put his arms round her waist from behind. 'But your investigations are part of you. What would we all talk about?'

'There are several months of each year when there isn't anything going on,' said Libby, switching on the electric kettle. The heavy iron one was retired for the summer while the Rayburn remained unlit.

'That's a nice contrast,' said Ben. 'Are you sure about this?'

Libby told him what she'd told Harry and Fran.

'I see.' Now Ben was looking thoughtful, as Harry had. 'Do you remember how Peter felt about writing his plays?'

'He was sure it was his fault there'd been murders surrounding them. In fact, it was nothing to do with him.'

'So aren't you doing the same sort of thing?'

'No.' Libby shook her head. 'I didn't start the murders, if you know what I mean. I've got involved and stayed involved long after I should have. And – well, it's upsetting.'

Ben nodded. 'OK.' He dropped a kiss on top of her head. 'Now make me that tea.'

Nothing more was said about the subject, and feeling slightly disconnected to the word, Libby got through the rest of the afternoon, cooked a stir-fry for dinner, and went up to the theatre for the penultimate rehearsal before transferring to Nethergate.

At various points in the evening she noticed Ben and Fran in conversation, Ben and Peter in conversation, and even Fran and Susannah in conversation. She correctly deduced that the conversations were about her. Why were they so concerned, she wondered? Everyone had been telling her for years not to get involved. Why were they not all cheering with relief?

Ian had already arrived at the pub and was sitting with Patti and Anne when the theatre crowd trouped in. He greeted everyone, including Libby, quite normally, and went to the bar with Ben for drinks.

'And guess who they're talking about,' said Libby gloomily to Fran.

'You have rather thrown the cat among the pigeons,' said Fran. 'It just seems so unlikely.'

'I know. Harry doesn't think I'll be able to resist if something comes up.'

'And will you?'

'I've no idea. But if I keep a low profile, nothing should come up, should it?'

Ian placed a half of lager in front of her. 'Is that what you've been keeping today? A low profile?'

Libby looked up at him warily. 'I kept the phone off.'

'I know. And when you turn it on, and listen to your landline messages, you will find several from me.'

'And Ben,' said Libby.

'And me,' said Fran.

'Well, I've seen you all now, so I can delete them all.' Libby buried her nose in her glass.

'May we ask what's going on?' Anne moved her wheelchair a little closer to the table. 'What's Libby done?'

'She's retiring from the investigation business,' said Harry, appearing behind them. 'And if you believe that, you'll believe anything.'

Chapter Thirty-five

It appeared that Libby's resolve was to be tested as soon as she turned on her mobile phone in the morning and played the answerphone messages.

Ian's message was the most tantalising.

'For all the good it will do, we traced Jean and Bob Burton to an address in Wales. Jean died fifteen years ago, and Bob followed her two years later. There is no trace of Gerald, who appears to have vanished completely. This, of course, will lead you to think he must be Alec Wilson. If so, there is a possibility that he knew Sally Weston.'

'Of course he did,' Libby said out loud in exasperation.

'What?' Ben came through from the kitchen.

'Listen.' Libby replayed the message.

'I thought you weren't going to have anything to do with it any more?'

'I'm not.' Libby sat down at the table in the window and scrolled through the messages on her mobile. 'I can delete your messages from yesterday, can't I?'

'Yes.' Ben came and sat down opposite her. 'Look, if you need to follow this up with Ian –'

'No,' said Libby firmly. 'I said yesterday.'

'What happens if someone else gets in touch with you?'

'Like who?'

'The estate agent?'

'He'll get in touch with Fran. Or Ian.'

'Are you sure he hasn't already?'

'Fran would have told me last night, even if Ian didn't.

Ben sighed. 'OK. But if you do have to do something – just don't feel bad about going back on your decision.'

Libby looked up in surprise. 'Do you think I would?'

'I think you might.' Ben stood up. 'I'm going up to the office. You know where I am if you want me.'

Libby stared, still surprised. Ben never said that. When he'd gone, she pulled the laptop towards her.

'I'd better email the others,' she told Sidney.

Just to let you all know, she wrote, *Walter Roberts was arrested here in Kent two days ago. He and Geoff Croker in Erzugan were involved in a people trafficking scheme, and the police are assuming that Alec Wilson's murder is connected, although Sally's seems to be a puzzle. Justin Newcombe was supposed to meeting someone also connected to the organisation whom we assume is the murderer. Walter Roberts denies being that person, and the police seem satisfied that this is the case. I don't suppose we'll hear any more about it unless we have to give any more statements to the police – although I can't think why we should!*

All the best to everyone, and hope to see you in Erzugan another year.

And that's that, she thought as she pressed 'send'.

The phone started ringing as soon as she set foot in the conservatory.

'Walter!' said Greta. 'I don't believe it! He never went anywhere!'

'Only when Betty was well out of the way, apparently,' said Libby. 'He went out to check up on his investment in the business.'

'Poor old Betty. Did she know, I wonder?'

'The police think she did but was too scared to say anything.'

The next to call was Neal.

'People trafficking? That's awful!'

'I know. Mainly girls for prostitution.'

'Oh, God! And was Alec in it too?'

'I don't think so, but I don't really know. I only know about Walter because Ben and I saw him in London and then Betty reported him missing.'

'In London? Did he kill Justin?'

'He says not.'

'Oh.' Neal paused. 'Well, I know you said you hoped to go back, but I don't think I will. I really thought I'd found a little bit of paradise, but ...'

'Lot of serpents in paradise,' said Libby.

'Yes,' said Neal with a sigh. 'Oh, well, I'll carry on looking. If I find another paradise, I'll let you know.'

Martha had replied to the email.

Well, that was a surprise! Thank you for telling us. Geoff and Christine have vanished – arrested, I suppose – and the Jandarma and British police have all gone. I haven't seen Jimmy, but I'll pop down this afternoon. I bet he's shocked. Betty and Walter have been going there for years.

Keep in touch, and hope to see you here again.

It was afternoon when Fran called.

'I've just had Richard Smart on the phone. The advert's gone live. Will you call Carol and tell her?'

Libby sighed. 'OK. Where do we look?'

Fran told her.

'Right. And after that we're not doing any more, OK?'

'If you say so.'

'I emailed Jimmy, Martha, Neal, and Greta and Tom just to bring them up to date about Walter. Greta and Neal both phoned and Martha replied. Apparently Geoff and Christine have disappeared, presumed arrested, and all the police have gone. So that's that, isn't it?'

Fran sighed in her turn. 'Yes, Libby.'

To Libby's relief, Carol's phone went straight to voicemail and Libby was able to leave a message, after which she looked up the house ad online. It had been made to sound far more appealing than it actually was, and Libby was impressed to see that somehow, Richard had got hold of original photographs and floorplans from when the small development had first been built. This, she realised, was an advantage, as if any prospective burglar thought it was empty, they might not bother to try and gain entry.

So actually, she thought, perhaps that isn't an advantage, because Ian was hoping someone *would* show up. Oh, well, it wasn't her problem any more.

Carol rang just as Libby and Ben were sitting down to supper.

'It looks quite good, doesn't it?' she said. 'Do you think anything will come of it?'

'I've no idea,' said Libby. 'I can't see what Sally had to do with anything so I don't know why anyone would want to try and break into her house. I don't know why Ian – I mean, the police – think anyone would.'

'I expect it's because of what she used to do before she went to Turkey,' said Carol.

'Eh?' said Libby.

'She was a policewoman.'

Catherine wheels were going off in Libby's head. No wonder she'd been so affected by her father's activities.

'I – er – I don't – um – I don't think I know why ...' began Libby.

'I wondered if she'd been undercover out there.'

Now Libby really was speechless.

'Sorry, perhaps I should have said before, but it didn't really occur to me. She left the force when she went out to Turkey, and I know she started doing cookery courses.'

'Yes, I heard that.' Libby had recovered the power of speech. 'Was she teaching English or Turkish cooking?'

'Both. Cooking was her hobby, and she started off by teaching some of the restaurant and hotel chefs some British recipes, and they in turn taught her, so she began teaching ex-pats and holidaymakers Turkish cooking. That's why I was a bit surprised you hadn't met her. She would do the rounds of the hotels at least once a week to see if she had any takers.'

'I never knew any of this,' said Libby. 'Did the Turkish authorities know she'd been a policewoman?'

'I've no idea. I can't see why they should.'

'No.' Libby sighed. 'Well, I'm sure the police or the estate

262

agents will keep you informed of anything that happens.'

'Oh, aren't you involved any more?' Carol sounded surprised.

'I never was, really, and now they've arrested someone here and in Turkey I won't be told anything else.'

'Oh, that's a pity, I was getting used to being able to talk to you.'

'You can always ring if you want to,' said Libby, feeling uncomfortable. 'If I do happen to hear anything, I'll let you know, of course.'

Ben had put her plate in the oven.

'At least that won't happen so much,' she said, as he placed it in front of her.

'What?'

'Interrupted meals,' said Libby, and tucked into her chilli.

Friday morning Libby, Ben, and some of the stage crew who had got the morning off began transporting scenery, costumes, and props to The Alexandria. Fran was on standby at the other end to help unload and sort everything out. The old theatre had been rescued from disintegration by a trust set up by the family of the original founder, Dorinda Alexander, overseen by Ben, who had made sure the dressing rooms and facilities were as up to date as they could be. As there was more room here than in the Oast Theatre, the company would have more room to spread themselves, which had come as somewhat of a relief in the past couple of years.

'Ian called,' said Fran, as she and Libby carried armfuls of Edwardian bathing suits to the dressing rooms.

'Mmm?' Libby kept her eyes on her burden.

'Someone has asked to view the house.'

'Oh.'

'Aren't you interested?'

'I'm trying not to be. Will they let Mrs Oxford know?'

'I don't know. I suppose so. Why do you ask?'

'So that I don't have to. She rang last night.' Libby opened the door to one of the dressing rooms.

'And?'

263

'She asked if I'd be letting her know.'

'Libby.' Fran almost stamped her foot in frustration. 'Will you stop being childish?'

Libby turned a surprised face to her friend. 'Childish? What do you mean, childish?'

'You're behaving like a child in the playground. All right, you don't want to be involved in any more investigations, but to a certain extent you *are* still involved in this one, whether you like it or not.'

Libby, her colour heightened, lifted her chin. 'Are we having a row?'

'Yes,' said Fran firmly, and began hanging costumes on the rail.

Libby glared at her back for a moment, before doing the same thing.

'Carol told me something last night,' she said eventually.

'And were you ever going to tell me?'

'Er – yes. I suppose so.'

'Well, what was it?'

'Before she went to Turkey she was in the police force.'

Fran swung round to face her. 'Good God, Libby, why were you hanging on to that little nugget? Have you told Ian?'

'I wondered if he perhaps would already know ...'

Fran was dragging out her mobile. 'Damn! No signal down here.' She made for the door with Libby following.

'Ian, listen. Libby's just told me Carol Oxford called her last night. Did you know Sally Weston was in the force?'

From the expression on Fran's face, Libby guessed that he hadn't. She turned and handed the phone silently to Libby.

'Hello?' said Libby cautiously.

'Why didn't you tell me this?'

'I thought you probably knew.'

'Why would I know?'

'Someone must have known. Wouldn't it have come up somewhere when she was murdered?'

'Perhaps it was one of those facts that I was not told by the Met,' growled Ian. 'What else did she say?'

'Nothing. Just thank you for the house business.'

She heard Ian take a deep breath. 'Right. Fran told you someone's asked to view?'

'Yes, but I don't see why you think …'

'You went poking around, didn't you? Someone else might want to. Especially if she was in the force.' She heard a muffled swear word. 'I'm going now. If you hear anything else – from anyone – let me know at once. I don't care if you don't want to be involved. Tough.'

Libby handed the phone back to Fran.

'Not pleased,' said Fran.

Libby perched on the low wall by the stage door. 'It must have come up when Johnny Smith started looking into it, surely? They look into all the antecedents, don't they? I mean, that's how we knew that Alec Wilson seems to have sprung fully formed into life ten years ago, or whenever it was.'

'You know something,' said Fran, perching on the opposite wall, 'I'm beginning to sense our Johnny's fine Italian hand in all of this.'

Libby looked at her suspiciously. 'Are you having a moment?'

Fran shook her head. 'No, simple deduction. He obviously knew about Alec Wilson – who he was – right from the start. And then he wouldn't confirm whether he was in witness protection scheme or what.'

'And Ian wasn't told much, either.

'Nor was Inspector James.'

'So what do we think?' said Libby.

'I think Commander Smith has known who the murderer is all along.'

Chapter Thirty-six

Libby gasped. 'How?'

'I think he knew a lot more about it all when we first met him than he told us. Look how quickly he turned up.'

'But he took us to search the houses.'

'Do you remember what we said at the time? Camouflage. I bet Alec Wilson – and probably Sally Weston – were there to keep an eye on the trafficking organisation.'

'Then why didn't he just arrest Geoff Croker straight away?'

'Perhaps he didn't want to let it be known that the organisation was under surveillance. And perhaps Croker didn't murder Alec and Sally.'

'Ah!' said Libby. 'He was trying to ferret out more links up the chain, you mean?'

'Well, it could be, couldn't it?'

'It could – and in her email, Martha said Croker and Christine had "vanished". Not been arrested. Do you think they've done a runner?'

'More likely that they've been put out of the way,' said Fran.

'You don't mean –' Libby looked horrified.

'No, no, I'm sure he hasn't had them bumped off, I just mean quietly spirited away. To keep the chain intact, so the bigger bosses don't realise it's been broken.'

Libby now looked dubious. 'I should think an organisation of that sort would know what's going on.'

'Yes, but you know how these things work. Three people report to one person who reports to another, who reports to another and by the time it gets there, that person has no idea who the three people at the bottom were.'

'Hmm. S'pose so.'

Fran smiled a sly little smile. 'Getting interested again, are we?'

Libby wriggled a bit. 'We-ell ...'

Ben appeared at the stage door. 'That would actually be a relief.'

'What do you mean?' Libby looked up, startled.

'Someone kidnapped my Libby and put someone else in her place. I'd quite like her back.'

Libby glanced at Fran. 'Is that right?'

'We were all wondering where you'd gone.'

Libby looked back at Ben. 'Ian told me off.'

Ben threw back his head and roared with laughter. Libby and Fran began giggling in spite of themselves.

'Well,' said Ben eventually, wiping his eyes, 'if that doesn't beat all.'

'Actually,' said Libby in the spirit of fairness, 'it's more because I got myself involved in the first place than anything else. If I'd kept out ...'

'But we couldn't,' said Fran reasonably. 'We were dragged into it in Turkey by Johnny Smith.'

Ben perched next to Libby. 'Come on, then, what's the latest.'

Between them, Libby and Fran brought Ben up to date.

'And now we'd better get on with unloading all this stuff,' said Libby, standing up.

'Not much more,' said Ben, 'then I'll treat you to one of Lizzie's ice creams.'

Later, sitting on the sea wall with ice cream that tasted as it used to, Libby contemplated the horizon.

'I'm still not sure how they managed to bring a boat all the way round from the eastern Mediterranean to here. Surely it would have been easier to land somewhere along the south coast? You'd hit that first.'

'Perhaps they did,' said Ben. 'We don't know what the situation was. If it's a large organisation they could be bringing people in all over the country.'

'How awful.' Fran wiped ice cream from her nose. 'Do you

think they're bringing people overland, too?'

'If it's that big an organisation I would think so.'

'Poor buggers,' said Libby. 'They pay all that money and are then forced to live like animals when they get here.'

'And yet they still want to come to England,' said Fran.

Ben shrugged. 'No one tells them the truth. Or if they do, it isn't believed.'

'Doesn't bear thinking about,' said Libby, sliding off the wall. 'Can't believe someone we met was involved.'

'Walter didn't strike me as full of human kindness,' said Ben.

'Nor was Geoff Croker, or his Christine,' said Fran, 'but they were more stereotypical types of criminal.'

'I could believe it of them,' said Libby.

Fran went into Guy's gallery and Libby and Ben went back to their cars.

'So you're back to normal, now, are you?' said Ben as he held the door for Libby to climb into her new pride and joy.

'Well, I don't see how I can completely back out of this one,' said Libby, buckling herself in, 'but I shall try not to get involved in anything else. You'd prefer that, wouldn't you?'

'I'm not sure. You were very odd over the last twenty-four hours. Not like yourself at all.'

Libby looked down at her hands guiltily. 'I felt very odd,' she admitted. 'As though part of me had gone.'

Ben leant in and kissed her. 'Well, now it's back. Go on. I'll see you at home.'

Her basket began burbling just as she was driving down the high street and by the time she'd parked it had stopped. Before getting out of the car, she had a look at it. One missed call. A newly developing sense of self-preservation prompted her to ignore it as she didn't recognise the number, but when she'd let herself into number 17, tripped down the steps and over Sidney, she saw that the answerphone light was winking.

'Mrs Sarjeant, it's Johnny Smith here. I believe you know about Sally Weston's house going on the market? DCI Connell may have already told you that there's been a request to view?

We're trying to check up on the prospective viewer, and we wondered if you could ask Ms Weston's mother if she recognises the name?'

Couldn't you do that, Libby muttered to herself as she made her way kitchenwards to make tea. And how am I supposed to ask when you haven't given me the name?

She waited until Ben appeared and asked him what he thought. Ben's eyebrows disappeared into his (receding) hairline.

'You mean you haven't rung back immediately?'

'Well, no. I wondered what I ought to do.'

'I suppose you'll have to ring back. Ian said you couldn't stay out of it now, didn't he?'

'Yes, but this is a bit odd. Why isn't he or Smith asking Carol? Why ask me to do it?'

'Because you're less scary? Because she's got used to you? You did say she sounded disappointed when you told her you wouldn't be in touch any more.'

Libby sighed. 'OK. Pour yourself some tea. There's some in the pot.'

As the number was withheld on the landline, Libby used the number displayed on her mobile.

'Mrs Sarjeant, good to hear from you.' Johnny Smith sounded as comfortable and jovial as he had when they first met in Turkey.

'Commander Smith.'

'Oh, please, call me Johnny. Now, you got my message?'

'I did, but I would have thought you or DCI Connell would have been the right person to ask Mrs Oxford.'

'Actually this was DCI Connell's idea. He though Mrs Oxford would speak more feely to you.'

'But all you've got to do is ask her if she knows someone by the name of – what? You didn't tell me that?'

'But you're in a better position to dig around a little. She might not immediately remember the name, but if you get her talking she might come up with some sort of a link.'

So much for staying out of it, thought Libby. Aloud, she

said, 'I suppose I could try. What's the name?'

'Hamilton.'

'Male or female?'

'We don't know. The way this works is that people fill in an online form. A space is provided for a phone number, but it's often not filled in. Apparently a lot of people don't like being pestered on the telephone.'

I know how they feel, thought Libby. 'So I just ask her if she's ever known anyone called Hamilton?'

'That's the ticket!'

'But why?' asked Libby. 'There's nothing in that house. Sally Weston hadn't lived there since she packed up and went to Turkey –' she hesitated, 'after she left the force.'

There was a silence at the other end.

'The force?' repeated Commander Smith eventually.

'Well, yes. She was in the force, wasn't she?' Libby's fingers were so tightly crossed they were beginning to hurt.

'Er – yes. Of course.'

'So you knew who she was? Right from the beginning?' said Libby, greatly daring.

Ben appeared before her, frowning ferociously.

'No, no!' said Smith hastily. 'It came up a bit later.'

Libby realised she couldn't very well ask him anything else.

'Very well. Is this the best number to reach you on?'

'This is the mobile. You've got my card, haven't you?'

'Have I?'

'Didn't I give you a card when I came to see you and Mrs Wolfe?'

'I don't think so,' said Libby, wracking her brains.

'I'll always answer this one, don't worry. When do you think you might be able to get back to me?'

'I don't know. I am rather busy you know.'

Ben raised his eyebrows.

'Soon as you can, then. Prospective purchasers don't like to be kept waiting. Ha!'

Libby switched off the phone and repeated the conversation.

'I don't see what harm it can do,' said Ben.

'No, neither do I, actually, but I do feel as if I'm doing their dirty work for them.'

'Do it now, then you don't have to worry any more and you can concentrate on our last rehearsal tonight.'

Feeling as though she was about to sit an exam on a subject she knew nothing about, Libby found Carol's number.

'Oh, hello, Libby! I thought I wouldn't hear from you again.'

'The police thought you'd rather talk to me than them,' said Libby.

'Oh? What about?'

'Somebody's asked to view Sally's house, and they want to know if you recognise the name.'

'I wonder why?' Carol was obviously puzzled.

'Honestly,' sighed Libby, 'I've no idea. You and I know there's nothing there, so what they're worrying about I really don't know. Anyway, do you know anybody by the name of Hamilton?'

'Hamilton? I don't think so. It's a very common name, isn't it? I suppose I might have done in the past. Would you like to me to look through my old address book?'

No! Libby wanted to shout, but instead said 'I'm sure the police would think that was very helpful.'

'All right. I'll have to dig it out – we don't use them much any more, do we, with emails and things. Can I ring you back?'

'Yes, of course,' said Libby tiredly. And I just hope Commander bloody Smith doesn't keep ringing before then.

The final rehearsal went well, despite the costumes and props being unavailable, and Susannah pronounced herself satisfied with both ensemble pieces and soloists. David the drummer made his first appearance and made notes of where he might be able to contribute to the comedy and at last, at ten minutes to ten, Libby let them all go.

'Your basket was ringing earlier,' Peter told her as she climbed down into the auditorium. 'I didn't like to interrupt.'

Libby groaned.

'Go on, who is it?'

Libby told him about Commander Smiths' request. 'So this will either be him asking why I haven't called back or Carol telling me she doesn't know any Hamiltons.'

'Libby? I finally found my address book! And guess what? We did know some Hamiltons!'

Chapter Thirty-seven

Libby sank down into one of the red plush seats. 'You do?'

'Yes! Well, we did. When I was still married – when I still lived in Cherry Ashton.'

'Ah.' Libby waited for Carol to go on. When she didn't, Libby sighed.

'Oh, sorry. Well, yes, they're in my old address book and at first I couldn't remember who they were.'

'And who were they?'

'They were friends of my friend Valerie – I think I mentioned her, didn't I?'

'Yes – you said you'd heard from her recently.'

'Not that recently. It was a few months ago, now.'

'So you're not in touch regularly and you don't really know the Hamiltons?'

'No.' Carol was apologetic. 'It was a long shot really, wasn't it?'

'Yes.' Libby sighed again. 'But just to be on the safe side, I'll tell DCI Connell.'

'All right. They used to live near Valerie after she married – that's how we met. We went to dinner a couple of times with them. I lost contact with them and practically everyone else after – well, you know.'

'Of course. You don't remember their names? Or the address?'

'Susan and – oh, what was his name? Simon, I think, but I've got the address, it's here in the address book.'

'Oh, good. Could you send that to me in a text? And does Valerie still live near them?'

'Oh, no!' Carol laughed. 'She and her husband moved to

London years ago. They've got a very swish flat in South Kensington.'

'Oh – money, then,' said Libby, million pound signs floating in her head.

'More money than they know what to do with,' said Carol. 'That's one of the reasons we never kept up with them. We couldn't, you see.'

Libby decided she didn't like Valerie much. 'Well, that's great, thank you, Carol. I personally don't see what this has to do with anything, as I said, but I'll pass it on. Sorry to have put you to so much trouble.'

'Oh, it was no trouble.' Now it was Carol's turn to sigh. 'It was good to have something to do.'

A minute later, the address of the Hamiltons came through.

'Maidstone again,' said Libby, levering herself from the scat. 'I think I'll give it to Ian, not smarmy Smith.'

'You're going to have to explain that, dear heart,' said Peter. 'Now, come on. Hal has some fizz on ice at the caff to celebrate the end of rehearsals.'

Ben and Fran joined them and they walked down the Manor drive together while Libby explained what had been going on with Smith, Carol Oxford, and the Hamiltons.

'And really, I can't see that people Carol knew vaguely twenty years ago, or whatever it was, has anything whatsoever to do with the murders or the trafficking.'

'Why don't you want to give the address to Smith?' asked Ben. 'He was the one who asked for it.'

'We don't trust him,' said Fran. 'He's known more than he's told everyone right from the start.'

Libby's basket began to ring again. She took the phone out with some trepidation. 'Oh, it's all right,' she said. 'Ian. Hello, Ian?'

'What's this address you just sent through?'

'Oh, sorry, I thought you'd know.'

'Know what? Who are the Hamiltons?'

'Didn't you know?' asked Libby, in some surprise. 'It was you who told me that there's been a request to view.'

'No, I didn't. Who told you?'

'Smith.' Libby explained how she'd finally obtained the Hamiltons' address. 'I don't see how it can help, and Carol hasn't seen these people for twenty years.'

'So why did Smith ask –' Ian suddenly broke off. 'Thanks, Libby. I'll see to it. Don't bother to call Smith.'

'It might have nothing to do with the Hamilton who's requested the viewing. It's a common name,' said Libby.

'It's a coincidence. Worth looking at. I'll be in touch.'

'Well!' said Libby to the others. 'Ian didn't know anything about it.'

'You see?' said Fran. 'Smith's not to be trusted.'

'I think,' said Peter, as they resumed their way down the drive, 'that he's in a very difficult position. He works for an undercover arm of the Security Services, presumably, and he's been thrust into the middle of a murder enquiry that he's trying to keep quiet, but which has slipped out of his control.'

'Because of Justin's murder.' Libby nodded thoughtfully. 'I hadn't looked at it like that.'

'You've still got the keys, haven't you, Lib?' said Fran as they reached The Pink Geranium.

'Yes, why?'

Fran shook her head slightly as Peter opened the door and ushered them all inside. On the coffee table in front of the sofa in the window stood two ice buckets from which foil wrapped bottle tops emerged. Adam appeared with a tray of glasses.

'Compliments of the chef,' he said with a grin. 'Save some for me.'

The champagne was duly opened, and the success of The End Of The Pier Show toasted.

'So what did you mean?' Libby asked Fran in an undertone, while Ben and Peter started talking about the lighting rig at The Alexandria.

'Not now. I'll call you in the morning.'

Libby sat back, a simmering bundle of frustration.

Harry joined them for a quick glass and Adam finished off the second bottle after ushering the final diners out of the door.

'And we'll go now,' said Ben. 'Come on, Fran, we'll walk you back up the drive.'

'No need,' said Fran. 'I'm parked over the road. Speak to you tomorrow, Lib.'

'What about?' Ben asked suspiciously as he and Libby walked slowly down the high street.

'She wanted to know exactly what Carol and Smith said,' Libby said, almost truthfully.

'Well, you certainly didn't stay away from the coalface for long, did you?' Ben tucked her arm through his. 'Just be careful.' He turned and looked at her. 'And don't say you always are.'

'No, Ben,' said Libby meekly.

Libby was in the middle of a full English breakfast when Fran called.

'Ben cooked it, not me,' she said through a mouthful of wicked fried bread. 'So what's up?'

'When is this viewing supposed to happen?'

'I don't know. Could you ask Richard?'

'And what about the Hamiltons? Are they still where they were?'

'I don't know, Fran! I just passed on the information.'

'What was that address? I'll look them up.'

Libby sighed. 'OK. I'll forward Carol's text to you. Why is it important?'

'I don't know. I'll call you if I find anything out.'

'Fran's got a bee in her bonnet,' Libby told Ben, turning back to her breakfast.

'Just hope it doesn't buzz over this way,' said Ben. 'More tea?'

Libby turned her attention to her rather neglected house and spent most of the morning dusting, changing beds, and wiping down paintwork. Feeling virtuous, she heated some soup at lunchtime and went to sit under the cherry tree. Ben had gone to the estate office and then to lunch with his mother.

Just as Libby carried her tray back into the kitchen there was a knock on the front door.

'Fran! What is it? I thought you'd be helping in the shop.'

'Sophie's down.' Fran perched on the arm of the chair. 'Listen – the Hamiltons, believe it or not, are still at their old address. I called them –'

'You did what?' gasped Libby.

'I called them. I said I was a friend of Carol's and did they know her daughter had died in Turkey.'

'Oh, Fran! What on earth made you do that? They must have been immediately suspicious.'

'They were just surprised. And said they did know.'

'Well, I suppose it was in the papers.'

'No. They said they'd been told by an old friend. Neal Parnham.'

'Neal!'

'And they knew nothing about the viewing. They actually knew very little about Sally, and only remembered Carol rather vaguely.'

'As she remembered them. So I suppose she might have known Neal, too?'

'She might, but it sounds as if she and Neal came from different sections of the Hamiltons' life.'

'So the police hadn't been on to them? I wonder what Ian did with the address?'

'I don't know. What I do know is that the viewing is set for this afternoon.'

'Are we going?'

'I don't know what we can accomplish, but I sort of feel ...'

'I'll go and get changed,' said Libby.

'I'm not at all sure why I feel we should go over there,' said Fran later, as she turned the Smart car towards Steeple Mount. 'I'm pretty sure the police will have the place under surveillance.'

'We might recognise someone that they don't.'

'Yes, but they won't have important policemen doing the surveillance, so they won't recognise anybody,' said Fran.

'In which case we can point them out,' said Libby.

'What do you think the brief is? Just watch? Intercept?' Fran

279

looked right and left and pointed the car across the crossroads to the Cherry Ashton road.

'No idea. We know, and Ian knows, that there's nothing in the house. So I suppose it's a watching brief. After all, it might be nothing to do with any of this, and a perfectly innocent Hamilton looking for their first step on the housing ladder.'

'And it'll be accompanied, Richard says, so there's no chance of any funny business.'

'I wonder if it'll be a real estate agent or an undercover cop?' said Libby.

Fran sent her an amused glance. 'Mickey Spillane rules, eh, Libby?'

'Where do we go?' said Libby. 'We can't sit outside.'

'Or go round the back,' said Fran.

'I know – Agnes!' Libby pointed. 'That's her house, and she's got an empty drive.'

'You nip out and ask her then. We're early, so hopefully no one will see you.'

Libby ran across the road and panted up to Agnes' door. The lady herself opened it looking surprised.

'Oh, I'm sorry, Agnes, but we need to park somewhere for a little while and –'

'Park here then. Come and have a cuppa after,' Agnes interrupted.

Libby gave her a grateful grin and within minutes, the Smart car was parked on the drive and Fran and Libby were watching out of the front room window while Agnes made tea.

'Not hardly hidden there, it isn't,' said Agnes coming in with mugs. 'Suppose you tell me what's going on?'

Fran told her a sanitised version of recent events while Libby kept an eye out for visitors to Sally's house.

'Well,' said Agnes when Fran had finished, 'if it helps catch whoever killed our Sally, you can do what you like.'

'There's a car coming,' Libby announced. 'Looks like it's stopping.'

Agnes and Fran joined her at the window.

A tall young man with a fresh face and an ill-fitting suit got out of the driver's side and looked at his wrist.

'Checking the time,' said Libby. 'Is he the viewer or the agent, do you think?'

'The police, I think,' said Fran, as the young man now checked a smartphone. Agnes looked at her sharply.

'How do you know?'

'I don't,' began Fran.

'Look!' said Libby. 'Another car.'

The second car drew up behind the first and the door opened.

Libby and Fran gasped.

'Neal Parnham!'

Chapter Thirty-eight

Agnes looked surprised.

'Young Neal? What's he doing here? He hasn't changed much.'

Fran and Libby turned to her open-mouthed.

'You know him?'

'Course I do! I told you I used to help with the children all those years ago? Neal's Valerie's boy. Lost touch years ago, they did. Valerie's husband made millions, so they say.'

'Oh, good grief,' said Libby. 'If only we'd known!'

'What do we do now?' said Fran. 'They've gone into the house.'

'And the policeman – or whoever he is – is coming out again, look,' said Libby.

'Let's go and tell him,' said Fran, making for the door.

'He might not be a policeman,' said Libby, falling over her feet in her haste.

But Fran had already laid her hand on the startled young man's arm.

As Libby arrived beside her, the door opened behind them.

'Let 'em in, son,' said a familiar voice.

Commander Johnny Smith stood aside to let the women pass him. Inside, standing in the sitting room as if poised for flight, stood Neal Parnham.

'Now then, young man,' said Smith, leaning against the door jamb and crossing his arms. 'Suppose you tell me who you really are. You aren't John Hamilton, are you?'

'Don't you recognise him?' Libby burst out. 'He was in Erzugan with us. He's Neal Parnham.'

'Oh?' Smith looked interested. 'I don't think I ever met him.

I wonder why not.'

'None of us were really of interest to you then, were we?' said Fran.

'No, of course not. So come on, son. Out with it. Why are you here?'

Neal's colour, which had faded to grey under his lingering tan became almost transparent. 'I – er –'

'You knew Sally as a child, didn't you?' said Fran gently.

Neal turned to her with relief and nodded.

'So why didn't we know this?' asked Smith.

'I should imagine because he was scared he'd been implicated in her death if he admitted it,' said Libby, and watched as Neal's face brightened.

'Ah. So why Hamilton?' Smith strolled over to stand in front of Neal, who shrank back against the mock fireplace.

'They were friends of his parents, weren't they, Neal?' said Fran. 'I suppose it was the first name that came into his head.'

'Yes,' said Neal, in a strained voice. 'I was visiting them … I even sent the request to the agents from their computer.'

'So you stuck with it,' said Smith. 'And why did you want to come here?'

Neal, with three curious faces turned towards him, crumpled. Smith caught him before he reached the floor. Libby went into the kitchen and filled a mug with water.

'Did you think there would be something here that would link you to Sally?' said Fran, on her knees beside Neal who was now sitting on the sofa.

Neal nodded.

'You killed her because you knew her?' Smith's voice was harsh.

Libby and Fran turned to him aghast.

Neal shook his head.

'Right.' Smith hauled Neal to his feet. 'You're coming with me, son. You stay here ladies. I'll see to you later.'

'Oh, I don't think so,' said a dark voice from the doorway. 'I think I'll take charge of Parnham, Smith.'

Ian walked forward and took Neal's other arm as Johnny Smith turned quickly to the window and then back towards the kitchen.

'No escape, I'm afraid,' said Ian, as the young policeman/estate agent came in accompanied by a burly uniformed constable. 'Take him back to the station.'

Fran and Libby watched open-mouthed as, with a policeman attached each arm; Commander Johnny Smith was marched out of the house looking furious. Neal sank back onto the sofa and put his head in his hands.

Ian glared at Fran and Libby from under beetling brows.

'I suppose there's no point in asking you what you're doing here?'

'Um,' said Libby. Fran said nothing.

'I'd like them to stay,' Neal said suddenly. 'I want to explain.'

'Then they can stay,' said Ian, in a gentler voice. 'You know the kitchen, obviously, Libby. Do you think you could rustle up some tea or coffee?'

'There's no milk,' said Libby dubiously.

'What about the lady who allowed you to park on her driveway?' Ian lifted an eyebrow. 'If I asked one of our nice policemen outside, do you think she'd let him have some?'

Libby sighed. 'I'm sure she would.'

Ian moved to the window, opened it a crack and signalled to someone outside. Standing up, Libby saw two squad cars and four large policemen. She shook her head and went to put the kettle on.

After a sheepish-looking constable had handed over a delicate jug, Libby brought in four mugs, the jug, and some sweeteners on a tray.

'No sugar,' she said. 'Carol didn't take it.'

'Now,' said Ian. 'Tell us all about it, Mr Parnham.'

Neal took a sip of tea and straightened his back.

'It was all because of my mother, you see,' he said to Fran and Libby.

'Your mother? Valerie?' said Libby.

285

'You should have got her surname,' said Fran.

'Ladies!' said Ian. 'Go on, Mr Parnham.'

'That wouldn't have helped. I have my father's name. My mother remarried. She's Valerie Nassar now.'

'Ah,' said Libby.

'I didn't know anything about this at first, but apparently she decided she wanted to find her adopted son.'

Fran and Libby looked at each other.

'Yes, you're right. He was Alec Wilson. He came to see her after Sally wrote to Mother –'

'Sally?' said Ian, Fran, and Libby together.

'My mother wrote to Sally's mother saying she was looking for him and he seemed to have disappeared. Sally's mother – Carol – told Sally in a letter. Well, of course, Sally knew where Alec – Gerald – was. She asked his permission to tell my mother. And that was that.'

'But –' began Libby.

'Ssh, Libby,' said Ian.

'So then my mother told me all about it.' Neal's face hardened. 'I couldn't believe it, especially as I'd almost grown up with the bastard.'

Fran nodded. 'And Agnes used to look after you when the mothers had lunch.'

'Yes. Of course Gerald was older than I was. But he was Aunt Jean's. I never knew he was adopted.'

'Neither did he,' said Ian. 'It was all hushed up by Jean and Valerie. She was engaged to your father, so she went away to stay with a relation, supposedly, had the baby, Gerald, and handed him over to Jean and Bob. But she never forgot him.'

'You've spoken to my mother?' Neal looked scared stiff.

'Yes. She rang us, actually. Because Carol Oxford –' he paused and looked at Libby, 'had called her to ask about the Hamiltons.'

'Oh.' Neal had slumped back again, and Libby had to rescue his mug.

'So Alec – or Gerald – was threatening your inheritance, was that it?' asked Fran.

Neal looked at her. 'My stepfather is a very rich man and has no children. his fortune goes entirely to my mother. And as he is almost eighty ...'

Ian stood up. 'Come along then, young man. Let's get to the station.' He looked over at the two women. 'Will you lock up?'

'But ...' began Libby.

'Yes,' said Fran.

He smiled. 'I'll call you as soon as I can. You'll want the whole story.'

'Today?' said Libby.

Ian shook his head. 'No, Libby. I've been up all night and I've now got another full night to do. Possibly tomorrow.'

Neal was ushered out and they saw him driven away in one of the squad cars, while Ian disappeared round the back and reappeared driving his own long low black saloon.

'If we'd gone round the back after all we'd have seen he was here,' said Libby.

'And perhaps we wouldn't have gone in,' said Fran. 'Come on. Let's wash up and take Agnes' jug back.'

Agnes, who had watched everything from her window was naturally agog. They told her what they could, and promised that Carol would be in touch with her.

'And we don't know anything about Johnny Smith,' said Libby as they drove away.

'We said he knew all about it right from the start, didn't we?' said Fran.

'You did. But he didn't apparently know the murderer.'

'But he had to find out if it was anything to do with the trafficking operation. I expect that's why he was here today. Why he asked you to find out about the Hamiltons.'

Libby shook her head. 'I don't understand any of it.'

'Don't worry. Ian will explain it all. Tomorrow, I hope.'

'I shall send him a text and invite him to Hetty's for lunch,' said Libby. 'Then he can do his Poirot gathering afterwards.'

'If he can spare the time, poor man.'

Ian could spare the time.

'I got home at four thirty this morning,' he told Libby the

287

next morning, 'and I'm having the day off. Are you sure Hetty doesn't mind?'

'Not at all, but she says save the story until afterwards.'

'Well, of course, or Harry wouldn't hear it, would he?' said Ian.

Ian arrived in a taxi bearing wine and flowers, and surprisingly clad in jeans and a T-shirt. Fran, who had also been invited with Guy, looked quite startled.

'Is Sophie looking after the shop again?' asked Libby.

'Yes. She's quite happy. Some boyfriend or other is coming down to see her,' said Guy.

'So it really is off with Adam?'

'I'm not sure,' said Fran. 'I think it might still be on.'

By the time they'd reached the coffee and brandy stage, Harry had joined them with Peter.

'Go on then, Ian,' he said, sitting down and pouring himself a large glass of red wine. 'We're all ears.'

Ian settled back cradling his brandy balloon.

'You all know by now what Neal Parnham told us yesterday. He was appalled by his mother's decision to leave half her fortune to his newly discovered half-brother. In fact, she was planning to settle money on him in the immediate future. Neal himself, who hasn't worked in years and has a habit of losing money, saw his chance of money dwindling away. So he found out where his half-brother lived and without telling his mother, booked himself a holiday.

'Of course, when he got there, he found not only Gerald living under another name, but Sally as well.'

'So did he kill Sally? And Alec?' asked Fran.

'He did. Alec Wilson's was planned, but then he realised, especially after you started saying the long-lost mother ought to be found, that Sally would immediately realise what had happened, so she had to go, too.'

'When he left Martha's that time, not long after he'd got there,' said Libby.

'And then he turned up later with Justin didn't he?' said Peter. 'Was he in on it, too? Is that why he was killed?'

'No,' said Ian. 'I was sure you would have figured that out, as well.'

'The trafficking?' asked Fran.

'The trafficking.' Ian nodded.

'And was it –?' said Harry.

'Johnny Smith!' said everyone together.

'Yes, it was. He really had put Alec Wilson, who was ex-Security Services, and Sally Weston, who was also undercover, there to keep an eye on the so-called problem, when in fact he was running it with the help of his friend in the Jandarma in Antalya. The Crokers were on the ground, and Walter Roberts was sent out every year to check up.'

'But Alec and Sally hardly did anything,' said Libby. 'We were told that.'

'No. They were almost like sleepers. Smith told them he would activate them as soon as he had any intelligence. He did a couple of times, we've now found out, but they were false trails.'

'So he was using us as camouflage,' said Libby.

'And he had to keep tabs on you over here because you were ferreting around where he wanted no ferrets,' said Ian. 'I, of course, was an additional nuisance. He couldn't keep me under control as he could Inspector James.'

'Why did Alec/Gerald have a false name and Sally didn't?' asked Harry.

'Gerald Burton was ex-Security Services, as I said, and had recently been involved in a very high-profile case – a secret one, of course. He was also left injured, so to protect him, he was given a new name and what appeared to be a cushy job in an idyllic Turkish village.'

'But what I don't understand,' said Ben, 'is why Smith risked having anybody out there who could have spoiled his racket.'

'Because nothing actually left Erzugan.'

There were expressions of astonishment all around the table.

'You mean it was all a put-up job?' said Peter.

'Yes. There were trafficking operations, but not from there.

A lot of it was organised from there by the Crokers, of course.'

'And Justin? What about him?' asked Libby.

'Oh, you said something about creative accounting to Smith, didn't you?' said Ian. 'Well, that was exactly it. He did all the Crokers' accounting, and several of their friends, too. He came over on business for them, but had to inform the police he was coming because of the ongoing investigation. By this time, he'd become suspicious of Smith, who he'd seen with the Crokers somewhere. We don't know the details of that, just that he decided it would be a good idea to ask Smith and see if he could get cut in on whatever it was. And that was that.'

'Poor Justin,' said Fran.

'I didn't realise Smith was back in the country by then,' said Peter.

'Oh, yes,' said Ian. 'Now, does that clear everything up? Can I have another brandy?'

Hetty silently poured him a large brandy.

'I'm sure I'll think of more questions,' said Libby, 'but you've more or less covered it.'

'Thank you.' Ian inclined his head. 'And, as usual, you two managed to be quite useful.'

'Even if you didn't want to be,' said Harry, giving Libby a dig in the ribs. 'What now, Miss Marple?'

Libby dug him back. 'I'm going to manage a nice gentle End Of The Pier Show,' she said. 'And I'm never getting involved again.'

END

Others in the Libby Sarjeant Series
by
Lesley Cookman

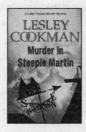

Murder in Steeple Martin

Murder at the Laurels

Murder in Midwinter

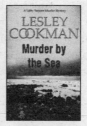

Murder by the Sea

Murder in Bloom

Murder in the Green

Murder Imperfect

Murder to Music

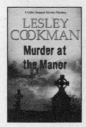

Murder at the Manor

Murder by Magic

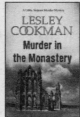

Murder in the Monastery

Murder in the Dark

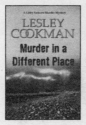

Murder in a Different Place

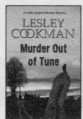

Murder Out of Tune

Murder in the Blood

For more information on **Lesley Cookman**

and other **Accent Press** titles,

please visit

www.accentpress.co.uk